Death Crosses the Border

Just past El Mirador, the spectacular viewpoint, the toll road suddenly rose directly along the edge of the coastal foothills.

"Hallelujah!" Zeke shouted . . . to the night and to the driver of the Caddie, who was still on his tail. His unseen companion must be enjoying the magnificence of the scene as much as he was.

As if in response, the old gas-guzzler accelerated and moved into the left lane. Zeke was aware of the car moving to pass him in the side mirror. Then the car swung into him . . .

Taking the risk of steering with one hand, Zeke grabbed his flashlight from the passenger seat. He shined it at the other driver, hoping to awaken him to the danger. But Zeke was wrong, he saw as he directed the flashlight toward his assailant. The driver was not the *borracho*—the drunk—he had assumed.

The Caddie hit him again, this time with nothing between highway and air but a narrow shoulder and a few tufts of grass. Zeke's Samurai sailed over them effortlessly.

For a moment, as his car shot off the highway, Zeke prayed for the other driver's soul. But as the Samurai arced sideways toward the cliff, his good intentions vanished. He wished retribution and suffering on the person he had glimpsed in the flashlight beam—the person he had recognized . . .

DEATH CROSSES THE BORDER

JANICE STEINBERG

BERKLEY PRIME CRIME, NEW YORK

DEATH CROSSES THE BORDER

A Berkley Prime Crime Book / published by arrangement with the author

PRINTING HISTORY
Berkley Prime Crime edition / November 1995

ISBN: 0-425-15052-6

Berkley Prime Crime Books are published by The Berkley Publishing Group, 200 Madison Avenue, New York, NY 10016.
The name BERKLEY PRIME CRIME and the BERKLEY PRIME CRIME design are trademarks belonging to Berkley Publishing Corporation.

PRINTED IN THE UNITED STATES OF AMERICA

10 9 8 7 6 5 4 3 2 1

In memory of Lynn Luria-Sukenick
Brilliant teacher, cherished friend,
and matchmaker extraordinaire

Acknowledgments

Although I share Margo's questions about the maquiladora industry as a whole, I have nothing but thanks for the people who graciously gave me tours of their maquiladoras: Bonnie Ann Kleffel, who clearly cares about her employees, and Herb Annetsman, who showed me the sophisticated waste treatment system he'd designed for the factory where he was a manager.

Thanks also to Victor Castillo for taking me to Tijuana's squatter colonias, Patricia LeSire for checking my Spanish, and the members of my writers' group for their insightful criticism: Ann Elwood, Judith Hand, Janet Kunert, Martha Lawrence, Mary Lou Locke, and Abigail Padgett.

Teresa Chris is the best agent any writer could hope to have. I am also fortunate in my editor, Karen Ravenel, and in the superb cover art of Robert Goldstrum.

And, as always, many thanks to Jack Cassidy.

1 / Unbeliever on Board

JESUS IS MY COPILOT
GOD SAID IT. I BELIEVE IT. THAT SETTLES IT.
SON OF GOD ON BOARD.
YO AMO JESUS.

Margo Simon grimaced as she scanned the dozen or so bumper stickers plastered on Reverend Ezekiel Holroyd's car, parked in the newly asphalted lot beside Revelation of God Church. The bumper stickers were a display not just of faith but of tremendous perseverance. With a spare tire covering half the back of Holroyd's tiny Suzuki Samurai, Margo was amazed Zeke had managed to fit so much vinyl there.

"Just a sec, I need to get my tape recorder from my car," she called out. She was grateful that journalistic principles limited the sentiments on the back of her Toyota Corolla to a plug for her employer—KSDR-FM, SAN DIEGO PUBLIC RADIO—and a proclamation that her child, actually her stepson, David, had been Citizen of the Month at his school. A show of her own opinions would no doubt have Ezekiel Holroyd haranguing her that she was headed straight for hell . . . not exactly the topic of conversation she would choose for the next several hours, while the minister served as her tour guide to Tijuana's poor.

Climbing into Holroyd's Samurai, Margo recalled her mother's annual refusal to buy a Christmas tree: "Calling it a Chanukah bush doesn't make it Jewish. It's not our religion." *Unbeliever on board,* she thought, fastening her seat belt.

Reverend Holroyd—Zeke, he'd said to call him—started

the engine and lurched out of the parking lot, grinding the gears and sending a jolt through Margo's spine; the car badly needed new shocks, as well as cosmetic repairs to the frayed convertible top. Zeke didn't appear to notice the bumpy ride. Too young to have ever thrown out his back, Margo thought enviously. Too young to be anyone's spiritual leader either, she would have surmised. With a cluster of acne decorating his chin and a lanky, not-yet-filled-out body, Zeke Holroyd looked barely out of high school. He drove like a teenager, too. Hitting the San Diego Freeway during the afternoon rush, he alternated between aggressively tailgating and then swerving around the offending slowpoke. Margo had seen just the bumper sticker to add to his collection: URBAN ASSAULT VEHICLE.

Thank goodness Zeke's church was in Chula Vista, a suburb some ten miles south of downtown San Diego . . . and therefore only seven or eight miles from the border; they'd get off the freeway soon. Then again, the Tijuana traffic would no doubt make the freeway look like paradise.

Zeke was intently tailgating a truck, enveloping them in diesel exhaust. *Damn Ray Fernandez!* thought Margo. She wondered if, in foisting Ezekiel Holroyd on her, Ray had been engaging in a bit of revenge. "Believe it or not," Ray had told her on the phone, "your best guide to the squatter neighborhoods of Tijuana is a fundamentalist minister. Especially," Ray had added archly, "since you'll need someone bilingual." She understood Ray's resentment: He had been giving her advice on doing the special report for which *he* had submitted the grant proposal, back when he and Margo were both half-time reporters at KSDR, before Margo had beaten him out for a full-time job. By the time the grant came through, Ray had taken a position—an exile, he called it—with a radio station in Fresno.

Ray needn't have been so envious. Margo's promotion had come with a three-month probation period (of which six weeks remained), and with no noticeable increase in respect from the new station manager. She had hoped to cement her position with a terrific story in an area where she had well-established contacts, such as the arts or the local homeless population. Instead, she'd gotten Ray's project dumped in her lap—a half-hour special report on the maquiladoras, the mostly U.S.-owned factories just south of the border. It was a story for which Mexican-born Ray was far better suited than she.

Any reporter could look up the statistics on the booming maquiladora industry, and Margo had. By the early 1990s, two thousand such factories had sprung up along the border from Texas to California, employing half a million Mexicans and manufacturing everything from televisions to furniture to hospital gowns; and once the North American Free Trade Agreement was fully in place, the industry was expected to change administratively but not in any substantive way. As for Margo's Spanish, it was serviceable if rusty. But, as Ray hadn't resisted reminding her, she needed help to capture the nuances of what people said, and even more, to gain entry into the maquiladora workers' world. It was odd help, at that. She'd have figured her interpreter would be Latino, whatever his religion, unless Ray had really thrown her a curve.

"How do you happen to speak Spanish?" she asked Zeke.

"When I was growing up, my folks had a mission in Peru. . . . Muggy weather we're having," he commented. "Must be some storms out in the Pacific. It's great for surfing."

"You surf?" Margo was aghast at the tone—incredulity verging on insult—she heard in her own voice. It struck her that her previous contacts with fundamentalists had consisted of firing questions at them while they were picketing women's clinics; she hadn't really dealt with a fundamentalist Christian as a person before. She'd assumed that Zeke Holroyd would be prejudiced against her, the reporter from the "liberal" radio station (at least, according to KSDR's critics). Now she realized that any obvious prejudice appeared to be on her side.

"I surf when I have time," Zeke replied to her question, not sounding at all offended. "Oops, here's our exit." He jerked the wheel and cut across two lanes of traffic. Margo grabbed the door handle to steady herself. Hadn't a consumer group charged that Samurais tended to flip over doing moves like that? The fact that the convertible top was up didn't reassure her. "You're probably used to crossing into Tijuana at San Ysidro," Zeke said. "I'm going east to the Otay Mesa crossing, where a lot of the maquiladoras are."

"Shee-it. . . . Uh, good grief, what *is* all this?" said Margo. Gleaming office parks lined the road. The last time she'd been out this way, she had seen nothing but open country and a few horse stables.

"A lot of maquiladora companies maintain their U.S. offices and warehouses here. Do you know what the word means? *Maquiladora?*" said Zeke. "It refers to the portion of corn a farmer used to leave a miller in exchange for the miller's grinding his corn. The idea of the maquiladora program is the U.S. companies bring raw materials for Mexican labor to assemble. What they leave is the workers' wages, like the farmer leaving some of his corn. At least, that's roughly how it works." He turned south toward U.S. Customs with a metal-on-metal of tortured gears. "Actually, my wife is the business expert. Why not come to dinner sometime and she'll fill you in?"

"Um," murmured Margo, thinking, *No way.* Zeke Holroyd might be challenging her stereotype of the rabid fire-and-brimstoner, but already she'd had to hold herself back from swearing, and she rarely ever swore when doing an interview. It was like being told not to think about elephants and then being able to think of nothing else.

They were waved through U.S. and then Mexican customs.

There should have been a sign, crudely lettered on torn cardboard: WELCOME TO THE THIRD WORLD. No matter how many times Margo went to Baja California, she was always stunned by how profound and immediate the contrasts appeared.

Instantly the road deteriorated, potholes replacing the

smooth pavement only yards to the north. Vendors selling chewing gum, blankets, and trinkets roamed the northbound side of the street, where cars waited in four carbon monoxide-spewing lines to cross to the U.S. At the first intersection, half a dozen of Tijuana's ubiquitous wind-shield washers—boys wielding spray bottles of cleaning fluid and rags—danced among the cars as if they each possessed a cat's nine lives.

Tijuana even felt sultrier than San Diego, a false difference born not of freak weather patterns but of the stop-and-go traffic. Speeding down the California freeway, Margo had felt comfortable enough in Zeke's convertible. South of the border, she became acutely aware of the July heat. She found a large barrette in her purse and gathered her mop of damp, wavy brown hair off her neck. Zeke, she noticed, kept shoving his thick-lensed eyeglasses up the bridge of his perspiring nose.

As he had remarked, this summer was unusually humid—the kind of weather that, in Margo's native Connecticut, would eventually find release in a storm. Here, months past California's winter rains, the thick air only stirred the thick dust with a more languid hand than in arid seasons. Through the Samurai's open windows wafted a dense cloud of grit and particularly noxious exhaust, an ironic switch from *el norte*. Unlike Southern Californians with their taste for Japanese and European cars, people in Tijuana "bought American" with a vengeance—big, decades-old Fords and Buicks that belched fumes, unrestrained by government smog controls.

Zeke offered her a soda from a cooler in back, in which a six-pack of cherry 7-Up floated in half-melted ice. She was relieved he didn't take a can for himself. He needed both hands to dodge through the choked traffic, his left steering and his right locked whitely on the gearshift, as he headed east, away from the central, bargain-filled streets that were the only Tijuana most gringos, including Margo, had visited.

"When do we get to Ciudad Industrial?" she asked. She had noticed several signs for the "industrial city," and already they were passing some factories, dingy concrete buildings disgorging people. They had purposely crossed the border just after five P.M., when the factories began to let out.

Zeke chuckled. "This is it. There are about a hundred factories here, on both the north and south sides of the main road." He turned right onto a long, drab side street lined with blocky buildings and added, not unkindly, "What did you expect?"

What *had* she expected? An impeccably landscaped drive leading to shining glass and steel buildings, twin to the U.S. industrial parks they'd passed en route to the border? If not *norteamericano,* however, the Ciudad Industrial didn't look Mexican, either. Rather, it seemed a sorry hybrid of the two cultures, U.S. functionalism wedded to Mexican poverty and resulting in unremitting ugliness. Even the street names—Siete Sur (Seven South) and Uno Oriente (One East)—were lifeless, out of place in the same city that offered Avenida de la Revolución and Paseo de los Heroes, names that sang on the tongue.

The workers, mostly young women in T-shirts and jeans, emerging from the factories made Margo think of songbirds escaping an airless cage. *Sentimental bleeding heart on board!* she chided herself. The women were laughing and chatting, evidently less depressed than she by the aesthetic shortcomings of their surroundings. Nevertheless, they had probably just put in a nine-and-a-half-hour day, for which they were paid nine dollars at best, higher than Mexico's minimum wage but nowhere near enough to get by. It wasn't sentimentality but good journalism to think that they might deserve better lives.

Zeke interrupted Margo's reverie, bringing the Samurai to a halt that hurtled her toward the windshield. She flung out her arm to stop the momentum.

"Rosalia!" Zeke called, leaning out the window.

A woman, walking with two others, looked up. The woman was young, with a Gibson girl figure in tight blue jeans and shiny black hair halfway down her back. She was probably lovely, when her face wasn't discolored by bruises.

"*Qué pasó?*" said Zeke. What happened?

"*Nada.*" Nothing. If they kept the conversation at this level, Margo would have no problem understanding what they said.

"Did Chuy do this to you?" demanded Zeke.

Rosalia shook her head, long hair rippling over her shoulders. Clearly, she was pretty without the bruises; she moved like a woman confident of her attractiveness.

"Can I give you a ride home?"

She shook her head again.

Resuming driving through the Ciudad Industrial, Zeke sighed. "Margo, guess how old that girl is."

"Twenty? Twenty-two?"

"Seventeen."

Only two years older than Margo's stepdaughter.

"Does she go to your, um, your church?"

"We don't have a church in Tijuana. We have prayer meetings in Rosalia's *colonia* Tuesday nights—so I was here two days ago—and she comes sometimes with her cousin, Anita. She lives with Anita's family. But Rosalia's young, all she really cares about is having a good time. That's fine, I'm not opposed to having a good time, regardless of the media image of fundamentalists." A brief but unembarrassed smile acknowledged he hadn't forgotten that Margo represented the media herself. "Problem is, Rosalia's been having a good time with her married boss."

"Is that who Chuy is? Her boss?"

"No, Chuy's Anita's husband. He beats Anita sometimes and I'm afraid he may have started on Rosalia. Did you know one reason women in Latin America are joining our church is that the Catholic priests, for all their liberation theology, let the husbands act that way? They say it's men's nature. We tell the husbands not to hit their wives. We also tell them to stop drinking, which is where a lot of the beating comes from."

Reverend Ezekiel Holroyd was certainly coming across

as more politically correct than Margo had anticipated. More savvy as well. Even though she found herself warming to him, Margo couldn't shake the feeling that she was hearing an evangelical public relations man "positioning" himself as a friend of women's rights.

Beyond the rim of the mesa on which the Ciudad Industrial was built, all human traces seemed to vanish from the landscape, roads and buildings giving way sharply to summer-parched Marlboro Country that looked no different in Baja California, Mexico, than in San Diego.

The dirt road dropped so steeply from the mesa that Margo wouldn't have seen it if Zeke hadn't turned there.

"There's still a little farming here," yelled Zeke, over the transmission's metallic groans. If he'd been rough on his gears in the city, it was nothing to what he inflicted on them on the thirty-degree descent, bumping over rocks and steering around several groups of Mexicans on foot.

Sure enough, they were entering a valley in which she saw a farm with cows and cultivated fields—although with the persistent criticism that many maquiladoras dumped their toxic wastes down the drain, she would hate to eat anything raised downhill from the Ciudad Industrial.

They continued along the rubbish-strewn road, which crossed a gully and then twisted upward, deeper into the hills. They came around a rise . . .

"Wow!" Margo gasped. No other response seemed adequate. They had entered a small city, with hundreds of houses built of scrap wood, tin, and who knew what else. She knew that Tijuana's population had tripled, from half a million people in 1980 to as many as a million and a half by the early nineties. And she'd seen photographs of the squatter communities in the hills. But a thousand photos couldn't have prepared her for the vastness of the settlement.

"Colonia Zapata," announced Zeke, stopping the car.

"How many people live here?"

"Ten thousand? Fifteen thousand? It's growing constantly."

"Wow!" she repeated, and then yelled, "Hey!" as a

rock smacked against the windshield.

"Get down!" Zeke cried.

Margo crumpled onto the floor in front of the passenger seat, landing on a small trash pile of candy wrappers and crumpled soda cans. She heard Zeke cry out. Another rock thudded into the side of the car and then there were people yelling in Spanish, chasing the attacker away.

She looked up. "Zeke, are you okay?"

Zeke had tried to fold his long body under the steering column, but he'd only partially succeeded. He was holding his hands over his face. Blood ran between his fingers.

2 / Casa Sweet Casa

"Zeke!" cried Margo. Was he even conscious?

"I'm okay. They just jammed my specs into my face." Wincing, he plucked off his glasses, which were badly bent, one lens cracked. "I think there's a towel . . . ?" He groped toward the backseat.

Margo found the towel and filled it with ice from the cooler in back. Zeke's bleeding, she saw, came from one gash above his eye and another on the side of his nose. She handed him the makeshift ice pack.

"Thanks." Zeke pressed the ice pack against his face. "Guess I'll have a real shiner."

Several Mexicans had gathered beside the car, three men and a woman. Zeke assured them he was all right, then asked, "*Quién lo hizo?*" Who did it?

The Mexicans shook their heads as they drifted away.

Zeke sighed. "If they saw, they're not going to tell. Probably just some kids reacting to a couple Anglo faces. Well, no real damage done." He gestured at the windshield. The rock had left a ding, a small spiderweb of cracks radiating from it, but the glass had held.

Margo offered to take him to a doctor, but Zeke insisted on continuing their tour. "Really, I've gotten worse than this playing soccer." His voice sounded strong. "But you'd better drive."

With Margo at the wheel and Zeke navigating, they went down a wide dirt road between long rows of connected dwellings, some made of nothing more than flattened cardboard boxes. Many of the houses had roughly fenced yards, where women were cooking at makeshift outdoor stoves—

the colonia lacked gas, electricity, and running water, Zeke informed her.

They had gone about a quarter mile when Zeke asked her to stop. He jumped out of the car.

"Rafael! Sandra!" he called, striding toward the nearest house, where two small children played in a fenced yard. Zeke swung his long legs over the fence and scooped up one of the kids, who squealed in delight. Margo followed through the gate.

From a lean-to beside the house, a man emerged. His beaming smile quickly changed to concern. "*Padre! Qué pasó?*"

"*Un accidente, Rafael. Pero no es nada.*" It's nothing.

Rafael ran inside. He came back in a moment with a clean towel and a bar of soap, and led Zeke to a large metal barrel of water in the yard.

"Zeke!" Margo thrust herself between him and Rafael. "Is that water safe?" The water barrel was marked POISON.

"Don't worry, it's fine." Zeke leaned down to let the shorter man reach his forehead.

People got the fifty-five-gallon barrels free from the factories, Zeke explained, while Rafael gently cleansed his cuts. The water, which came from a standpipe in the colonia, was used primarily for bathing and washing dishes, not for drinking. There'd been only one problem, when some dozen families complained that the water from their barrels was burning their skin. The water was tested and only one barrel contained any caustic chemicals. The rest of the complaints were attributed to mass hysteria.

"*Muchas gracias,*" Zeke said, as Rafael tied a clean rag bandage around his head. Zeke introduced Margo and continued in fluent Spanish, "Rafael is my mechanic. He works at Sanyo, assembling television sets, but he's got a nice little car repair business on the side. You should ask him about his job. Did you know Tijuana has become the television assembly capital of the world?"

In English, he added, "Are you following so far?"

"As long as no one talks too fast."

"Good. Just let me know any time you need a translation."

Rafael invited Margo to sit on a crate and shushed the children fondly, if not one hundred percent effectively. Margo smiled; the kids' occasional giggles would provide a great background to Rafael's story.

He and his wife had come to Tijuana four years ago from a small village in Sinaloa, Rafael said. They'd found maquiladora jobs almost immediately. Things weren't so good, however. They made more money than at home, but everything here cost more, and Rafael always felt sick from smelling the chemicals at the furniture factory where he worked. And after Sandra had the first baby, she could no longer handle the forty-eight-hour week at a factory that packaged plastic fingernails. So Rafael crossed the border illegally and did farm labor in California. He couldn't always get money back to Sandra, however, and he missed his family. He had returned to Mexico two years ago and taken the job at Sanyo, where he earned some thousands of pesos a week—about forty dollars, Zeke converted quickly. Starting the car repair business last year had helped a lot. Rafael now brought in another fifteen or even twenty dollars a week, enough that he'd been able to buy one of the television sets he made.

"A television? Here?" Margo had primarily needed Zeke's assistance to state her questions, rather than to understand Rafael's replies. But how could someone have a television in a place with no electricity?

"I'll show you," Rafael said proudly. He started for the house, but hesitated, frowning.

Zeke, ignoring Rafael's confusion, stooped under the doorway. "*Buenas tardes,* Sandra," he called out. Good afternoon.

"*Buenas tardes,*" came a woman's voice.

The house was lit by only a small window and the flickering television, broadcasting a Mexican soap opera. But Margo required no illumination to know that, unlike her husband, Sandra hadn't greeted Zeke Holroyd with a smile.

"Sandra," Rafael said nervously, "this is a reporter who's a friend of the Padre's."

Sandra came forward, polite if not welcoming, wiping

her hands on her skirt. Margo's eyes, adjusting to the dim interior, saw that Sandra had been folding meat, vegetables, and corn meal into husks for tamales, sitting at a table on one of the house's two chairs. The only other furniture in the one-room, dirt-floored home was a double bed and of course the television, perched atop a crate and powered by a car battery.

"Sandra, were you able to use the clothes I brought last week?" Zeke seemed determined to break through the woman's resistance.

"Yes. Thank you. Are you going to help us with this?" Although Sandra spoke with characteristic Mexican courtesy, she thrust a piece of paper at Zeke. Something in the gesture made Margo think of the rocks thrown at Zeke's car. Apparently, not all the residents of the colonia loved *el Padre*.

"With children playing and people in the street socializing, Colonia Zapata, if hardly luxurious, has the air of a real community." Margo, strolling with Zeke, talked her impressions of the bustling colonia into her tape recorder. "There are savory cooking odors from the outdoor stoves. At an outdoor table, three men are playing a lively game of dominoes. Another half dozen kibitzers are standing around."

One of the dominoes players half-stood as they passed, a thin man with a fine-boned face and almond-shaped eyes, and Margo had the feeling he wished to speak to her. But the game was intense and his friends made him sit down.

"Diego Torres." Zeke followed her gaze. "He's trying to recruit people for a maquiladora workers union. All he's recruited so far is dominoes partners. No one wants to get in trouble at their jobs." Zeke steered her around a corner. "We're close to Anita's. I'd like to see if Rosalia's at home."

Rosalia wouldn't leave the bedroom and she was supposed to be helping with dinner, griped Anita Cruz, biting a lower lip that looked gnawed with a chronic sense of injustice. And no—are you joking?—Chuy hadn't hit Rosalia. As a matter of fact, Chuy thought sweet, pretty Rosalia could do nothing wrong. Well, just wait nine years until Rosalia was Anita's age and you'd see if Chuy still felt that way.

Margo tried not to show her astonishment: Anita, only twenty-six? Rosalia's cousin was not just thin but desiccated, as if all the life force had drained from her, leaving a residue of pure resentment. Margo would have guessed her age at forty, in spite of the bawling infant she held in her arms.

"Will Rosalia talk to me?" asked Zeke.

Anita thrust the baby at Margo and left the room, muttering.

With both Chuy's and Rosalia's maquiladora incomes, Zeke said, this was one of the biggest places in the colonia. There were two bedrooms in addition to this main room, which Margo described on tape: The room was furnished with a table and six chairs. An open, blue-painted wooden cabinet held bags of flour, rice, and beans, two pots, various cooking implements, and half a dozen ceramic plates, painted bright yellow with a design of tiny blue and white flowers. Had Anita brought the pretty plates with her from her home village? Margo wondered, as the woman dragged her cousin into the room.

"You think by hiding your face you can hide your shame?" Anita grasped Rosalia's arm so hard she was probably adding to the girl's bruises.

Rosalia put up no resistance, other than to state sulkily, "I'll only talk to the Padre. Alone."

"I have to go to Carmen's, anyway. Watch Manuel." Anita plucked the baby from Margo's arms, deposited him in Rosalia's, and stalked to the doorway. She paused, clearly waiting for Margo to accompany her.

"Some people, my husband Chuy for instance, are good even though sometimes they act like sinners," said Anita, as she led Margo down the street. Margo couldn't completely understand the strong village accent, but Antia could have spoken Urdu and no one would have mistaken the malice in her voice. "You can pray for someone like that, you pray for the good in them to be stronger than the sin in them. But Rosalia doesn't have any good part, she is nothing but sinner. What do you do then? How do you pray for someone if there is nothing good to pray for?'' She clutched at Margo's sleeve.

Margo realized that, although Zeke had introduced her as a reporter, Anita had been too absorbed in her grievance against Rosalia to listen. She must have assumed Margo was part of Zeke's church.

''I'm sure there's a good part to everyone,'' Margo improvised. She didn't recall any journalistic prohibition against giving religious advice under false pretenses. Not that Anita seemed at all likely to believe her. If Anita ever said prayers for her young, pretty cousin, they had probably been answered by the bruises on Rosalia's face.

Carmen's, Anita's destination, turned out to be a small store where colonia residents could augment the purchases they made at the *supermercado.* The store also seemed to be a communications center, at least for the women of the colonia.

''Ana told me Rosalia got beaten up,'' said Carmen. Taller than most Mexican women—close to Margo's five six—Carmen looked quite capable of hoisting the cases of canned goods and toiletries on her shelves.

''That Jaime gives her so many presents.'' Anita picked over a box of onions. ''Well, he really gave her something this time.''

''Jaime. Right,'' Carmen said. It occurred to Margo that Anita might have beaten Rosalia herself; she suspected Carmen had the same idea.

''You work at that factory sometimes,'' said Anita. ''You know he can't keep his hands off the women.''

''None of them can. That reminds me, tell Chuy there's a union meeting tomorrow night.''

So much, thought Margo, for Zeke's assertion that no one wanted to join the union.

''Diego Torres!'' Anita selected three onions, then sniffed at one and put it back. ''How can anyone believe what they said about—what did they call it, hysteria? When the Garcias and their neighbors got burned from their water? Everyone knows Diego Torres put something in the water, so he could call a big meeting about the danger of chemicals in our water and get people into his union.''

''Ai, Anita! I suppose that's why the scientists couldn't find any chemicals in the water! Like I said, tell Chuy about the meeting, okay?''

''Did you find out what you wanted?'' said Zeke, as Margo inched the Samurai forward in the line of cars waiting to cross the border. Zeke's eye having swollen nearly shut— not to mention his glasses being useless—she was driving him to his apartment in Imperial Beach, not far north of the border; she'd get a lift back to her car from his wife.

''I got a great start. Thanks.''

With sunset, the temperature had gentled. Except for the exhaust fumes from several hundred vehicles, the forty-minute wait was almost pleasant here, the wandering vendors creating a carnival atmosphere with their cheap bright ceramics and striped blankets for sale.

Margo's initial resistance toward Reverend Zeke Holroyd had loosened considerably. Both of them sipping lukewarm sodas from his cooler, she found herself chatting easily to him about Jenny's teenage sulks and the recent strains at the dinner table from eleven-year-old David's militant vegetarianism and Barry's determination to lose twenty pounds; Margo ate healthily herself, but the two of them were almost driving her to chili dogs. Zeke was remarkably easy to talk to. Maybe that was why, when Margo had returned from the store, Rosalia was laughing . . . as if she felt much better for whatever she had confided to the minister.

''Say,'' said Margo, inching forward in the traffic; the Customs station was only three cars ahead. ''What was that thing Sandra gave you?''

Zeke fished through his pockets and found the piece of paper. ''It's not important, Sandra just worries,'' he said, handing the paper to Margo when the traffic halted again.

The printed notice, from the Baja Nueva Development

Company, stated that the company owned the land on which the colonia was situated and that the residents had been ordered to leave by the end of the previous month. The notice contained no specific threat, but it implied that if people didn't leave willingly, they would be removed by force.

"Do they have the right to do that?" said Margo.

"Theoretically, yes. But no government official wants to authorize mass evictions and get thousands of colonia residents mad at him. And if they do make people leave, these people were squatters to start with. It doesn't take much to find another empty hill and squat there."

Margo snagged her tape recorder from behind the seat and hit Record. "But these are people's homes. If this company *is* insisting on its right to the land, can't it give people some money to help them move? And what about the companies these people work for? They profit from the cheap labor. Why don't they help provide decent places for the workers to live? With running water or, at the very least, sanitary water barrels?"

She jumped, hearing a sudden metallic sound—Zeke crushing his soda can in one fist.

"Why . . ." —he drew out the word— "do you reporters always think someone owes these people? You get all up in arms about the miserable squatter settlements and how the maquiladoras exploit the pathetic Mexicans. What you never seem to understand is, the Mexicans are grateful for the maquiladora jobs, those jobs are a lot better than most jobs they could get in Mexico. And running water? Forty percent of the population of Tijuana doesn't have running water!"

Margo had feared he would preach at her about religion. She had struck a nerve with politics, instead.

"Look at it this way," Zeke said. "As squatters, these people don't have to pay rent, they don't pay utilities. They're getting a free ride. When they built on that land, they were taking the risk that someone might claim it someday. That's the trade-off for squatting.

"Anyway, that's my soapbox," he said, with an uncomfortable chuckle. "You're not going to put that on the radio, are you?"

"It's up to you. If it's how you really feel . . ." Margo reminded herself she wasn't doing an exposé on Reverend Ezekiel Holroyd. But she thought again of the rock that had blacked Zeke's eye. Was it really thrown by a naughty child, aiming at just any Anglo? Or had the rock hit the exact target for whom it was intended?

3 / Ezekiel's Fiery Chariot

Thank the Lord Mila had cleared up that problem with her boss at the hotel, thought Reverend Ezekiel Holroyd, climbing into his Samurai shortly after ten, following his Monday night prayer meeting in Rosarito. The town, some seventeen miles south of Tijuana, had for decades been known for a single tourist attraction, the pink stucco Rosarito Beach Hotel. Before easy air travel, the hotel had attracted Hollywood celebrities driving down to Mexico to get wild. In more recent years, an entire vacation industry had sprung up in Rosarito, new high-rise hotels pulling in scores of middle-class tourists coming to Mexico to get wild. It had also lured scores of Mexicans from the countryside to work as maids, waiters, and the like. Rosarito was fertile ground for people in need of spiritual guidance, as the simple country folks taking jobs at the hotels came face-to-face with the material wealth of *el norte*, and with the morals that many North Americans seemed to think loosened automatically the moment they crossed the border.

Six new people had attended the meeting tonight! Ernesto had brought a man who worked with him in maintenance, Veronica came with two other maids, and Pilar had brought her brothers and a teenage daughter whose sweet voice had soared on "De Colores." Zeke hummed the tune as he got onto the toll highway heading south.

He hadn't wanted to drive to Ensenada, another fifty miles south, but once on the road, he didn't mind that the person he was going to see had insisted on meeting there. What a perfect night God had created. Southern California usually turned chill the instant the sun set, a reminder of

its semi-desert climate. But the muggy summer was offering one benefit: balmy evenings like this, when it felt
blessed to step on the gas, the ocean wind whipping over
his body through open windows. The breath of the Lord.

About twelve miles south of Rosarito, Puerto Nuevo's
local lobstering industry had spawned two dozen or more
restaurants, all serving the same fare—broiled lobster,
beans, rice, tortillas, and pitchers of potent margaritas.
Thronged on the weekends, the place was quiet on a Monday, especially at ten-thirty. And south of Puerto Nuevo,
the traffic thinned to almost nothing. Zeke stepped harder
on the gas. It was amazing what the little Samurai could
do, Ezekiel's winged chariot.

USE THE LEFT LANE FOR PASSING ONLY, the signs said.
He pulled over to pass once or twice, but there was virtually
no one else on the road, except for one of the old U.S. gas-
guzzlers that Mexicans drove. Liking both cars and Mexicans, Zeke had given it some thought and decided
Mexicans didn't just buy the thirty-year-old American cars
because they were cheap, but because they loved those big
babies with their fins and rusted chrome.

He passed the car, a Caddie. Quite an engine this one
must have. Zeke was pushing eighty and the Caddie stayed
right behind him.

Much of the toll highway was separated from the ocean,
first by the old highway, which was slightly downhill. Beyond the old highway was a stretch of land, occupied in
some places by Mexican shantytowns and, in distinctly different places, by new communities being built for North
Americans, each white stucco townhouse with its satellite
dish linking it to the rest of the developed world. But just
past El Mirador, the spectacular viewpoint, the toll road
suddenly rose directly along the edge of the coastal foothills.

"Hallelujah!" Zeke shouted . . . to the night and to the
driver of the Caddie, who was still on his tail. His unseen
companion must be enjoying the magnificence of the scene
as much as he was.

As if in response, the old gas-guzzler accelerated and

moved into the left lane. Zeke was aware of the car moving to pass him in the side mirror. Then the car swung into him, just where the road dropped two hundred feet down the cliff!

Zeke wrestled the steering wheel back. He would have gone over except that the Samurai's right wheels rode up an escarpment. Praying out loud, he guided the car back onto the highway and pushed the gas pedal to the floor.

The other driver sped up, too, cutting Zeke off from switching to the left lane. The Caddie driver must be so drunk he was barely conscious. Taking the risk of steering with one hand, Zeke grabbed his flashlight from the passenger seat. He shined it at the other driver, hoping to awaken him to the danger. But Zeke was wrong, he saw as he directed the flashlight toward his assailant. The driver was not the *borracho*—the drunk—he had assumed.

The Caddie hit him again, this time with nothing between highway and air but a narrow shoulder and a few tufts of grass. Zeke's Samurai sailed over them effortlessly.

For a moment, as his car shot off the highway, Zeke prayed for the other driver's soul. But as the Samurai arced sideways toward the cliff, his good intentions vanished. He wished retribution and suffering on the person he had glimpsed in the flashlight beam—the person he had recognized.

The car smashed into the cliff, then rolled over and over, shattering bit by bit, as did Zeke Holroyd, on their descent to the sea.

4 / Porsche Man

What did it mean, anyway, to go around a church widdershins, and what was supposed to happen to you? thought Margo, walking from the parking lot to the back of Revelation of God Church early Tuesday evening. Did you have to go all the way around or was it enough to make a partial circuit, as she was doing, skirting the handsome faux-stone edge of the church and heading for the utilitarian aluminum trailer where Zeke Holroyd had his office? (As assistant minister, Zeke got the Spartan digs. Margo assumed the head man was housed inside the church proper.)

Although Zeke, calling yesterday, had arranged to meet her at six-thirty, the only other car in the parking lot was a few leaps up from Zeke's Samurai—a shiny new black Porsche.

Funny, Margo had an impression of activity as she approached Zeke's trailer. Her knock got no answer, however, nor could she say why she had thought there was someone inside. It was her night to fix dinner and she needed to get home, but the favor Zeke had offered was worth at least a few minutes' wait: information about various maquiladora companies, with notes indicating owners and managers Zeke knew who might be willing to be interviewed.

The spot was inviting, a well-tended lawn where, beside the trailer, ten child-size chairs formed a circle under a flowering magnolia tree. Folding herself into one of the chairs, Margo picked up a book from the ground—*The Faces of Satan*. According to the colorfully illustrated volume, the Prince of Darkness was ever-vigilant, waiting to pounce on the soul that didn't shun the world's temptations.

Curious to imagine what it must be like to regard Satan—
or evil, or whatever one named it—as a vivid presence in
one's life, as real as a neighbor or the checker at the corner
convenience store. Margo shuddered. In spite of the charming scene, the sweet little chairs beneath the fragrant magnolia, she felt as if she'd come into contact with something
twisted and ugly.

Again she sensed someone was in Zeke's office. She
even felt that she was being watched. Widdershins indeed!
Refusing to be spooked, she strode to the trailer and
pounded on the door. "Zeke, are you there?" But again
there was no response.

Zeke was now fifteen minutes late, and Margo returned
to the parking lot, still occupied by the black Porsche.
(Didn't the Porsche count as a worldly temptation?) She
started her car and drove half a block . . . but then turned
and came back to the parking lot. If the Porsche owner was
at the church, Margo might be able to get into Zeke's office;
maybe he'd left the information out for her. That way, she
would never have to set foot near Revelation of God again.
She started walking toward the main church entrance. A
man was approaching her from the back of the building.
Thirtyish, tall, and slender, the man wore a polo shirt and
slacks. She'd swear he jumped half a foot when he saw her.

"Hi. I was looking for Reverend Holroyd," she called,
nervous herself. Where could the man have come from except Zeke's trailer? And if so, why hadn't he answered her
knock?

"He's not here." The man nearly ran past her; she could
smell his sour, anxious sweat.

"He was going to leave something for me," said Margo.
"If I could just get in to see if it's there?"

He threw open the door of the Porsche and slid in, saying, "I'm running late," before slamming the door. He
ground the gears—couldn't anyone here drive a stick?—
and took off with a squeal of expensive tires.

Probably just a hard-core fundamentalist who could spot
a heathen at twenty paces, Margo told herself. Nevertheless,
the man had made her uneasy. She went back and checked

Zeke's trailer. The door was locked, with no sign of forced entry. Around the other side of the trailer, however, the sliding glass window was open and the window screen lay on the ground. One of the kiddie chairs stood against the trailer, perfectly placed for someone to climb in the window. Standing on the chair, Margo peeked inside. A desk, facing the opposite wall, had most of its drawers pulled open, as were the drawers of two metal file cabinets. Some two dozen file folders were scattered over the desktop and floor.

What now? she asked herself. Call the police? Probably the Porsche man was just a parishioner with a few problems that the church would prefer to keep "in the family." And did she really want to stick around the church until the police arrived? She was cooking tonight not just for Barry but for the kids, and there would be a minor mutiny if she showed up with Thai take-out one more time.

She settled for calling Zeke at home . . . but not until she had driven home herself and started water boiling for pasta. Zeke's line was busy. Margo tried calling again after dinner—still busy. How far was her responsibility supposed to extend? Why didn't Zeke have "call waiting"? At ten, she dialed the number one last time. An unfamiliar voice answered, a man who announced in hushed tones that Brother Ezekiel's earthly remains had been found in his car in the ocean that morning, his soul having been "called to God" from a cliff in Mexico the night before.

"Oh, shit," said Margo, hanging up the phone.

"What is it?"

She turned to Barry and opened her arms for a hug, then poured a glass of white wine and went to sit with him on the lumpy couch on the patio. She kept wanting to stroke her husband's hair or lean against him, her thoughts drawn less to the dead minister than to the sweet, timid young woman she'd met less than a week ago, the sweet young widow, now that Zeke had flipped his Samurai into the Pacific.

"*Are you a Christian?* No kidding, Barry, that was the

first thing Zeke's wife said to me when I gave him a ride home last week.''

In the dark, the patio's clutter—Margo's pottery wheel, several bicycles, garage sale furniture, pots of fresh herbs— faded into shadow and she saw again the Spartan, neat-as-a-pin apartment where the Reverend and Mrs. Ezekiel Holroyd lived. They had to be that, ''the Reverend and Mrs.,'' just as she and Barry were ''Margo Simon and Barry Dawes''—both couples responding to the changes in marriage of the past decades, but one embracing the changes and the other trying to turn back the clock. Except the Holroyds hadn't been as simple as that.

''It took me by surprise,'' Margo continued her recollection. ''Both the question, and the fact Zeke *hadn't* asked it, even though he and I had just spent hours together. I think he was a lot more confident in his beliefs than she was.'' A lot more confident in everything, she thought, recalling the young woman who scarcely seemed to possess an identity of her own. ''His parents were missionaries and so were their parents. He was so embedded in the church, I think he couldn't be threatened by someone who didn't believe exactly what he did. But his wife's a new convert. She's a senior at San Diego State and she just got involved in the church during her sophomore year. Zeke was doing a campus ministry, that's how they met. She even took a new name then—Lael, it means 'devoted to God.' ''

''What happened when you revealed you were of the Hebrew persuasion?'' Sticking to his diet, Barry was quaffing a mineral water with a slightly injured air. ''Did she make the sign of the cross? Offer to pray for you?''

''Actually, when I said I was Jewish, Zeke said, 'The people of the Book,' like that was a terrific thing. And they insisted on giving me dinner. I didn't understand at first, but when they talk about someone being a Christian, they only mean a fundamentalist. I got the feeling it's worse to be an Episcopalian or Lutheran than to be Jewish.''

''So they might have prayed over a lapsed Catholic like me.''

''Or me, if I'd admitted the only Jewish things I do are

lighting the Chanukah menorah and having a Passover seder once every three or four years. Hi, Grimalkin." Margo stroked the cat that had jumped into her lap. "As I said, I doubt Zeke cared one way or the other. Lael was the dogmatic one, but not because she's certain she's right; it's more like she's terrified she's not. A scared rabbit. Zeke was just the opposite; there was no fear in him. I guess that's why he drove the way he did. Damn." She knew the highway Zeke had gone over. It twisted up and down the coastal foothills between Tijuana and Ensenada, offering spectacular views. Spectacular drops, too.

"Sounds like a reckless streak in a spiritual leader," said Barry.

"Zeke wasn't the main minister, there's someone above him, probably suitably white-haired and godlike. Zeke was the one they sent on the road, doing the campus ministry and then the mission in Tijuana."

Barry wandered over to the herb pots and came back chewing on delicate fronds of dill. After dining on pasta with oil-free marinara and salad with lemon juice dressing, he clearly felt deprived. He would have loved the dinner the Holroyds served: chicken thick with barbecue sauce, salad with ranch dressing, and ice cream for dessert. Everything out of a 1950s sitcom about a happy American family, down to the nearly invisible wife. Lael had seemed so fuzzy, so out-of-focus . . . except for the odd scene that had happened in the kitchen, the one Margo recounted now.

"I went to ask Lael if I could help her with dinner," Margo said, sipping her wine. "She was standing at the sink washing lettuce and at the same time doing these incredible pliés—perfect turnout, not a vertebra out of place. I came up behind her and . . . Barry, it wasn't just that I startled her. She looked terrified. I said pliés were always murder for me, I was always too pigeon-toed to get a good turnout. Her eyes got huge and she said, 'Do you dance?' Whispering. I whispered, too, somehow it felt necessary. I told her about my improv class and how it's just for fun since we're too old to be serious dancers. For a minute, she and I were really connecting." And for that moment, Lael

Holroyd had seemed more real than at any other time. "I asked if she was a dancer—she looks like one, thin and wispy, with this glorious long blond hair. She got this look on her face, like the kids when they've really screwed up, and she said no. Do you think the church forbids dancing?" Margo lifted her bare feet into Barry's lap and wiggled her toes until he complied with the demand for a massage. "Ah . . . Wasn't it Emma Goldman who said she didn't want to be involved in a revolution if she couldn't dance? I'm with Emma."

"Margo." Barry kneaded the ball of her foot in a way that made her purr. "What if Zeke was abusing her? Not necessarily physically, but emotionally?"

Margo closed her eyes, took herself back to the Holroyds'. "I don't think so. Of course, with emotional abuse, it's hard to know." Not like the bruises on the young maquiladora worker's face—what was her name? Rosalia?

"If she's a new convert and not so established in the church's beliefs, maybe she wasn't supposed to talk to anyone who wasn't a church member. Say it was one thing for Zeke to invite you to dinner, a way to show how open-minded he was. But you weren't supposed to corrupt the help."

Margo shook her head vigorously. "They weren't like that. In fact, every time I thought I had her pegged or had their relationship pegged, it turned out I was wrong. For instance, she's majoring in marketing at San Diego State, so she can help Zeke with his ministry. Well, I figured she hated marketing and she was just studying it out of self-sacrifice. But then she talked about her courses, and she obviously enjoys them. The church lets her have a computer and she puts together fund-raising appeals for Zeke's mission in Mexico. She showed me a brochure she did, and it was excellent. She even studies the maquiladora industry to identify fund-raising prospects. In fact, she offered to put together a list of owners Zeke knows, who might be willing to let me see their factories."

Which had led to that afternoon's strange encounter with the Porsche man . . . a thought that was blasted from Margo's mind by shattering decibels of rap music.

"Should we flip for it?" sighed Margo.

"No, I'm sure I'll burn up five or ten calories telling her to turn it down." Grumbling, Barry hoisted himself up from the couch and went inside.

Margo took another sip of wine, trying not to feel more culpable than she already did. Seeing Barry in a bathing suit a few weeks earlier, she had found his teddy bearish body chunkier than the summer before, heavier, somehow, than without clothes. Still as sexy as ever—she preferred men who looked like grown-ups, rather than exercise fiends clinging desperately to physical (and often emotional) adolescence. With the thought, however, of averting heart attacks and other ills, she had gently asked if Barry had put on a little weight, a question that was not heard in the loving spirit in which it was posed. Margo had judiciously refrained from mentioning the subject again, but she *had* shifted to lower fat foods—as much as she could control the meals in a household where everyone, including the kids, took turns as the chef. She wondered if Zeke had ever done the cooking, and assumed he hadn't; but then, she'd been wrong each time she had made assumptions about Zeke and Lael.

A murmur of voices came from inside, Barry's calm, Jenny's petulant. Jenny had the last word, but the volume of the music decreased.

"Mission accomplished," said Barry, returning. "Are you going to go to Zeke's funeral?"

"I'll send a card, but it's Friday and there's a big maquiladora conference at the convention center. Besides, I didn't really know him. And no matter how much they like us 'people of the Book,' it doesn't mean they want us in their church."

As Margo spoke, she understood why the man in the black Porsche had seemed out of place at Revelation of God. As much as she detested being told she "didn't look Jewish," the man really had reminded her of the nice Jewish boys her mother used to urge her to date: crinkly dark hair, intelligent brown eyes behind horn-rimmed glasses, and fingers so slender and sensitive-looking that if he didn't play the violin already, it might not be too late to learn.

She drained the last of her wine and leaned back, breathing the summer perfume of sage and skunk. The patio overlooked one of San Diego's canyons and the smells, along with the danger of fire, were among the mixed blessings of living in a canyon house.

Even if the man were Jewish, Margo cautioned herself, he could be a "Jew for Jesus." But then why did no fundamentalist bumper stickers decorate his car, nothing but a decal for the San Diego Padres baseball team and a personalized license plate, "CALTI," which had no religious significance she was aware of?

Barry came over with a handful of pungent mint leaves and gave her one to nibble as he stroked her bare leg. She hadn't heard of mint being an aphrodisiac, but someone should add it to the list, she thought . . . no longer worrying about Porsches, dead ministers, or frightened women who danced in their kitchens in secret.

5 / These Pumps Weren't Made for Running

Margo had a soft spot in her heart for picketers. No matter that picketing as a political tactic had largely been appropriated by the religious right. Whenever Margo spied milling protesters, it was like hearing a favorite Joni Mitchell tune on the radio—a trip down Nostalgia Lane, back to candlelight marches at the University of Wisconsin and the heady conviction that she could win equal rights for women, or stop people buying lettuce at Safeway and help the farm workers, or end not only the war in Vietnam but the insane jockeying for power among nations that caused war in the first place. Just like Joni could promise eternal romance. Well, even Joni was married now. Older herself and arguably wiser, Margo's second, trained response to seeing a picket line was to turn on her tape recorder and get the story. But for a few seconds, when she drove up to the convention center for the maquiladora conference and spotted a cluster of people carrying signs outside, she felt that old twinge of excitement, the sense of having discovered kindred souls.

She parked in the underground garage, took the elevator to the first floor, and went outside. JUSTICE FOR MAQUILADORA WORKERS, said the first sign she read, edging past the police officers keeping the picket line away from the convention center entrance. It looked like light duty, since there were only a dozen or so picketers and none appeared poised to storm the barricades, or rather, to board ship, since the convention center's postmodern architect had played up the harbor front location by suspending hundreds of yards of canvas over the second floor terrace to suggest sails.

Among the picketers, Margo noticed Harry Rusk, a prominent local union leader, carrying a sign that said, U.S.–MEXICO LABOR UNITED. Rusk, known as "Mr. San Diego Labor," was the group's most likely spokesman, but Margo had interviewed him in the past and found him a world-class bullshitter. She scanned the rest of the protesters, hoping for another interview, and spotted a Latino whose strong, rather arrogant features looked familiar. At first glance, he reminded her of Antonio Gades, the brilliant dancer in Carlos Saura's flamenco films; the man walked as if his feet struck sparks. Then Margo realized she had actually seen him before—in Colonia Zapata, playing dominoes.

She fell into step with him. "Diego . . . Flores?" she said, fishing her memory for the name of the union organizer she had heard about in the colonia.

"Torres." He regarded her warily and said in Spanish, "Didn't I see you last week with Ezekiel Holroyd?" Not, from the way he said it, his favorite evangelist, dead or alive.

"Zeke was giving me a tour for a story I'm doing. I'm Margo Simon, KSDR Radio. Tell me why you're picketing."

Having replied in Spanish, Margo figured she'd passed his test. But Diego Torres didn't look any friendlier.

"There is a Mexican proverb," he said. "Poor Mexico. So far from God and so close to the United States." Fluent and barely accented, his English suggested a far better education than that of the workers he sought to represent. "U.S. businesses have been getting a free ride on the backs of Mexican workers. The maquiladoras don't pay people enough to live decently. They don't follow safety procedures, like giving the workers face masks or special clothing when they work with dangerous chemicals. They've created a crisis at the border by enticing people to move there for jobs but providing no housing or infrastructure.

And they're notorious for dumping toxins, which pollute both sides of the border, since air and water don't need green cards to get across.'' He waved his picket sign: AMERICAN MEDICAL ASSOCIATION CALLS BORDER ''VIRTUAL CESSPOOL.''

Torres continued, ''We—U.S.-Mexico Labor United— say if a U.S. company wants to locate a factory in Mexico, it has to meet U.S. standards of worker and environmental safety, and it should pay a living wage. In fact, why not hold this conference in Tijuana and show the real conditions in the maquiladora industry, instead of bringing people to this fantasyland?'' His sweeping arm took in the convention center, the neighboring high-rise hotels, and the quaint shopping center further down the harbor front, and seemed to accuse Margo by association.

Bravo! thought Margo, but wished she liked the messenger better. Torres had stepped out of the picket line and stood facing west, forcing her to squint into the morning sun, already brutal at eight A.M.

''I thought American labor opposed the maquiladoras because they take jobs from the U.S.,'' she said. ''I'm surprised representatives of U.S. unions are marching with you on behalf of maquiladora workers.''

''That's what the capitalist media want people to think, that U.S. workers and Mexican workers are enemies. You U.S. reporters, you say you're so objective. But who owns the radio station you work for, señora? General Electric? Standard Oil? The same people exploiting maquiladora workers, those are the people paying for your pretty clothes.''

Margo considered telling him about public radio, but she doubted a list of NPR's corporate sponsors would convince him she was untainted. Besides, she could do without his eyes traveling down her pale yellow linen suit and lingering on her legs. Hardly a new experience in the life of Margo Simon, Girl Reporter, and definitely not confined to interviews with macho Mexican men. Nevertheless, she felt a desire to place the two-inch heel of one of her pumps on Torres's instep, and grind.

"Thanks for your comments." She turned to leave.

"Your friend Zeke Holroyd, for instance," said Torres. "He screwed the people the same way they're getting screwed by the maquiladoras." The rage in his voice seemed undulled by the fact that his enemy was being buried that day.

Margo had started to walk away, but she stopped and switched the tape recorder back on. "What did he do?"

"Some of the women in Colonia Zapata used to do sewing for a U.S. maquiladora owner who brought the work to their homes. This man didn't file any papers with the government, he paid no taxes or benefits. And he leased the women these lousy manual sewing machines and deducted the leasing fee from their wages. Holroyd knew about this injustice. So what did he do? Just talked to the man, very friendly, you know, gringo to gringo."

"Did it help the women? What Zeke did?"

Torres scowled. "It happened before I came to the colonia, I don't know the details. I think the owner filed papers and stopped making the women pay for the sewing machines. Later he took the machines back; he went out of business, I guess. The point is, the case should have been pursued, it could have illustrated the abuses in the industry."

Whether the women benefited or not, thought Margo.

"You're a fighter, that's how you would have done it," she said. "It sounds like Zeke did make things better. He just didn't fight, he was a conciliator."

"Oh, Holroyd was a fighter. Only he didn't care about fighting for the people, getting them the money they deserved. The only money he ever fought for went to his church."

Hearing Torres's pelting syllables, the fluent English delivered with the urgent rhythm of Spanish, Margo had an image of the rocks pelting Zeke's Samurai the week before.

"Did you ever try to stop him?" she said.

"Stop Ezekiel Holroyd? The only thing I had to do was help the people open their eyes and look at the truth of their lives. Truth is a powerful weapon."

So, thought Margo, is a well-thrown stone.

A hearty "Damn!" came from one of the stalls in the women's bathroom inside the convention center, followed by, "Anybody got any clear nail polish?"

"Dorothy!" Margo called out with pleasure. She had first heard that two-pack-a-day bray nine years ago, telling her how to change her plugs in an auto maintenance class offered at a local women's center.

"Who is that? D'you have nail polish? I'm supposed to parade onstage at the start of this thing and I just got the Mother of all Runs in my panty hose." San Diego County Supervisor Dorothy Troupe emerged from the stall. "Margo, my love! How are you? How's life in the radio biz? I don't have time now, but I'd love to catch up. Clear nail polish?" she queried two other women at the sink, who shook their heads. "You don't have any, Maggie, do you? No, look at these." She grabbed Margo's hand. "Do you bite these scraggly things?" Dorothy's own fingers were tipped in a businesslike shade of muted coral.

"God, it's good to see you, lady!" Margo gave her a hug, glad that neither the glossy manicure nor a tailored suit in a stylish teal could make her old friend look like she had just breezed in from a political image-maker.

Dorothy may have had her long hair styled in a neat frosted coif and she'd replaced her dangly earrings with little gold circles, but she would always be more Janis Joplin than Nancy Reagan. Several of her nails were chipped and the suit bunched on her plump body. (Margo remembered how lovingly Dorothy used to put away pizza and jug wine, back when they'd both had more time to socialize.) And the snag in the supervisor's panty hose was prodigious; nail polish might stop the run from spreading, but it couldn't hide the gap where freckled skin showed through the off-white hose.

"To tell the truth," said Margo—Dorothy had always been someone she could tell the truth to—"I can't stand manicured nails."

Dorothy hooted. "Neither can I. They remind me of those Chinese emperors in *Ripley's Believe It or Not*, the guys with fingernails two feet long as a symbol they never had to wipe their own asses. I swear, someday I'm going to chuck all this and get a job as a forest ranger. Plain nails, let my hair go gray, and for Chrissake, no more panty hose."

"But not right away. I hear you're planning to run for Congress in the special election this fall."

Dorothy developed an intense interest in the lipstick she was applying; she smooshed her lips together, snagged a fleck off her tooth.

"Let's talk, Maggie," she said. "Really talk, like old times. Look, I'm out of here after I make my appearance this morning. What about tonight, will you come to Craig's party? Promise?"

"Who's Craig?"

"Craig LaBerge, King of the Shelter Companies, he's speaking this afternoon. He's giving a post-conference bash tonight and I want to see you there. You can get the address from Sean, he'll be here all day. Yeah, he works for me now, my own kid, all grown up. Just a volunteer internship while he's in college," Dorothy added quickly. "I wouldn't be dumb enough to put my son on the payroll these days, even if he was Bobby Kennedy." She hoisted up her skirt, wriggled out of the torn panty hose, and stuffed them into the trash. "Better than the run," she said, stepping barefoot into her beige pumps. Definitely Janis Joplin, thought Margo, accompanying Dorothy back to the conference hall.

Margo hoped the rumors about Dorothy running for Congress were true. In the three years Dorothy had served on the Board of Supervisors, she had learned to operate within the power structure. At heart, however, she remained the blue-jeaned activist who had led neighborhood groups to demand better police protection, decent parks, and community clinics. Sitting on the Board had only made her upgrade her wardrobe, not shift her loyalties. If anything, Dorothy could be too loyal, thought Margo, remembering Dorothy's third husband, an addict whom Dorothy had defended against all criticism. Only a fatal overdose had loosened that bond.

Sean was the son of Dorothy's second marriage, to a race car driver. Sean had had his own problems with drugs back then. Dorothy's son still didn't come across as a solid citizen, thought Margo, when she found him during a break. His hair a little greasy and his manner vague, Sean had grown into his dad's good looks, the kind that called for black leather and a Harley, not the sport jacket he uncomfortably wore. Margo wondered if the internship was Dorothy's way of propping Sean up, just as she had propped up Husband Number Three. Didn't she know that there was now a name for that kind of behavior, "codependency," and it was considered unhealthy? Thinking of how Dorothy would respond to such psychobabble, Margo almost interrupted the next talk, about prime industrial sites, by laughing out loud.

The conference lunch was alfresco, a buffet on the convention center terrace. Months ago, when someone was planning the event, it must have seemed lovely to imagine lunching under the canvas sail-roof as it billowed with the breeze from San Diego Bay. Today, however, the ship had hit the doldrums and the swabbies started drooping after just a few steps out of the air-conditioned building.

Margo draped her jacket over her arm and dragged herself to the buffet table at the far end of the terrace, too hot to appreciate the perfect view of the steel-blue bridge to Coronado Island arching across the bay. She eyed the spread, which seemed to eye her back, daring her to consume anything that had sat in the heat for even five minutes. She plucked a few mango slices from a carved pineapple, half-listening to the discussion taking place next to her, about the stricter regulation of maquiladoras promised by Mexico's environmental agency. Did the harsh fines recently levied against several companies signal a genuine change in policy, or were they only window dressing by a government that still couldn't afford the kind of environmental policing the border needed?

The speakers sounded knowledgeable. Margo looked up to ask if she could interview them . . . and met eyes, across the table, with the Porsche man from the church three days ago.

With a look of panic, the man took off into the crowd.

There was no reason a member of Zeke's church couldn't be involved in the maquiladora industry, Margo told herself, even as she abandoned jacket and plate (but not her tape recorder) and dashed around the table after him. Still, if the Porsche man *hadn't* broken into Zeke's office, why run?

He was tall enough that she could spot him running out the door to the bay side of the convention center. But when she got outside, he was nowhere in sight. He must have taken one of the long flights of stairs to the harbor. Left, toward the park? Or right, to lose himself among the buildings and crowds? Margo chose the crowds, racing down the steps and searching for the ripple the tall runner would make among the strolling tourists on the bay front walk. She didn't see him, but took off down the harbor front anyway. She got half a dozen steps before, hobbled by her narrow skirt, she tripped and sprawled.

Damn fashion!

She picked herself up with the help of an elderly couple from Michigan and sat on the low wall beside the walk, taking stock of the situation and her injuries. Her quarry must be long gone, she reflected, removing her shoes and rubbing her screaming toes . . . which had felt the impact of each concrete stair, her feet canted awkwardly in her pumps. She'd also scraped her knee in falling *and* landed on her tape recorder. The tape machine had survived, thank goodness, but her knee had bled onto her best skirt and she was going to have a monster bruise on her right hip.

What could the Porsche man have stolen from Zeke, anyway? she thought, squeezing her feet into her shoes and limping back toward the convention center. Had he snagged a dozen illustrated guides to identifying Satan in our midst? Maybe he'd behaved so strangely because he feared Margo was an emissary from the old Prince of Darkness, the way she had showed up asking for Zeke Holroyd just hours after his body had been found.

"Holy shit," she said under her breath. *She* hadn't known Zeke was dead when she went to the church three days ago. Had the Porsche man already heard the news?

She half-ran, half-limped into the convention center parking structure, hunting for the black Porsche with the CALTI license.

She passed Mercedeses, Cadillacs, and plenty of top-of-the-line trucks—*someone* was making money from the maquiladoras—but no black Porsche. Somewhere in the garage an industrial-strength car alarm went off. Shrill whistles filled the air . . . like the whistles going off in Margo's head about the late Zeke Holroyd, who was seeming less and less a simple preacher lending a helping white hand to the brown wretched of the earth.

What had Zeke been up to, that Diego Torres's hatred was unabated by his death? That Zeke's office had been ransacked only hours after his body was found? Was he taking money from someone in the maquiladora industry—for instance, from the Porsche man?—to encourage people not to fight the developers who wanted to kick them out of their homes? Ample reason for Torres's rage, and for the Porsche man to want to remove any evidence of Zeke's real purpose in the colonia.

She heard a groan.

Oh, come on! she told herself. It was just the last gasp of the car alarm.

Someone moaned again, this time she was sure of it.

"Who's there?" she yelled.

The moan, louder, answered.

She found Sean, Dorothy Troupe's son, lying on the ground between a Lincoln and a Mercedes. His jacket was torn and one of his teeth was lying, bloody, on the ground beside his bruised face.

6 / King of the Shelter Companies

The mariachi band was playing "Guantanemera," an ironic accompaniment—to anyone who knew it was a song of the Cuban revolution—for the well-dressed guests quaffing champagne at Craig LaBerge's post-conference party.

"*Con los pobres de la tierra, quiero yo mi suerte echar,*" sang the mariachis. *With the poor of the earth, I want to cast my luck.* Dorothy would appreciate the irony. Dorothy would be singing along with the band. She had picked up a lot of Latino culture over the years, out of genuine interest in her Mexican-American constituents as well as a pragmatic concern for getting them to trust an Anglo from New Jersey. Where the hell was Dorothy, anyway?

"It looked worse than it really is, the dental bill's going to be the worst part of it," Dorothy had insisted when Margo reached her at the hospital earlier. "And I'll be damned if I'm going to let an accident of Sean's make me miss a chance to see you. That kid! Can you believe he tripped over his own feet and then cut his head open on the door handle of a car!" Actually, Margo didn't believe it. Dorothy was talking fast. "Remember the time he sliced his foot open at the beach and you and I sat in the emergency room and snuck tequila from a bottle in my beach bag? God, I could use a drink now! I'm getting my ass over to Craig's as soon as I get Sean settled with some videos and a coupla burritos, and you'd better be there."

Margo had nearly protested that her own injuries cried

out for as quiet an evening as Sean was having. But Dorothy was persuasive, as always. Margo had settled for a quick shower and a change of clothes into a long, gauzy flowered skirt, a cotton sweater, and flat sandals. She'd left Barry, Jenny, and David arguing over what kind of pizza to order. David was pushing for not only no meat but no cheese because of the way dairy cows were treated, and Jenny was moaning that she didn't care what they got as long as they did it fast because she had to go to a friend's, but they'd better not even consider onions! At least Margo had escaped that domestic drama, she thought, biting into a piece of sushi.

The sushi was fantastic. And the setting! Framed by purple bougainvillea and cooled by the evening breeze, Craig LaBerge's exquisitely tiled patio could be the set for one of those soap operas about the rich and powerful, something with a title like *Captains of Industry*. Almost everyone Margo met was either a corporate executive or married to one.

As if from central casting, a lovely young girl floated by in a white dress, offering a tour of the garden. Margo's knee had stopped throbbing, helped by the two glasses of champagne she'd downed. She joined the ten or so people trailing the magic child onto a path down the lushly landscaped hillside. She had never thought of San Diego's southern suburbs as a high-rent district, but LaBerge's place in Bonita could have been plunked down in any of the pricey enclaves on the county's north coast, especially those where the houses occupied extensive grounds.

"A lot of plants that do well in Southern California originally came from Australia, South Africa, or the Mediterranean countries," said the poised young tour guide, who had introduced herself as LaBerge's twelve-year-old daughter, Miel—both French and Spanish for "honey," she informed them. "For instance, this tritonia, with the clusters of orange flowers, is native to South Africa, but it grows here like a weed."

Two waiters in embroidered *guayabera* shirts had followed them from the patio, bearing trays of champagne,

Mexican beer, and a delicacy Miel identified as shiitake mushroom pâté. Margo helped herself to a Carta Blanca beer and a cracker heaped with pâté. LaBerge was sparing no expense; the last time Margo had seen shiitakes in the market, the big, earthy-tasting mushrooms had cost twelve dollars a pound. Of course, the King of the Shelter Companies should make enough to feast on shiitakes and caviar nightly, if even one of the guests signed on as a client.

What LaBerge's and other shelter companies did, Margo had learned at the conference that afternoon, was establish and operate maquiladoras for businesses that were nervous about venturing into Mexico on their own. A client paid the shelter company a fixed amount per employee, out of which the shelter paid wages and benefits, rented factory space, and administered the paperwork and permits required by the U.S. and Mexican governments. LaBerge was vague about figures, except to emphasize that, with forty clients, his company was the biggest in the industry. However, shelters typically charged three to four dollars per worker per hour, Margo had learned; a little rough math suggested that with forty companies, employing perhaps fifty workers each, LaBerge must be bringing in some seventeen million dollars a year . . . out of which he paid only six million in wages and benefits. That left plenty of pesos to cover rent, paperwork, and incidentals like designer hors d'oeuvres.

Another waiter materialized with spicy Thai chicken satay on skewers. Margo helped herself. She didn't know how the Pacific Rim cuisine was going over with the other guests, many of them prospective maquiladora owners from the Midwest. But she was in food heaven.

"Enjoying the satay?" Craig LaBerge emerged from another path. Margo got out "Delicious" from a mouth full of chicken. He handed her another skewer of satay and took one for himself. Accompanying him was one of his clients, the president of a shoe company in Chicago or Pennsylvania who had a Tijuana factory; the man had spoken at the conference that afternoon.

"I told Miel she had to let me do part of the tour." LaBerge put his arm around his daughter, who smiled up at him, Beauty to his Beast. Both had the same thick, tawny hair, Miel's held prettily off her face with a schoolgirlish pink band. But where she looked charming, Craig La-Berge's shaggy thatch, echoed in thick eyebrows and a wiry goatee, made Margo think of the play *Hair*. She had a feeling LaBerge would laugh if she told him. For all the opulence of the party, the host seemed as comfortable kneeling in the dirt to display his agapanthus plants as he was lifting a glass of expensive California bubbly. Maybe that was the key to his success in a business in which he had to serve as a bridge between Harvard-educated CEOs and Mexican peasants drawn to Tijuana by the maquiladora jobs.

Father's and daughter's voices rose over the talk and music from the patio and the twilight chitter and rustle of the canyon. Something in the mix of sound struck Margo as foreign, however, as if she'd wandered off the set of *Dynasty* and stumbled into the kind of film where danger lurked around the next bend. "Stumble" was the operative word. Her sandals were scarcely walking shoes and she tripped, catching herself on the very friendly box manufacturer from Portland who had left "the little wife" at home.

Returning from the garden tour, she found Dorothy settled on a tiled bench, a half-full champagne glass in her hand.

"Dorothy, when you're elected to Congress, make a law requiring shoes women can walk in, will you?" said Margo, grabbing a fresh beer from a passing waiter and sitting beside her old friend.

"Sure thing. Anything else you want?"

"Yeah." Margo massaged her knee, which was aching again. "The Equal Rights Amendment. A ban on selling weapons to volatile governments that end up using them against us. And instead of wasting millions of acres producing grain to feed beef cattle, we should eat the grain ourselves." David's vegetarian politics must be making a mark. "When are you going to announce your candidacy?"

Dorothy took Margo's hand. "Friend to friend? Not politician to reporter?"

That she had to ask—and that Margo hesitated a beat

before answering—said a great deal about how both of them had changed. Margo thought back to what she and Dorothy were doing almost a decade ago, when they'd first met. Jobs, certainly, not careers. Margo, newly arrived in San Diego, had been waitressing, a skill acquired after she had dropped out of the University of Wisconsin; it was several years before she enrolled at San Diego State and finished her B.A. And Dorothy managed an auto body shop . . . or was that when she had crewed on fishing boats?

"Friend to friend," pledged Margo. "As long as I get a few exclusives along the way."

"Deal. Honestly," said Dorothy, "I don't know. The party's been courting me ever since Bryson got the judgeship and left the House of Representatives. They're making all kinds of promises about the money they can put behind me, but you know what you can buy with promises." She drained her glass and twisted it in strong, tense fingers. "I've always been partial to that slogan, 'Think globally, act locally.' What I really care about is dealing with issues that affect neighborhoods, not screwing around with national policy. Of course, lately a lot of neighborhood issues are national issues. Like community clinics—we used to be able to get real results working at a local level or at most going to the state. Now you talk about community health and you're dealing with national health care reform."

"That's why we need you in Washington."

"Whoa!" Dorothy tried to drink from her empty glass and went back to fingering it. "It's one thing to sit on the County Board, a good old gal like me. But everyone in Congress is a lawyer. All I've got is a high school degree. And face it, I wasn't paying much attention in high school, with Jerry sitting next to me." Jerry was Dorothy's first husband, whom she'd married right out of high school; seven months later she'd had her first child. "But enough about me, Maggie. Tell me what you were doing at the conference today."

Margo explained about the story on the maquiladoras.

"By the way," Margo added, "did you know Zeke Holroyd?"

"That little shit! I've shocked you, haven't I?"

"You know he's dead, don't you?"

Dorothy lit up a cigarette, coughed vigorously for a moment. "Ah, that clears the lungs. Look, I wouldn't wish anyone dead. Well, a broken leg, maybe. But that church is in my district and the old minister and I always understood we were diametrically opposed on every significant issue. I didn't waste time trying to win him over and he didn't waste energy on me—a picket line outside my office once a year, maybe."

"What do you mean, the old minister? Isn't he still there?"

"Zeke was taking over. And *he* didn't ignore me. All smarmy friendliness and pancake breakfasts and twisting my arm to appear on panels where I was the only person to the left of Ronald Reagan. I don't know how well he knew his Bible, but he could quote chapter and verse on the number of fundamentalists in the district, and he knew exactly how it would look if I kept turning their invitations down."

Dorothy tried to drink from her empty glass again.

"Let me get you a refill," offered Margo. "More champagne?"

"Actually, tonic water, and I'd love more, thanks."

"I thought you were dying for a drink, after all the hassle with Sean."

"I was. I am. But I stopped drinking about a year ago. No shit. I did it out of vanity. A twenty- or even a thirty-year-old woman can be real cute when she's had a few, especially if she knows how to keep her pants on. And at forty, you kinda get off on drinking the guys under the table. But I turned fifty last year and believe me, there's nothing attractive about a fifty-year-old broad with a snootful."

The same might apply to fifty-year-old men, thought Margo, noting Harry Rusk, the union leader, in a boozy and somehow illicit-looking huddle with Pete Demetrides, a partner in a local law firm that had created a special department to aid maquiladora owners. Not that political foes couldn't drink together. But what would Diego Torres and the rest of U.S.-Mexico Labor United think if they knew how Mr. San Diego Labor was spending his Friday night?

Barry and David had just finished a game of chess when Margo got in. She made a bowl of popcorn (no butter) and offered it to them, along with the part of her evening she thought her stepson would enjoy.

"We were walking deeper into the canyon, Davey, and I heard these very weird sounds. I couldn't place them, but I kept thinking of jungles. I saw this wooden structure ahead of us and I thought the sounds were coming from there. Squawks and shrieks! But I still couldn't figure out what they were."

"Tropical birds," said David.

"Excellent deduction, Watson." She hoped David's frown was only a facial reflex to hearing anything from an adult. "The structure turned out to be this incredible aviary. Craig collects parrots—did you know the term *parrot* includes macaws and various other birds? He has about two dozen, and we could only go in a few at a time so we wouldn't upset them. You should have seen the plumage! There was one whose tail was two feet long. In fact, he said if you ever wanted to see them, Davey, I could bring you over. What is it?" She was unable to ignore the boy's grimace any longer.

"They belong in the wild. Putting animals in captivity is torture."

Oh, Davey! she almost groaned. It had been a long day and she'd hoped to please him with the aviary. And although he had a point, she wasn't up to a fresh tale of animal abuse tonight. She slipped away to take a very long bubble bath.

7 / God's Will

"Remember, this is your public radio station." Although Margo heard the words, she was barely cognizant of speaking them herself. "We depend on the support of our listeners to broadcast 'Weekend Edition,' the outstanding National Public Radio program you're hearing this Saturday morning, the first day of our pledge drive. Please give us a call at eight seven three, fifty-four hundred and become a member of KSDR."

She had been doing the on-air fund-raiser for two hours—pitching for ten minutes each half-hour—and she felt as if she were talking with a pillow in front of her face. No, actually the pillow was embedded in her brain, thick feathers spilling from her mouth instead of coherent speech. (Didn't that happen to a princess in a fairy tale? Or did she utter toads?) If Dorothy had quit drinking at fifty out of vanity, Margo at thirty-eight had discovered her own reason to say no to booze: a fear of rampant stupidity. After the mix of beer and champagne at Craig LaBerge's party the night before, this morning she could barely recall the station phone number, much less deliver it with the combination of warmth and urgency that got listeners to call and pledge money. And, of course, she was pitching with her tough new supervisor, rather than with a buddy to whom she could confide her sorry condition and who would take up the slack.

Claire De Jong didn't believe in slack. Sitting across the table from Margo, her sleek little blond head bent toward the microphone, KSDR's news director exuded—to Margo's sense of smell, which was nauseatingly acute at the moment—the odors of styling mousse and chlorine. Claire had probably leaped out of bed at six and swum two miles before coming to work. "Blond Ambition," as Margo privately called her, was training for a triathlon.

Not, Margo reproached herself, that it was Claire's fault she had impressed Alex Silva, the new station manager, when they had worked together at National Public Radio in Washington, D.C., or that Alex had recruited her for KSDR. Alex was the one who'd made everyone miserable in the eight months since he had become manager, dangling promotions in front of some and axing others. Claire was simply an outstanding reporter, with a never-take-lunch dedication that Margo attributed to her being only twenty-five, a child of the get-ahead eighties, just as Margo was shaped by the idealistic years earlier. (In her opinion, much of the sixties had actually happened during the following decade. People who maligned the seventies as the "Me Decade" were just sore because a lot of women had said "me" for the first time.)

Nevertheless, Margo wished Claire were a little less perfect. Or at least, she wished her supervisor weren't closer in age to her stepdaughter than to herself.

"There are volunteers here at the station waiting to take your call," boomed Claire. Like a surprising number of women in radio, she was petite but had a BIG voice.

Claire looked up—Margo's cue? No, thank goodness, it was time for their break. Margo intended to spend the full twenty minutes in her office, the door closed and her throbbing head on her arms. When she entered the hallway, however, a volunteer handed her a message: Lael Holroyd had called.

Margo took two aspirin, then returned the call.

"I heard you on the radio this morning," Lael said softly. "I just wanted to thank you for the sympathy card."

"Sure, you're welcome. How are you doing?"

"Oh, everyone's been really nice. The funeral was yesterday and a lot of people came over after." Tentative, as if she wanted something.

"If there's anything I can do . . ."

"Oh, no. I just wanted to thank you. I don't know, maybe you have to work all day. Well, people are coming today, too, if you'd like to."

"Um . . ." All Margo wanted to do, when she finished her four-hour shift at KSDR, was escape to her patio and lose herself in the soothing rhythm of throwing pots. Her hands itched so much to plunge into Black Mountain clay, she could almost feel it coating her fingers.

"I get off around one," she heard herself say. "Is that okay?"

"Oh. Oh, yes, one would be fine. And don't worry about lunch. Everyone from church has brought over tons of food."

Margo took another aspirin. Why had she agreed to go to Lael's? Had she really heard, in the voice of Zeke Holroyd's widow, not just invitation but need?

At least Lael hadn't exaggerated about the "tons of food," thought Margo, loading a paper plate with assorted salads and a turkey and avocado sandwich. Fortunately, she was able to concentrate on chewing—yum, the turkey was the real thing, not slimy processed slices—without having to say much. It was sufficient to nod from time to time as the Reverend Paul van den Moeller emoted from the room's fattest chair.

A big man, the head minister of Zeke's church fully, joyfully occupied his bulk; no thin man struggling to get out, but a spiritual CEO whose authority demanded a stout earthly vessel. Fat, pink, well-groomed hands alternately punched and glided through the air, as van den Moeller larded his outpouring of sadness with Bible quotes. The Bible had plenty to say about untimely death, some of it quite beautiful, especially delivered in the minister's stirring bass. He reminded Margo of Ronald Reagan—grandfatherly, theatrical. Tears glistened in his eyes but never interfered with the resonance of his voice. A cynic might opine that van den Moeller felt less grief than he was expressing, especially a cynical unbeliever who suspected the deceased had coveted his boss's job. (What had Zeke said the night she'd had dinner there? That the fund-raising he was doing on behalf of his mission in Tijuana was a lot more successful than what the church did for itself? Zeke had implied that the old guard might be satisfied with saving a few souls, but the minister of the nineties had better keep the money coming in.)

Van den Moeller was hooking most of this audience, at any rate. The half dozen people sitting around the small apartment sniffled away, calling out occasional amens.

Except for Lael.

Pale, wearing a black cotton dress so big on her it made her look like a child costumed for Halloween, Lael sat on the couch with her eyes closed, grasping an older woman's hand. Several times the woman handed her a small brown paper bag that Lael held over her nose and mouth for several minutes; "the poor thing" had been hyperventilating, Margo was told during a lull in van den Moeller's oratory. The woman attending to Lael was Reverend van den Moeller's wife, Judy, and the other visitors were all members of the church. Zeke's folks were trying to get back as soon as they reasonably could from their current mission in Africa.

"What about Lael's family?" Margo asked the man who was filling her in.

He looked startled to be reminded Lael had a family, but then recalled that her mother and a brother had flown in from somewhere outside Sacramento earlier in the week and stayed through the funeral yesterday.

"But they're not Christians," he said, as if that explained everything.

Margo remembered that to Zeke and Lael, "Christian" only referred to fundamentalists. In fact, even among the fundamentalists, it must be tough to keep track of who was on the bus and who was off. For instance, Margo was certain some groups prohibited smoking, but two people were puffing away as van den Moeller orated about the Will of God.

Margo had just helped herself to a piece of carrot cake when Reverend van den Moeller lifted his bulk from the chair. There was a flurry of hugging and saying "Praise the Lord" and covering salads with plastic wrap; and in moments everyone else had gone.

"I guess I should take off, too," Margo said, swiftly forking in the carrot cake.

"Oh, no." Lael grabbed for the paper bag and breathed into it.

Margo rubbed Lael's back, feeling the thin body quivering. She had no idea why Lael had requested her company in the first place, a quasi-heathen she barely knew. But it was easy to understand Lael's fear of being alone. Didn't anyone from the church, anyone close to her, have the sense to know that? What was Margo supposed to do now? Although she was empathetic—and often in danger of getting too emotionally involved in stories—she had never been the Earth Mother type. A lost child was more likely to run instinctively to Barry for comfort than to her.

"Do you want to walk on the beach?" she asked. Hardly a contender for the Earth Mother prize for aid to the bereaved, but Lael nodded.

The apartment was only a few blocks from the ocean, even though you couldn't go in much, Lael said, what with the frequent sewage spills from Tijuana that contaminated the water here in Imperial Beach. She and Margo took off their shoes and skittered over the sand, scorching in the mid-afternoon, to the cooler, damp water's edge. Lael walked listlessly, the overlarge black dress billowing around her thin calves. She didn't seem the type to use makeup, but someone had put blusher on her; around the pink oblongs on her cheeks, her face was bloodless, that of a porcelain doll. Margo pulled out the paper bag for hyperventilation that she had tucked into the waistband of her slacks. Lael shook her head no, her long blond hair blowing across her face. She looked more ephemeral than ever, like one of the characters in *Star Trek* dematerializing on the transporter pad.

"What are you studying in school? Besides marketing?" asked Margo. If Lael talked, it might force her to breathe normally.

Lael didn't seem to hear.

"Are you into science? History?" Margo wondered what subjects wouldn't clash with church doctrine. Geology involved the formation of the planet, in considerably more than six days. Literature had to be a mine field of sin.

"Spanish. You know, for doing missionary work."

A scared rabbit, Lael had seemed when Margo met her ten days ago. A hunted rabbit now, panic in her eyes. No wonder. If you believed in a God whose Will would smack your husband off a cliff in Mexico, wouldn't you be terrified He'd cross the border and come after you next?

"Lael?"

Lael had taken off, dashing across the sand. Margo didn't go after her. Better to give her some space. And whatever had made Lael run, it was the first sign of life and energy she'd displayed.

Feet pounding, the same rhythm as the words in Lael's head:

> For your hands are stained with blood,
> your fingers with guilt.
> Your lips have spoken lies,
> and your tongue mutters wicked things.

Lael hit the hard, hot pavement, still barefoot, and kept running.

> Your hands are stained with blood.
> Your hands are stained with blood.

The pavement burned the soles of her feet, but she didn't feel a thing.

8 / Atonement

Margo put on her shoes and walked back to the apartment, thinking she had better round up someone to keep Lael company, someone motherly.

Lael already had another visitor. A tall, slender black man was talking to her outside the door of her apartment. As Margo came up, the man reached into his breast pocket and handed Lael a card—Margo saw that the card was embossed, as elegant as the man's dove-gray suit.

"I wish I could delay this, Mrs. Holroyd," he said. "But you understand, the sooner I get all the information I need . . . If I could just come in for a few minutes?"

Lael looked dazed. "He's from the insurance company," she told Margo, unlocking the apartment door.

"Lael." Margo made sure Lael was looking at her. "You don't have to see him right now. I'm sure this could wait a few days."

"Mrs. Holroyd, it's very important," the man said.

Pop psychologists had probably written books about the kind of dynamic the three of them had established so rapidly. The insurance agent would be called something like "the Persecutor" and Margo would play "the Rescuer." Lael could never be anything but "the Victim."

"It's okay, Margo," murmured Lael.

"I sure would appreciate a glass of something cold, Mrs. Holroyd." The man took the big chair Paul van den Moeller had occupied. In it, however, he managed to look smaller than he really was, less authoritative. It occurred to Margo that he was being intentionally disarming.

"Hi, I'm Ashley Green," the man said, while Lael was

in the kitchen. "Are you Mrs. Holroyd's sister?"

"Just a friend. Margo Simon." She shook his proffered hand, mentally kicking herself. She wouldn't have shook hands if the insurance man were white. But her whole family had taken part in the first civil rights march cosponsored by her synagogue when she was twelve, and she had kept on marching for years. All right, it was reverse racism, but she couldn't snub Ashley Green.

Lael came in with glasses of iced tea for Green and Margo, then sat in a straight-backed chair, a schoolgirl ready for a quiz.

"We just need to go over a few facts, Mrs. Holroyd." Ashley Green's voice was soothing, with a hint of a Southern accent. "Last Monday night, the night of his unfortunate accident, I understand your husband was at some kind of meeting in Rosarito Beach, that's just south of Tijuana?"

"A prayer meeting, he led a prayer meeting in Rosarito every Monday night."

"From when to when?"

"Usually it started at eight and ended around nine-thirty." Lael had pulled herself together, a good student giving concise answers in a clear, soft voice—a poise belied by her bare feet, which twisted around each other under the chair.

"Any reason he'd be driving south afterward?"

"South?"

Green nodded. "Toward Ensenada. Instead of coming straight back to the U.S."

"Is that where he crashed?" Margo demanded. Lael might docilely cooperate with the insurance man, but Margo believed in questioning authority.

"Yes, just beyond a point called El Mirador. About thirty miles south of Rosarito." Green answered Margo's question, but he addressed Lael. "As I said, Mrs. Holroyd, would your husband have gone in that direction after his meeting?"

"I don't know," said Lael. "I guess, if someone was sick or they had some kind of problem and wanted him to visit."

"Is that something he did quite often? After the meeting, went to see someone?" The questions came leisurely, as if Green were shooting the breeze on an old wooden porch. A real pro.

"I don't know. Sometimes."

"Mrs. Holroyd, where do you think he was going?"

"Like I said, one of the people from the Rosarito meeting might have asked him to come see them. Maybe someone brought him a message that night, asking him to visit a family."

"What does it matter?" Margo broke in.

"Just a few technicalities. You wouldn't believe the forms we have to fill out."

He proceeded to ask in a friendly way if Zeke ever used to put away a few beers or tequilas with his Mexican friends after the prayer meeting, or if he ever used drugs.

Lael looked shocked, and Margo declared, "Reverend Holroyd was on a twisting road in the dark, driving a car that had a reputation for turning over when the driver did evasive maneuvers. Obviously, an animal ran across the road or maybe there was a drunk driver. Zeke swerved. The car flipped over." Another factor was the daredevil way Zeke drove, but there was no reason to reveal that to the insurance man.

"Well, you know how it is." Green again spoke to Lael. "A consumer group made those charges about the Samurai, but turns out the charges were never proved by U.S. government testing. Now, that's not to criticize the consumer group. Believe me, my wife and I always follow their recommendations when we buy a toaster or anything like that. It's just that my company has to consider every possible reason the reverend might have lost control of his car. I'm very sorry, Mrs. Holroyd, for having to bother you with these questions at such a difficult time. Just a few more minutes, if I may? It will help us expedite the claim."

Lael nodded, but her feet writhed.

"Was your husband a cheerful person?" Green smiled cheerfully himself.

"Oh, yes. Very."

"Anything bothering him lately?"

"Mr. Green!" objected Margo.

Either too numb with grief or too innocent, Lael didn't seem to understand what Green was getting at. "Zeke was really excited," Lael said. "The Tijuana mission was going so well. If anything, he was more excited than usual."

"So there was no reason," Ashley Green said very softly, "that your husband might have taken his own life?"

Lael swayed on her chair.

Ashley Green jumped to catch Lael as she fainted. After making sure she was breathing, he lifted her onto the couch and elevated her feet onto a pillow.

"Give me a couple of those ice cubes?" he said to Margo. She fished two cubes out of her glass and handed them to him. Rubbing the ice over Lael's temples and neck, he asked Margo to get her something to drink.

"Isn't there anything stronger?" he said, when she returned with a glass of apple juice. "Brandy or something?"

"That's what she was trying to tell you. They're fundamentalists. They don't drink, they don't do drugs." As capably as Green was dealing with Lael's faint, he had provoked it by badgering her.

Lael opened her eyes. "What happened?" she gasped, trying to sit up.

"You just passed out for a minute, honey," Green said kindly. He took the glass from Margo and supported Lael as she drank.

"I'm sorry," she said. "I'm okay now. Really."

"No rush," said Green. "You just lie here awhile. Have you eaten anything today?"

"I don't know."

He directed Margo to see what she could find in the kitchen. She felt like a nurse being ordered to produce surgical implements. Scalpel. Clamp. Potato salad. But the doctor was damn good and she compliantly assembled a plate of sandwiches and salads from the copious leftovers in the refrigerator.

"Have you done this before?" she asked Green. Lael, at his urging, was managing to eat most of the food.

"I've got kids." Evasive, a professional questioner who disliked answering questions himself. "Are you going to be able to stay with her?"

"I don't need . . ." said Lael.

"Sure you do," said Ashley Green.

"I really can't," said Margo, but offered to call Judy van den Moeller. Following Lael's directions, she found the Holroyds' phone—with the van den Moellers' number programmed in—on the desk in the bedroom, along with a computer, two Bibles, a college dictionary, and a directory of maquiladora companies. She reached Judy van den Moeller right away and received a cheerful promise that someone would be there within an hour.

Solicitous as he had been, Ashley Green clearly hadn't lost sight of the information he desired. When Margo returned to the living room, he was gently holding Lael's hyperventilation bag to her face . . . and asking whether Zeke could have been taking any medications—antihistamines for hay fever, for instance—or if he had a history of epilepsy.

"For God's sake, let her alone!" Margo snapped.

"Just one more little technicality," he said. He got Lael to sign a release so he could retrieve Zeke's car from the Mexican police.

After Green had left, Margo went back to the bedroom to phone Barry and tell him she was waiting for the church sympathy squad to arrive. Again she noticed the maquiladora directory. Of course! She brought the directory into the living room.

"Lael, have you ever heard of a maquiladora called . . . CALTI?" she asked, finding in the directory the name she had seen on the license of the black Porsche. "Or Robert Kohler?" Kohler was listed as the company's owner.

"I don't think so. What do they do?"

"Manufacture women's clothing." Margo skimmed the entry in the directory. "Established two years ago. Eighty employees. Did Zeke ever mention them? . . . Lael, are you all right?'' Margo had rebuked Ashley Green, but here she was pushing her own questions at Lael, who was white-faced, holding a half-full pack of cigarettes in her hand.

"Oh. Yeah. I guess someone must have left these." Slowly Lael put the cigarettes down on the end table. "What were you asking about?"

"A company called CALTI. But it's not important."

"It's all right. I don't think I've heard of them. Oh, did you ever get the list of maquiladora owners I prepared for you? The ones Zeke knew, who might let you look around?"

"No, but you don't have to . . ."

"I bet it's right on the desk." She went into the bedroom and came back with a manila folder. "You can borrow the directory, too."

"Thanks, I'd like to."

Lael picked up the pack of cigarettes again, shook it so a couple of filter ends stuck out, and extended the pack. "I should have asked if you wanted one. Do you smoke?"

"Not anymore."

Lael took the cigarettes to the wastebasket, but hesitated. "So many people have been coming over, I'm sure someone would like these."

Margo recognized the signs. "Y'know what I hated when I first tried to quit smoking? I used to dump half a pack of cigarettes into the trash, this was when I lived in Santa Fe. Then I'd go outside, even in the middle of winter, and rummage through the trash for them. In fact, even worse, sometimes I'd take a scissors and cut a whole pack of cigarettes in half and throw them out. Two hours later I'd go looking for the filter halves and I'd smoke those."

"I used to roll my own," Lael confided. "No filters." She was still clutching the pack.

Margo hesitated a moment, then said, "You know, I would never, ever encourage anyone to smoke, but you're under enormous stress. And that brand has really low tar. I think at the moment you should do anything that makes you feel a little better."

"Oh, I shouldn't. . . . Really?"

"Yeah. I'll take the cigarettes with me when I leave, so you won't have them around." Margo felt like Satan tempting an innocent, but Lael seemed like an innocent who needed permission to brush her teeth in the morning.

Lael took out a cigarette and placed it between her lips. A pack of matches was slipped under the cellophane of the wrapper. She pulled out the matches and lit the cigarette, inhaling deeply. She giggled nervously. But she looked more relaxed.

"I guess just one is all right. I've already been atoning," she said on a long exhale.

"Atoning?" Margo's personal knowledge of atonement was limited to "Day of . . . ," the annual twenty-four-hour fast in which Jews worldwide cleaned the slate collectively. Her understanding of how the concept worked in Christianity was that one expiated one's sins on an individual basis. But that meant one had to sin first. "I didn't think your church opposed smoking."

"It doesn't. But we have personal contracts with the Lord, in addition to following the standards He sets for all of us." Lael reeled off the words as if she'd learned them by rote.

"And if you violate your personal contract, you have to atone?"

"Uh-hmm." Lael leaned back, eyes closed. Margo knew the feeling. She'd taken an occasional drag after having quit and it was dizzying, a little like being high.

"Lael, how did you atone for smoking?"

"Stopped dancing." Lael was still leaning back, as if half-asleep; Margo wondered how much she *had* slept since Zeke's death. "I started as a dance major at State, before I was called of the Lord. I switched to marketing then, to help Zeke, but I kept going to my ballet class. Zeke didn't like it, he said it was part of my old life I needed to cast away. But I really did cast away a lot, I saw how sinful it was. . . . " She paused, her face white, and Margo started looking for the hyperventilation bag. But Lael regained color and said, "But with dance, well, you're a dancer, you understand. I started dancing when I was seven, I thought I couldn't live without it.''

The combination of grief, irregular eating and sleeping, and nicotine must have lowered Lael's barriers. She'd probably feel uncomfortable with Margo later, the stranger on the airplane to whom she had revealed too much. But she seemed to want to talk. Maybe that was even why she'd wanted Margo there—as someone outside her normal life, whom she didn't have to see later on.

"I can't imagine not dancing." Margo was appalled at the picture of Ezekiel Holroyd that was emerging.

"See, you do understand. And I agreed with Zeke that modern dance and jazz were too wild. But not ballet. You know,'' she appealed. "Ballet is so disciplined. And I thought I'd do something with the children in my Sunday school class, teach them a dance for the Christmas pageant.''

"Was it your idea, to atone for smoking by giving up your dancing?''

"Zeke's and mine. He helped me.'' Her eyes filled with tears.

Margo felt like crying as well—in rage at the thought of Zeke Holroyd manipulating Lael to drop her former interests, no differently than any jealous husband . . . but under the guise of leading her to spiritual salvation.

9 / Gringa in Mexico

It was only a partial eclipse, a corner of the moon passing over the sun. Still, it subtly altered the quality of the light on Monday afternoon, just at the time Margo crossed the border into Mexico. Maybe that was why she felt uneasy, the quiver of difference in the light, a blood-memory of primitive ancestors who had fled screaming from the eaten sun. More likely and prosaically, she was nervous because she had never before driven into Tijuana alone. With the exception of her tour with Zeke, all previous trips to Mexico had been for pleasure—jaunts to seafood restaurants, camping trips down the coast, the kinds of things one did with friends. Today her purpose was purely business, a visit to one of the maquiladoras recommended by Lael.

After leaving the radio station, she had filled the gas tank and checked everything she could think of: oil, water, tires, battery. And she made sure to stop for Mexican auto insurance, driving to the main San Ysidro border crossing, where half a dozen offices sold the short-term coverage. Zeke hadn't bought any insurance when they'd crossed at Otay Mesa, but he used to go to Mexico so often he must have had some kind of binational policy. Except, didn't Mexican law stipulate that only Mexican insurers could cover drivers there? Margo had heard horror stories about U.S. citizens who'd had accidents and landed in Mexican jails if they weren't carrying the Mexican insurance . . . and sometimes even if they were. Funny, she wondered if Ashley Green represented a Mexican insurance company.

Holding her breath, Margo negotiated one of Tijuana's notorious traffic circles. *Glorietas*, the traffic circles were called, in some kind of surreal joke, since the same word, *glorieta*, means a "peaceful arbor." Held up in traffic, she glanced nervously at the directions she'd written down. Not only was this her first solo trip, she had to drive further into Tijuana than she ever had before; the factory she'd arranged to visit was five miles south of the border.

More breathlessness: Tijuana economized on stoplights. There were virtually none. Instead, the front lines of cars at each packed intersection jockeyed for the right-of-way, courteously—with very few blaring horns—but never completely predictably.

How ironic, she thought, that Zeke hadn't crashed in crazy traffic like this but on the Ensenada highway, which must have been relatively empty on a weeknight. What *was* he doing, thirty miles south of his prayer meeting? But that was no mystery, even if Ashley Green had made it sound like one. As Lael had said, Zeke was probably going to see someone from his prayer group. The real mystery, Margo realized, was why it made the slightest difference, in terms of Zeke's auto insurance, where he was going or whether he'd taken antihistamines or even cocaine. He'd had an accident, he died, the insurance should pay up. Unless taking drugs nullified the policy? Or maybe Green suspected the accident was a fake and Zeke was now lolling around someplace tropical—Cabo San Lucas, Mazatlán—waiting for Lael to collect on the insurance and join him? That was even more ludicrous than the notion of Zeke committing suicide. His body had been recovered from the wreckage of the Samurai and buried three days ago.

Margo pulled over for a moment, checked her directions again, let out a sigh of relief. One more turn and she reached her destination.

During the next hour, at least eighty-five percent of her mind focused on learning about the workings of a factory that produced the majority of books of carpet samples used by retailers throughout the U.S. Another pesky fifteen percent, however, kept whispering insistently: What was Ashley Green really looking for? Why did Green want Zeke's wrecked car? Could there possibly be a black insurance agent named after the slave-owning Southern gentleman in *Gone With the Wind*?

And Green wasn't the only person who had displayed a suspicious interest in the late Zeke Holroyd.

"Have you ever heard of a maquiladora called CALTI?" Margo asked at the conclusion of the interview. "Owned by a man named Robert Kohler?"

"Sure, Bob Kohler. Young guy," the factory owner said. He added, "CALTI's right on the next street over from here."

Fate, in the person of the chubby maquiladora owner missing half a finger (a casualty of one of his own machines) couldn't have spoken more clearly if it had screamed in her ear.

Margo didn't see the black Porsche when she drove into the parking lot at CALTI, and she felt relieved. She had no idea what she would have said to Robert Kohler. *I just happened to be in the neighborhood and I wondered what you were searching for in Zeke's office?* Better, she thought, entering a brightly decorated lobby, to find out whatever she could about Kohler before confronting him.

"I'm sure I was supposed to come interview him this afternoon!" she improvised to the receptionist, when told that Kohler was at sales meetings in Los Angeles all day.

"I'm so sorry," said the receptionist, a heavily made-up young woman who wore a brilliant red dress—one of CALTI's products? Women's clothing manufacture, the directory had said.

"Darn, I really wanted to see the factory. I made a special trip."

"I'm sorry," the receptionist said again.

Margo didn't leave.

The receptionist got on the phone and produced Beth-Ann Gilling, the company's senior designer.

"Oh, man, it's an awful day." Beth-Ann Gilling looked it, tugging at the short blond curls that stuck out damply and unevenly from her head. Slender and youthfully dressed in a mid-thigh-length T-shirt and print leggings, on a good day she probably looked no older than thirty-five. At the moment, however, it was clear she was in her forties, her smudged attempts at makeup emphasizing the circles around her eyes.

"If you could just take ten minutes and show me around, answer a few questions?" coaxed Margo.

Beth-Ann leaned against the reception desk, pulling at her leggings. "Hell, it can't get any worse. Come on. Just be warned, don't think today is normal."

Beth-Ann led her through a small courtyard with several newly painted picnic tables to a padlocked gate. Even though the shackle was in place, the padlock wasn't actually locked—a typical feature of doing business in Tijuana, Beth-Ann sighed. She opened the door to a high-ceilinged, warehouse-style factory building in which sewing machines and cutting tables stood in rows. Many of the places were unoccupied, however, and none of the workers looked very industrious. Margo wondered if CALTI had hit hard times.

Unlike the carpet sample factory, which employed primarily men to operate its heavy equipment, CALTI was more typical of the maquiladora industry—all of the workers were women. Margo was struck by the way they were dressed. Looking out over the factory floor was like surveying a field of red poppies. Some of the women wore red shirts with jeans or skirts, there were scarlet tracksuits, and some women had on red dresses, ranging in style from gauzy Mexican cotton frocks to shiny Kmart synthetics.

"Is the red some kind of company uniform?" Margo asked . . . although you would think a uniform would look more, well, uniform.

"A uniform!" Beth-Ann emitted a sort of yelp, either a laugh or a sign of incipient hysterics. "It's the eclipse. They're all wearing red because of the eclipse today. I'm not sure I've got this right, but it's totally illogical anyway, so who cares? They believe that if they're pregnant and the light from the eclipse goes through their stomachs, their baby will be born retarded, *loco.*" Beth-Ann seemed unable to go for a minute without grabbing at her hair or clothes, or rubbing some part of her body. She had just massaged a shoulder and now switched to her elbow.

"Wearing red," she went on, "is supposed to protect them from the eclipse. They wear special bracelets, too. Half the girls didn't even show up today and the ones who did should have stayed home. They're producing a quarter of what they usually do. Now, even if you believe this eclipse superstition, only a few of the girls are actually pregnant. So why are they *all* wearing red? Well, they say, they might be pregnant, you never know." Beth-Ann groaned. "I was at the top of my class at design school, fifteen years ago. I should be Anne Klein by now. Or Calvin Klein. Instead I'm working in the armpit of the universe. God, Mexicans!" She spoke loudly, unconcerned at being overhead or else unable to contemplate the possibility that any of the workers understood English.

"Can I ask the workers a few questions?"

"You *habla español*?"

"*Sí.*"

"Bob does, too, he listens to the Mexican radio all day. Drives me nuts. Sure, talk to them if you can get any sense out of them today. I'll be in my office if you have more questions for me. Just ask Maria at the desk."

So Kohler listened to Mexican radio, mused Margo, as she received a demonstration at one of the sewing machines. Had the discovery of Zeke Holroyd's body been picked up by a Mexican station that day? Had Kohler known, when he searched Zeke's trailer, that the minister was dead?

Returning to CALTI's front office, she was told that Señora Gilling was involved in a phone conversation and Margo should wait there. The receptionist handed her a black portfolio: Señora Gilling had thought she might like to see some of the photographs Señor Kohler took of his workers. Scenting scandal—did Kohler force the women to pose nude, a nasty form of harassment for which the disgruntled Beth-Ann was seizing the opportunity to expose him?—Margo opened the portfolio. And smiled in admiration.

Robert Kohler was an artist. The photographs he took,

primarily in black and white, showed several dozen women, all fully clothed. The photos appeared to have been taken just outside the factory or at people's work areas. Although there were a few group shots, Kohler favored individual portraits, each of which captured something essential about its subject: a woman's narrow back bent over a cutting table, her shoulder blades visible through the thin fabric of her blouse; a shyly smiling girl with broad Mayan features. Looking at the lovingly photographed faces, the close-ups of working hands, Margo realized that the framed prints on the wall—beautifully composed shots of Mexican street scenes and children—must be Kohler's as well.

"He tries to take a picture of everyone," said Beth-Ann, beckoning Margo into her office. "He gives them prints, in addition to a bonus, for Christmas. Bob really cares about the girls." Beth-Ann sounded astonished at the idea. "He has a nurse come in once a week to do a clinic for them. When he first started doing it, they brought their whole families. You would've thought he'd tell them to leave the kids at home. But instead, he just contracted for an extra nurse." Whatever Beth-Ann despised about her job, it wasn't her boss.

"He's young to be a factory owner, isn't he?"

"Yeah. Family business." Beth-Ann pulled at her right ear, taking out an earring and briskly rubbing the lobe where it was pierced. "Bob's grandfather started a garment factory in New York. Then Bob's father struck out on his own by opening a factory in Los Angeles. Now Bob's doing it here. Me, if my folks could hand me a company on a platter, I wouldn't feel I had to prove myself by starting fresh somewhere else. But the Kohlers are Jews," she said, much as she'd exclaimed "Mexicans!" earlier.

Margo considered trying to make the designer squirm by mentioning she was Jewish herself. Beth-Ann, however, who was stretching her earlobe and jabbing the earring back through it, seemed squirm-proof.

"Beth-Ann, do you know if Bob knew Reverend Ezekiel Holroyd?"

"Uh-uh. But a reverend? I wouldn't think so. Like I said, Bob's Jewish."

Margo had been perusing the rest of Kohler's photographs. She stopped at one of a young woman holding an infant. The baby's face was in shadow and the focus was on the woman, scarcely more than a girl, her lower lip caught bashfully between her teeth. The building behind her looked more like the rough wood of the shacks in the colonia than the stucco of the factory.

"Who's this?" She held out the photo toward Beth-Ann, who was massaging her forehead in the place yogis called the third eye. Maybe this was some new kind of therapy.

"She's not one of the girls here now. But CALTI's been in business for two or three years and I've only had this job ten months. I started last fall in the rainy season. God, you should see when it rains here. None of the workers even get here, because the roads in Tijuana are impossible. It takes me four times as long to drive here in the rain, I have to keep getting out of the car and checking the water in the road with a stick. Sometimes you think you're about to drive through a tiny puddle and it's a four-foot-deep hole."

Margo nodded in the right places to Beth-Ann's story of woe. She was thinking that the woman in the photo could be Anita Cruz, Rosalia's cousin—Anita a couple of children and several hundred disappointments ago.

Leaving CALTI, Margo started driving toward the Otay Mesa border crossing. But when she reached the intersection she turned instead toward the Ciudad Industrial, thinking:

Bob Kohler took photographs of his employees.

A woman in one of Kohler's photographs looked like Anita.

Zeke Holroyd had interceded with a clothing manufacturer who was operating without papers in Anita's colonia.

Kohler had searched Zeke's office the day Zeke's body was found and had run from Margo a few days later.

Then there was Mr. Ashley Green's claim that the Samurai Zeke was driving hadn't merited its unsafe reputation, and his curiosity about what had made Zeke go off the road.

Margo didn't know what all that added up to, but it was only five o'clock, leaving over two more hours of daylight. Reaching the edge of the Ciudad Industrial and turning down the rough dirt road to Colonia Zapata, Margo reflected that the Reverend Ezekiel Holroyd had been a complex—and an extremely ambitious—man.

10 / Tijuana by Starlight

Driving along the road to the colonia, it was impossible not to think about the rocks hitting Zeke's car the last time, not to get a feeling that the people she passed stared at her hostilely. But the rocks, Margo had convinced herself, had been thrown at Zeke Holroyd specifically, not at just any Anglo. She became less sure of that when she passed a group of half a dozen boys and one shouted in English, "Yankee, go home!" Rattled, she considered turning around, retreating. But she'd just have to drive by the kids again . . . and how did she expect to talk to Anita? Wait ten or fifteen years until there were telephone cables to the colonia so she and Anita could chat on the phone? *Get a grip!* she commanded herself. The boys looked David's age, and David's mouth was the meanest thing about him. These kids had rougher lives, but they were still children.

When the road turned a bend and dipped into the gully, however, Margo wished she had gone back past the gauntlet of boys. The road at the bottom of the gully was blocked by three big metal drums, the kind in which the colonia residents stored water. Four men stood sentry duty, two of them gripping baseball bats. The other two held rifles, which they pointed straight at her.

Margo put the car in reverse, hoping to back up the narrow road until she had room to turn around. But one man had already approached her, demanding to know who she was. Was it good or bad to tell the truth? Margo had little time to ponder the question—the man was pointing a rifle in her face.

"*Soy reportera.*" Thank God her Spanish hadn't deserted her. Her breath was another matter. She could have used Lael Holroyd's hyperventilation bag.

"*Reportera americana?*"

"*Sí. De San Diego.*"

The man called the information back to his buddies, one of whom came over. This guy had a club.

"How do you know she's a reporter?" he asked Señor Rifle. "Just because she says so?"

"I am!" Being a reporter had to be better than whatever else they suspected. "See, I've got a tape recorder. And I'll show you my press card."

"Wait!" order Señor Club as she reached for her purse. "Open it so we can see."

Did they think she was packing a pistol? She was opening the purse slowly, holding it up to the car window, when she heard someone call her name.

Margo hadn't anticipated, the last time she had talked to Diego Torres, that she would be overjoyed to see the union organizer again. Her breath returned to normal as Torres held a brief conversation with the sentries, assuring them she was telling the truth.

"My car's right behind you," Torres told her, inclining his head toward a dusty but relatively new brown Volkswagen Jetta. The guards were moving the barrels to let them by. "I'll follow you into the colonia and then I can fill you in on what happened today."

Driving up the hill toward Colonia Zapata, Margo told herself sternly that there were members of her profession—those she envied as born reporters—who would have only one response to this situation: *Hot damn! I'm onto one hell of a story!* "Hot damn!" she said out loud, trying to drown out *her* refractory inner voice, which sounded like her mother and was pleading that she turn around immediately and get away from here, get out of Mexico. Now!

To her immense relief, no legions of angry Mexicans awaited her at the entrance to the colonia. In fact, everything looked much the same as when she'd come here with Zeke, except that where the first ten or fifteen houses had stood was rubble. It was as if a freak earthquake had leveled that small area.

Margo pulled over, out of the main roadway, and stepped out of her car. Diego Torres stopped his car and came to stand beside her.

"What happened?" she asked him, turning on the tape recorder.

"This morning," said Torres in his fluent English, "about ten o'clock, three men showed up with a bulldozer and demolished these houses, contents and all. They didn't say anything, except to make sure anyone inside the houses got out, but they had to be working for the Baja Nueva Development Company. You know what that is?"

She nodded.

"It's not clear," he said, "whether they planned to raze the entire colonia. They had only the one bulldozer, so my guess is they were going to destroy fifty or a hundred homes, to show what they *could* do if people refused to move."

"But they didn't succeed," said Margo, surveying the damage. "This can't be more than ten or fifteen homes."

"Just twelve." He chuckled, but didn't smile. "Whatever they were planning, they thought they could get away with it while the colonia was virtually empty, with everybody at work. They forgot about something—the eclipse. You've heard of our Mexican superstition, that an eclipse can harm an unborn child? Well, because of the eclipse, many women stayed home from work today. When these men started to destroy the houses, the women fought back."

Hot damn! said something inside Margo, this time meaning it.

"How did they fight?" she asked.

"Threw rocks. A few women had their husbands' guns and fired over the men's heads. These guys were just hired hands, you know, they didn't want to get shot. They took their bulldozer and left."

Torres, who had learned of the incident later that morning, had spent the rest of the day hounding government officials. No one would admit having sanctioned the demolition of people's homes, and, for the time being, he thought the colonia was safe.

"The important thing now," he said, "is to put pressure on Baja Nueva." He looked at her intently, angrily, as if to emphasize that he was cooperating with her only because it helped his cause, and not because he would ever consider her, an agent of the capitalist lackey media, an ally.

"What do you know about the company?" she asked.

"It's privately held, but we assume most of the investors are North Americans. Their agent is a San Diego attorney, Pete Demetrides."

"I think I can get an interview with him," said Margo, who had met Demetrides at Craig LaBerge's party after the maquiladora conference.

Exchanging tit for tat—Margo doubted Diego would have done her any favor without receiving a "tat"—he offered to take her to some of the women who had chased off the bulldozer. In her own car, she followed his to the heart of the colonia. He introduced her to a woman, Elena, who proceeded to act as her escort. She spent the next hour taping fantastic material: the woman whose two toddlers had stood beside her hurling rocks, the sixty-year-old grandmother who'd taken the family's rifle from its hiding place behind a sack of corn meal.

Passing a house that looked familiar, Margo realized it was Rafael's. At that moment, the late Zeke Holroyd's mechanic came out and greeted her. Wasn't it tragic about the Padre! he said, adding, " 'Precious in the sight of the Lord is the death of His saints.' "

She nodded, sorry she didn't have a quote of her own to contribute. But all she could think of was "In the beginning . . ." and a few lines from the Song of Songs that seemed less than felicitous.

"I guess the last time you saw the Padre was when he came here with me," she said.

"Rafael!" His wife, Sandra, strode into the yard where they were talking.

Margo tried to say hello, but Sandra said, "I heard what you were asking, señora—when was the last time my husband fixed the Padre's car? The same thing the other *norteamericano* asked on Saturday, pretending he wanted Rafael to fix his car, and he took up half an hour of Rafael's time and didn't give him any work.''

''What *norteamericano*?''

Sandra was on a roll, however, her volume increasing as she went on, ''Señora, my husband is an excellent mechanic, ask anyone here in the colonia. Anyone who says Rafael would miss an important problem with the Padre's car, so later the car would crash . . . If anyone told you such a thing, that person is a liar!''

From within the one-room house, one of the children started wailing, and Sandra ran back inside to tend to the crying child.

''What *norteamericano*?'' Margo whispered to Rafael.

''*Un negro*.'' he mumbled. A black man.

How had Ashley Green known where Zeke had his car repaired? And had Green really thought Rafael had botched something? Zeke must have carried a lot of insurance for the company to be investigating his death so closely.

''You'd better go,'' said Rafael.

Margo needed no encouragement. She had no desire to tangle further with Sandra. And she still hadn't gotten to the purpose for which she had come to the colonia.

To her amazement, Anita greeted her like an old friend, inviting her to take the best chair in the house. Anita sharply instructed her oldest child, a girl of six or seven, to put the baby to bed. She then turned back to Margo, with as wide a smile as she seemed capable of, and insisted on serving her guest a warm Coke.

''What happened to you?'' said Margo. Handing her the Coke, Anita had tilted her face into the light of the kerosene lamp on the table, flaunting her bruised left eye. Had the bulldozer men fought back?

''That Rosalia! That *puta*! I'm sorry to use a bad word in front of you, señora, but that's what she is, a *puta*, a whore.''

''Did Rosalia hit you?''

Anita sat down, leaning forward eagerly. "Chuy, he says I made her leave. I never did, I tell him. Wasn't I the one who let her stay here, even though she never did anything to help and she was out every night until one A.M., two A.M., some nights even three A.M., and then coming in and waking my little ones, and they can smell the liquor on her and the perfume and the smell of that boss of hers, a married man?"

A toddler clutched at Anita's leg. She shoved the child away, calling to the oldest to take him. The girl shot her mother a look as resentful as Anita's own.

"Rosalia, she's always saying to me, 'Ai, Anita, I never sleep with him.' Does she think I have my nose cut off? Does she think I can't smell him all over her? And that Jaime Galván, when he goes home to his wife and children, does Rosalia think they don't smell her, the stink of a *puta*? Señor Galván, he should think about his wife, too, but he's a man, men can't control themselves. A pretty young girl like Rosalia, she smiles at him and she walks around in her tight jeans, what else can he do?"

Margo held her tongue. This was not the time to try to raise Anita's consciousness.

"Listen to this, you see how crazy she is." Anita gripped Margo's hand. The woman's fingers were small, dry-skinned, and strong. "Rosalia, she's out until one A.M.—last Tuesday night, it was. She comes in and I'm still awake. How could I sleep, I tell her, because the Padre is dead in a car crash, I hear it on the radio that afternoon. Rosalia, she starts to scream. 'When did you ever care about the Padre?' I ask her. 'I'm the one who should be screaming, not you.' Rosalia doesn't listen, she keeps screaming, all about something she told the Padre and did the Padre tell he heard it from her, she's screaming until I have to slap her. Not hard, but it's the only way to make her stop. All our neighbors are yelling, 'Be quiet! We have to sleep!'"

"What did she tell the Padre?"

"Big secret! Nothing the whole colonia doesn't know, about her sleeping with her boss. The next morning the *puta* is gone, her bed isn't even slept in. And Chuy, he says that's my fault! As if I could make her do anything. Rosalia never did anything except what she wanted to do. Well, Chuy's a man, he can't see that Rosalia is so bad. I pray for my Chuy. Like I tell you, he acts like a sinner sometimes, but he's a good man. But Rosalia, I can't pray for her. Maybe you can. Are you going to lead the prayer meetings now that the Padre is dead? I don't know about having a woman do that."

No wonder the sour-faced woman had welcomed Margo enthusiastically. Anita had gotten it into her head that Margo was one of Zeke's fellow missionaries.

"I just came to see how you were doing." Margo let the misunderstanding ride. Like the members of Zeke's church, Anita probably figured you were on the bus or off the bus. If she believed Margo was on this particular bus, she'd be more likely to answer questions about Bob Kohler.

When Margo asked about the owner of CALTI, however, Anita's garrulousness disappeared. Yes, she used to do a little sewing at home. But it was two, maybe three years ago, she couldn't remember the man's name or anything about him. Bob Kohler? Robert Kohler? She didn't know, all those Anglo names sounded alike. A young man? Who was she, a married woman, to notice if a man was twenty or if he was eighty-five and had a beard down to his knees? And let some *jefe*, some boss, take pictures of her! *Por supuesto no!* Of course not!

"That's the kind of thing Rosalia would do, pose for pictures for her boss with no clothes on. Chuy, he doesn't believe me, what kind of person Rosalia really is. All he sees is the pretty young face and the pretty figure, and he thinks he's seeing an angel. Well, now that angel is walking the streets, I think." The corners of Anita's lips rose at the thought. "Because if she ran to Jaime Galván and thought he would take care of her, him with his own wife and children, she's stupider than I thought."

Diego Torres had cautioned her to leave the colonia before dark. But it was already dusk when she'd gotten to Anita's.

From Anita's house, she stepped out of the glimmer cast by the kerosene lamp into the profound darkness of a place that had no electricity. She heard a rumble of angry male voices somewhere to her right, and the words "Baja Nueva." Slightly farther away, a group had chosen oblivion instead of anger; there was drunken laughter and the strum of a guitar. No women or children seemed to be outdoors, as if they had ceded the night to the men.

Margo had parked perhaps a tenth of a mile from Anita's, a negligible distance during the long summer dusk. Now, tendrils of fear stirring in her stomach, she wished she had driven directly to Anita's door. She almost broke into a run when she saw a dog, her old phobia of canines making her heart pound. But like every Mexican dog, this one ignored her.

"Señora! Lady!" someone whispered.

Margo spun around, crouching in the stance she had learned in a self-defense class years ago—though she couldn't recall what she was supposed to do if attacked. One of the moves was called the "eye gouge." At the time, she'd wondered if she could possibly do that to anyone. Now she just wished she remembered how.

"Señora!" Coming up to her was Anita's daughter, the seven year old who had glared at her mother.

Margo shifted out of defense mode.

"My mother told you no one took her picture," said the girl. "She lied. I remember the man who took her picture."

"Do you know why your mother said it didn't happen?"

"No. You could ask Carmen. At the store. He took her picture, too."

They were at Margo's car. "Could you show me the way to Carmen's store?"

"Yes!" The girl eagerly hopped into her car. "Señora," she said as Margo drove, "are you going to look for Rosalia? I miss her."

How to tell the kid that, for all her mother's venom, Anita was probably right—Rosalia was off with her boyfriend, or worse?

"Yes, I'll look for her," said Margo. They arrived at the store.

"When you find her, tell her Beatriz says she has to come back. Or else to take me with her." The fierce child ran into the dark.

11 / Nose for News

Three men were sitting on the covered porch outside Carmen's store, sharing a six-pack. One of them called out something to Margo as she passed, but he spoke softly and glanced over his shoulder. Inside the store, Carmen sat on a crate by the counter, drinking a beer and listening to rock music on a small boom box. She pulled up another crate for Margo.

Sí, Carmen remembered the man who took photographs—Señor Roberto, he used to come to the colonia with sewing that some of the women did at home. He had taken Carmen's picture, too, but not a regular picture. He'd insisted on photographing her from the back while she lifted a big carton of canned goods, she said, shaking her head at the eccentricities of gringos.

Margo, having seen Robert Kohler's stunning photographs, understood exactly why he had requested the unconventional pose. Kohler had been drawn to Carmen's strength, which was not at all evident in her face, the unremarkable, lined brown visage common to hundreds of Mexican women of her age—late thirties, Margo guessed—and social class. Carmen's true character resided in her tall, sinewy body. The storekeeper got up to sell beer to two men. The men joked with her, even flirted a little, but Carmen seemed able and willing to slap them across the room if they gave her any guff.

"Would you like a beer, señora?" she asked Margo, after the men left.

"Sure, thanks."

Carmen plunged her hand into the ice-filled cooler,

pulled out a dripping Tecate, and swiped the bottle dry with a towel. Margo bought a bag of tortilla chips to have with it—dinner.

Taking another beer for herself, Carmen explained why Anita would have denied having her picture taken. Chuy hadn't liked it. Señor Roberto was young and *muy guapo*—very handsome—and when Chuy had found out about the photo session, he'd beaten Anita up.

"Poor Anita, she didn't know how lucky she was. At least Chuy cared who looked at her in those days. Now he works two shifts in a row, two different factories, and all he does when he comes home is shove some beans in his mouth and go to sleep. Anita could walk around the colonia naked and he wouldn't notice."

"Did Señor Roberto know Reverend Holroyd?"

"Why do you want to know?"

It was the voice of the no-nonsense body, not the ingratiating face, and Margo told Carmen the whole story: of suspecting that Bob Kohler had searched Zeke's office after his death, hearing Zeke had intervened with a man doing business illegally in the colonia, and finding Anita's photograph among Kohler's prints.

"It's like knowing something smells bad in your kitchen," she told Carmen, "and you have to keep sniffing around until you find out what it is. Something doesn't smell right about Reverend Holroyd."

"I thought you were from his church." Sharply.

"No, I'm a reporter for a radio station."

"KSDO?" Carmen named one of the biggest San Diego stations.

Margo picked up the transistor radio from the counter and found KSDR, which was broadcasting the weeknight jazz show. The signal came faintly, staticky; KSDR didn't have the kind of power most of the commercial stations did.

"I just met Zeke the day I came here," she added. The preacher had clearly inspired intense feelings in the colonia, both pro and con.

"Ai, that Anita! She thinks she knows everything." Carmen picked up Margo's empty bottle from the floor. "Another Tecate?"

"Fine." Actually, a second beer struck Margo as unwise, given her relatively empty stomach and the fact that she had to drive back to San Diego. But Carmen seemed to take her willingness to drink as additional proof she wasn't in fundamentalist cahoots with Zeke Holroyd. Margo accepted the bottle and made a point of taking a long first gulp; she could nurse the rest.

"I don't know anything about the Padre and Señor Roberto," said Carmen. "But I can tell you what the Padre did to people here. Most people in Mexico are Catholic, and in Catholicism, if you do something wrong you tell the priest in confession. Some people here in the colonia thought of the Padre the same way they were used to thinking of their priest in the village at home. They confessed to him. Only the Padre didn't just tell them to say some prayers. He used the things they told him for *chantaje.*"

"*Chantaje?*" Margo repeated the unfamiliar word.

Blackmail, Carmen explained. Margo had guessed that Zeke's work in the colonia might involve more than just saving souls. But blackmail?

"Did he make people pay him?" she asked. How could Zeke have profited from people who earned no more than forty or fifty dollars a week?

"Sometimes, yes."

"What people?"

Carmen went over to a carton of beans and ripped it open. Stacking the cans on a shelf, her strong back to Margo, she said, "A woman who used to tell her husband, just one or two times a month, that she was late getting home from work because the van she rode in broke down. Really, she went to a disco with other women from the maquiladora where she worked. The Padre made her give him money. Not a lot of money, but something every week. Another person, a man, started a small car repair business here using tools he found at his factory, things lying around that no one wanted. The Padre made this man fix his car for free." Carmen was carefully avoiding revealing any names, and Margo didn't let on that she knew one of Zeke's victims.

Carmen looked up. "*Hola*, Diego. Want a beer?"

How long had Diego Torres been standing in the doorway?

Ignoring Carmen, he snapped at Margo, "Didn't I tell you to leave here before dark?" Was Torres angry just because she had "disobeyed" him? Or had he overheard Carmen spilling the beans about Zeke's blackmail? He said, "I'll lead you as far as the Ciudad Industrial. You should be safe enough from there to the border."

Margo almost protested on principle—she hated being given orders—but she realized she'd welcome a guide out of the colonia.

"*Adios, señora.*" Carmen's tone warned her to say nothing of what they had discussed.

"Thanks for the beer," Margo said. She went out to her car, got in, and turned the key. She heard a feeble clicking sound. She tried again, with the same result. Damn!

As if he'd known this was going to happen, Diego Torres hadn't yet gotten into his car. He came over and gestured to her to unlatch the hood. She did. She had a feeling Dorothy had covered this particular problem in the auto repair class, but that was nine years ago.

"Do you have a hammer, anything like that?" Diego asked.

She shook her head.

He got one from his own car. Margo got out and saw him pound on something behind the carburetor. "Try starting it now," he said. She did and the engine turned over. "You've got a bad solenoid," he said, the word jogging her memory—that's what Dorothy had called it, and she had said to carry a hammer or something similar until you got it fixed.

"Thanks," said Margo.

"You learn a lot of things growing up in Mexico City," he said. "A little car repair. A little street fighting. And"— Torres leaned into her window, inches from her, his breath beery—"what turf you'd better stay away from." He got in his own car and led her out of the colonia.

Hot damn! What a story! she thought, driving to the border. *A holier-than-thou preacher who fleeced his flock.*

You plan to report on that? This time her internalized maternal voice didn't sound protective. It was as if Alice Simon were initiating one of those ethical discussions that had often occupied the dinner table when Margo was growing up, during the turbulent years of the civil rights movement and the Vietnam War, not to mention—and Alice mentioned it plenty, with three teenagers—the sexual revolution. For a woman who was "only a housewife" and helped with the family dry cleaning business, Alice could have sat down and debated with Talmudic scholars. (She was currently, at the age of sixty-five, studying for her Bat Mitzvah.)

Waiting in line at the border crossing, Margo continued to hear her mother—her conscience—in her mind. If she'd been tracking a bad smell, as she had described it to Carmen, then hadn't she located its source, the sack of rotten potatoes in Reverend Ezekiel Holroyd's pantry? *Chantaje*, blackmail. Forcing his wife to give up her beloved dance as "atonement" for smoking. Biting into Rafael's tiny auto repair business by making Rafael fix his car for free.

Whatever Zeke's nasty game had been, continued her maternal voice, it no longer mattered, did it? His death had liberated his victims; especially, it had freed Lael. Was there really anything else Margo needed to know, any reason to cause these people further pain?

After answering the Customs officer's questions satisfactorily, Margo crossed the border into the U.S.

Something still smelled.

Ashley Green had said there was no conclusive evidence that Samurais tended to roll over and he'd requested authorization to take possession of Zeke's car . . . and he had questioned Rafael. Did he suspect Rafael had tampered with the car he was compelled to work on for free? (Could Green have known about Zeke's blackmail?) Maybe Rafael had never intended to kill Zeke, but what if he'd bungled a repair on purpose—something minor, just so the Padre would quit taking advantage of him—and it was sheer rotten luck that whatever failed on the Samurai had done so when Zeke was speeding along a cliff edge? Was that why Sandra had blown up?

Or did Sandra have her own cause to act defensive? With Rafael running his auto repair business from right beside their home, Sandra must have picked up some knowledge of cars herself. And it was she, not her husband, who resented the Padre.

There was more, Margo realized as she drove across Otay Mesa—the industrial parks deserted at night—toward the San Diego Freeway. She had no proof that Zeke had "expanded" his practice to wealthy nonbelievers, but Zeke had known that Robert Kohler was operating illegally and he'd talked to Kohler—"gringo to gringo," Torres had said. Maybe blackmailer to blackmailee? Margo was now sure that Kohler had broken into Zeke's office last Tuesday, the day the minister's body was found. Had Kohler heard about Zeke's death on Mexican radio and hoped to remove any evidence of the blackmail he'd been paying? No wonder, when he'd spotted Margo at the maquiladora conference, he had run away.

And what about the warning Diego Torres had given her, before she left the colonia? Was he simply telling her not to meddle in colonia affairs . . . or did he know, maybe more than Carmen, what Zeke had been up to?

Margo got to KSDR and called Barry to let him know she was working late. For the next three hours, she produced the story of the victorious battle against the bulldozer fought by the women of Colonia Zapata . . . and thought about the Reverend Zeke Holroyd's death. No matter how hard she tried to wrap her mind around the idea, she couldn't believe Rafael or Sandra or anyone from the colonia had enough at stake to kill Zeke. The big, juicy target for blackmail, thus the person with the far greater motive, was someone like Robert Kohler. There was one major flaw in that theory, however. If Zeke had collected large sums of money from Kohler—or any other well-off maquiladora owner—why hadn't he lived in a nicer place, driven a newer car?

Her attention returned to her story; she was splicing in Diego Torres's comments. It struck her that even when Torres was laughing about the bulldozer operators forgetting the eclipse, his voice on tape expressed not amusement, but rage. Rage, Margo sensed, was his natural emotional habitat. She recalled the first conversation she'd had with the union organizer, at the maquiladora conference . . . and realized that he had answered her question about how Zeke spent his blackmail proceeds.

She even had it on tape. She ran to her office and scrabbled on her desk for the first cassette tape from the conference—found it! She fast-forwarded, until she heard Torres complaining that even though Zeke had gotten the clothing manufacturer (Kohler, as it turned out) to clean up his practices, Zeke hadn't fought for any financial compensation for the workers. Maybe, Margo had suggested, Zeke just wasn't a fighter.

"Oh, Holroyd was a fighter," Diego Torres had shot back. "Only he didn't care about fighting for the people, getting them the money they deserved. The only money he ever fought for went to his church."

12 / The Collection Plate

AMERICA NEEDS A FAITH LIFT, asserted one of the bumper stickers on a car outside Revelation of God Church the next afternoon. Reverend Paul van den Moeller looked as if he'd had more than his faith lifted, thought Margo, noticing the taut, slightly frozen way the pink skin stretched across the minister's pudgy cheeks.

Margo had hoped she could find out something about Zeke's fund-raising by asking his senior minister. However, she was quickly learning otherwise. Not that van den Moeller didn't have plenty to say. KSDR could have put him on the air during a pledge drive. As long as he remembered to give the station phone number every couple of minutes, the man would never run out of steam.

"In many of our Bible colleges nowadays," the big, white-haired minister expostulated, "they give courses on financial management and accounting, the very same things taught at the Harvard Business School." Befitting a Southern California clergyman, van den Moeller was dressed in a baby blue polo shirt and khaki slacks, as if he'd just breezed in from the golf course. "Now, I'm not saying those things aren't necessary in the church of today. Of course they are. Of course they are. But I think some of the young men get the wrong idea. They start to feel those worldly concerns are more important than they should be. They rely on financial expertise, when they should be relying on faith. On faith. Didn't Jesus Christ say, 'Therefore I tell you, do not worry about your life, what you will eat or drink; or about your body, what you will wear. Is not life more important than food, and the body more important than clothes?' Matthew six, verse twenty-five."

If Paul van den Moeller had studied anything besides Scripture in the course of his ministerial education, it wasn't financial management, it was acting. Against the handsome wood-paneled background of his office, he used his hands expertly, making no unnecessary gestures.

"Can you give me an idea how much Zeke was raising in donations? Eight thousand dollars a year? Ten thousand?"

"Oh, my goodness, no. Two or three thousand." He spoke as if the presence of actual dollar figures in his mouth created a bad taste there.

"I'd gotten the idea from Zeke that it was quite a bit more."

" 'Pride goes before destruction, a haughty spirit before a fall.' Proverbs sixteen, verse eighteen." He sounded as genial as before, and Margo had to consciously register the hostility of his words, the implication that, in going over a cliff, Zeke Holroyd had taken a "fall" he'd been asking for.

"Quite a few of the younger men, like Zeke, come to the ministry through their families," he went on. "A good Christian life is all they've ever known. Now, I wish that were true for everyone, that every child had the benefit of a good Christian upbringing. But I can't help but wonder if those among us who have fought our own battles with Satan haven't gained a deeper understanding of what's really important and what's not. Myself, I was such a hellion when I was a youth that they told me, when I graduated high school, they said to me, 'Paul, you have a choice. You can serve your country in the Army or you can go to jail.' Well, I chose the Army, got sent over to Korea. That's where I was called of the Lord, on a battlefield with men dying in my arms and Communist gunfire all around me."

Margo murmured appreciatively but not, she hoped, encouragingly. The story sounded as if it could go on forever.

"Could you give me any of the names of Zeke's donors, people who have factories in Tijuana?" she said. "I'd like to interview them about their efforts to help the workers through helping Zeke's mission."

"As I said, I don't count the nickels and dimes." Van den Moeller beamed, an innocent unsullied by filthy lucre. Finally, however, he gave her one solid piece of information. "The records you're asking about are handled by Zeke's lovely wife."

Lael Holroyd smelled.

Margo had done many interviews with the homeless, and she recognized the stench of unwashed skin and slept-in clothing as Lael faced her in the doorway. Lael's blue cotton dress was grease-spotted, and her blond hair hung dully, half covering her face.

Bad smells assaulted Margo when she stepped into the apartment as well.

"Has anyone been here to see you, Lael? Anyone from the church?" she asked.

Lael shook her head listlessly. "I told them I wanted to be alone for a little while."

"Have you eaten?" Lael's breath had the sour odor of someone who'd been fasting.

Another head shake.

The apartment kitchen reminded Margo of the movie *Repulsion* in which a woman's descent into madness was mirrored by an uncooked rabbit rotting on the counter. Lael had left out some of the food brought by the church ladies. Deviled eggs and cold cuts were decomposing in the heat. An overflowing garbage pail added to the stench.

Margo opened all the windows, then found some unspoiled cheese and fruit in the refrigerator and brought them to Lael in the living room. She realized she shouldn't condemn the church members for their neglect. Lael had sounded all right when Margo called to say she had a few follow-up questions from her discussion with Zeke. Anyone who had only spoken to her by phone couldn't have known how badly she needed help.

"Have you been out at all?" asked Margo.

"I wanted to go to work, I'm a counselor at the church summer camp," murmured Lael, as she ate a few bites of cheese. "But they said not to come this week."

"Why don't I run a bath for you?"

"Okay." Lael seemed likely to agree to anything.

Margo got the water going and looked for some bubble bath. But bathing in the Holroyd household was clearly not meant to be a sensual experience. Shampooing, however, was. The one hint of self-indulgence Margo had seen in the modest apartment was the shampoo and conditioner sitting on the side of the tub, the same expensive brand Jenny insisted on using. Zeke, Margo was sure, wouldn't have minded shampooing with cheap bar soap; the fancy products had to be Lael's. So the church hadn't demolished that little bit of vanity. Good for Lael.

While Lael obediently soaked, Margo filled a giant-sized trash bag with rotted food and took it downstairs to the building's Dumpster. She scrubbed the kitchen sink and counter, even the trash can, and surveyed what remained in the larder: more fruit and cheese, half a dozen cans of soup, and a box of crackers, as well as plenty of baked goods. The trick was making sure Lael ate any of the food. Margo figured she'd better enlist Mrs. van den Moeller's help again before she left.

She took a bite of a brownie, put some more brownies and cookies on a plate, and checked the milk in the refrigerator—sour. She poured out the milk, rinsed the carton, and threw it away. But there was apple juice; she poured two glasses.

Lael, having finished her bath, had put on a pair of loose slacks and a gauzy Mexican embroidered blouse. She held a ledger book in one hand. With the other, she combed her long wet hair, the comb gliding through, no tangles; maybe Margo ought to try the expensive conditioner herself. Lael looked slightly less fragile now, mere glass instead of the thinnest crystal.

"You were interested in people in the maquiladora industry who donated, weren't you, Margo?" she said.

Margo repeated the conversation she had had with Reverend van den Moeller.

"Two or three thousand dollars a year!" Indignant on

Zeke's behalf, Lael showed a spark of life. "Zeke raised forty-six thousand from the time he started the Tijuana mission just two years ago! I know it's not Reverend Paul's fault. He can't pay attention to all those financial details, he has so many other things to worry about. It's just that Zeke worked so hard, he ought to get some credit. Of course," she said, looking confused, "that shouldn't matter, should it, whether he gets credit? All that really matters is he was working for the Lord." Margo had a feeling church doctrine often conflicted with Lael's most basic instincts.

With a sigh, Lael opened the ledger book. "Anyway, Joseph Ollman is a member of our church, he owns a factory in Ciudad Industrial. He donated fifty dollars. And Craig LaBerge runs a big shelter company, called Mexican Assembly Brokers; he gave one hundred dollars. What Zeke did was, he'd find out where people worked, people who came to his prayer meetings. Then he'd ask their employers for donations. That way they knew they were helping their own workers."

"Was that the only way he decided who to ask for donations, by identifying employers of people who came to his prayer meetings?"

"Oh, no! There are quite a few Christian business organizations in San Diego. He asked people in those groups for help, whether they did business in Tijuana or not. Do you want their names, too?"

"I don't think so." Not unless Zeke's capacity for digging up dirt was more extensive than Margo could imagine. "Just the ones involved in the maquiladora industry."

Lael mentioned a dozen other names, factory owners and managers. None of the names were familiar, however, and, other than Craig LaBerge, there were no donors of over fifty dollars.

"What about Bob Kohler? Robert Kohler? Can I take a look?" Margo reached for the ledger.

Lael hesitated a moment, but handed the book over. Margo wondered if Lael ever said no. She'd broken down donations to the Tijuana mission on a month-by-month basis, she explained, resuming combing her hair, an act that obviously gave her pleasure. She deposited the individual donations into a special account and each month transferred the money from that account to the main account for Revelation of God. No matter how much Zeke raised, apparently it didn't affect the amount of money the mission received; everything went into the church's common pot. No wonder Revelation of God looked so spruce, the parking lot newly asphalted and the grounds attractively landscaped.

Looking through the ledger, Margo saw a number of larger entries, from five hundred to as much as fifteen hundred dollars.

"What's this? Unity Assembly, *S*?" Margo indicated a donor of $980.40.

"Unity Assembly is another Christian church. The *S* stands for *speech*. It means Zeke gave a talk to them about the mission."

"And the church gave him a donation?"

"He passed a collection plate, actually a woven basket he got in South America." Lael pointed to the basket on a shelf.

"That's a lot of money to get, just from passing a basket."

"Zeke was a wonderful speaker. That's how I saw him the first time, giving a speech at San Diego State." Lael was actually animated. "He used to come home from doing one of his talks about the mission and he'd give me that basket just filled with twenty-dollar bills. It was like everyone ran to their automatic teller, you know the way those machines only give you twenties? I asked him if they had automatic tellers outside all the churches, because it looked like people got so inspired by his talk, they all went right out and withdrew sixty or a hundred dollars and put it in the basket."

There were some thirty ledger entries similar to that for Unity Assembly and they constituted the bulk of the donations, Margo would guess as much as forty thousand of the forty-six thousand dollars Zeke had raised. Automatic tellers outside the churches, indeed! Zeke must have instructed his blackmailees to pay in twenties. Then he could slip the money, several hundred or a thousand dollars at a time, into the basket every time he gave a speech.

Eyes shining, Lael smiled as sweetly as *Rebecca of Sunnybrook Farm,* apparently reflecting on Zeke's ability to motivate folks to reach into their pockets. Did she really have no clue as to what Zeke was up to? But why would she suspect Zeke of fabricating the story of the fabulously generous audiences moved by his oratorical gifts? Lael was, after all, only twenty or twenty-one, and she'd seen her husband as being just a couple of steps down from God. Whatever unsavory practices Zeke engaged in, he must have kept them secret from his wife . . . unless he had so cloaked them in his particular flavor of religion that Lael knew what he was doing but believed it was holy?

"Lael, Zeke must have talked about the people in his prayer meetings and the things he saw in Tijuana. Did he ever tell you about people he found doing things that were wrong?"

"You mean sinners? People in the service of Satan?" Lael whispered.

"Um, sure." Margo thought of the children's book she'd seen at the church, *The Faces of Satan,* and wondered again what it was like to see evil as a vibrant part of one's life, a constant threat to be battled . . . a constant temptation. She said, "Would people tell Zeke if they'd done something wrong?"

"Oh, yes." Through sudden tears, Lael said, "He'd be so happy when someone who had been living a life of sin repented. People would stand up in prayer meetings and confess their sins and accept the Lord into their hearts."

Anyone willing to broadcast his or her sins probably made a lousy candidate for blackmail. But Margo assumed not everyone cared to make a confession publicly.

"Lael, are you okay?"

The young woman was rocking back and forth with sobs. Margo reached out to her, but although Lael let herself be held, she remained rigid. Her weeping seemed not to release her grief but to intensify it.

"I'm sorry," she said, the sobs subsiding to sniffles. "It's just so many questions—you and the insurance man the other day."

"By the way, did you ever hear back from him?" said Margo. Maybe *she* would atone for turning inquisitor again by giving five dollars to the next homeless person who asked her. "Ashley Green, wasn't that his name?"

"Was I supposed to? Hear back from him?"

"I don't know. Would you mind if I called and asked him a few questions?"

"I guess not." Lael found the business card Green had given her.

Calling the number on Green's card connected Margo with the San Diego office of a major national insurance company. After ten minutes on the phone, however, and being transferred to four different departments, she hung up the phone and turned to Lael.

"The insurance company has never heard of Ashley Green."

13 / The Antichrist Ashley Green

Lael wished she could snap her fingers and make Margo vanish. Instead, she had to look interested as Margo asked her for the white pages. For a moment, Lael didn't know what the words meant—"white," "pages"—but then she understood and got the phone book.

"Are you all right?" Margo said to her.

"Yes. Fine." Anything to get Margo out of there quickly.

Margo had stopped at a page of the telephone book. "There are no Ashley Greens listed, but there are three A. Greens," she said.

Fool! Did she think the Antichrist would be listed in the telephone book? For surely that was who Ashley Green was. Lael said nothing, however, just sat quietly while Margo telephoned the three A. Greens . . . none of whom, of course, was the right one. Please, let her leave soon!

"I'm going to call Mrs. van den Moeller, all right?" said Margo.

"Oh, no, thanks. I just have a headache. I want to take some asprin and lie down." Lael hoped she was smiling. It must have worked, because Margo said okay and left.

At last! Lael grabbed the Bible and hugged it to her, tears filling her eyes. The Antichrist Ashley Green had come to her house. The Antichrist knew all the terrible things she had done. She opened the Bible and read:

For God will bring every deed into judgment,
including every hidden thing,
whether it is good or evil.

The words on the page should have blurred through her weeping. But instead each word shone brightly, as if meant expressly for her. *Every hidden thing*, she repeated to herself, and thought for a moment of the file Zeke had hidden on the computer. He'd asked her to set up the password for him; he had known *she* wouldn't violate his secret file. For a moment, she felt so profoundly evil she thought of turning on the computer and looking at the file. She ran into the living room, away from the computer, to escape her evil thoughts, and turned again to the Bible. Lael felt as if some force outside of her—God? Or Satan?—was turning the pages and drawing her to each passage it wanted her to read.

Instead of fragrance there will be a stench;
instead of a sash, a rope:
instead of well-dressed hair, baldness;
instead of fine clothing, sackcloth;
instead of beauty, branding.

As if you could telephone the Antichrist Ashley Green! But he would come back for Lael whenever he was ready. She heard noise in her head, as of a thousand horses stampeding, a million bees buzzing.

For your hands are stained with blood,
your fingers with guilt.
Your lips have spoken lies,
and your tongue mutters wicked things.

Lael threw the Bible away from her, feeling unfit to touch it. The words buzzed again and again in her mind: *Your hands are stained with blood.* The terrible, terrible things she had done.

Wildly, she looked around the room. Had the Antichrist returned already? Her gaze took in the small television, sofa, chairs, the table with magazines. Why wouldn't Ashley Green show himself? Was he waiting for her to make some kind of sign?

Her sewing kit lay on the couch, where she had been fixing a rip in the seam of the black mourning dress she was borrowing. Her eyes went to her good sewing shears, sitting all sharp and shiny on top of the bunched black dress. Brightly, through her weeping, Lael saw herself reach for the shears.

14 / Bird Man

"Margo, two minutes!" Les Trumbull, KSDR's chief engineer, called into her office on Wednesday morning. They were scheduled to go together in the mobile van to do a report live.

"Just five minutes!" she bargained, paging through the maquiladora company directory for the number of Craig LaBerge's company.

One hundred dollars scarcely sounded like a major black-mail payoff, she cautioned herself. Nevertheless, Craig LaBerge's hundred-dollar contribution made him the biggest of Zeke's maquiladora donors. Furthermore, as a significant player in the cross-border industry, LaBerge was a legitimate interviewee . . . and Margo preferred to slip in her questions about Zeke surreptitiously, at the same time she pursued her official story. The alternative was to share her suspicions with Claire De Jong and solicit the news director's blessing to look into Zeke's demise. Claire would undoubtedly jump on the tale of the fundamentalist preacher/blackmailer; whereas Margo had little stomach for pursuing the story unless she found proof that Zeke's "fund-raising" had actually led to his murder.

She found LaBerge's number, phoned his office, and obtained an appointment to interview him that afternoon.

"Hey, Margo, ready to roll?" repeated Les.

"One more minute, okay?"

She called the office of Pete Demetrides, Baja Nueva's lawyer. Demetrides was out of town all week and his secretary had put Margo off when she'd called the day before. But Demetrides must have heard about Margo's story on the Colonia Zapata rebellion and instructed his secretary accordingly. With a solicitude no doubt reserved for corporate clientele, the secretary booked Margo for Monday, the first day Demetrides would be back in San Diego.

"Margo!" Les demanded.

"Coming!"

Dashing out to the van, Margo felt more than just the high of going to cover a big story. They were on their way to Dorothy Troupe's eleven A.M. news conference, where the county supervisor was expected to announce her candidacy for the House of Representatives.

A stage draped with red, white, and blue bunting had been set up on the north side of the Horton Plaza shopping center downtown, and all the local Democratic politicos were on hand. Those higher in the pecking order—like the labor leader, Harry Rusk—skillfully shouldered each other for the most visible spots on stage. The rest of the pols milled around the edges, all vying for the brass ring, three seconds on the television evening news.

Margo wondered if Dorothy had really been undecided about running for Congress when they'd had their supposed heart-to-heart less than two weeks before. She felt a bit hurt to think that her old friend had strung her along. But any hurt was quickly overshadowed by excitement when Dorothy stepped up to the podium and the crowd roared.

Dorothy didn't just announce her candidacy and get in a few sound bites for the meager attention span of TV news. Instead, characteristically, she spoke for twenty minutes about who she was and what she stood for. Margo always cautioned herself to be scrupulously objective any time she covered Dorothy. But she couldn't keep from grinning when the candidate caught her eye. She went up to the stage afterward and returned Dorothy's hug warmly.

"Got time for a few questions?" Margo asked, signaling to Les to wait for her with the station van.

"For you, of course. Walk me back to my car." Any other politician would have commandeered a special parking spot right beside the stage. It was just like Dorothy to have parked in the shopping center garage.

Margo asked Dorothy about her campaign plans as they walked through the shopping center, trailed by Dorothy's son, Sean. Someone had taken Sean in hand for his appearance next to his mom on stage; he'd gotten a haircut and his clothes looked fresh from the cleaners. The injury he had received, falling in the convention center parking lot, showed only as a fading bruise on the side of his head. One thing about Sean, Dorothy always used to say, the kid might be accident-prone but he healed damn fast.

"Do you think being a congresswoman, rather than a county supervisor, will change your views about U.S.-Mexican trade?" asked Margo, as they entered the parking structure.

"I'll still be concerned with helping the San Diego economy and at the same time balancing that with my concerns for the environment and for the humane treatment of workers on both sides of the border. In other words, I'm not going to make anybody completely happy. How's your report on the maquiladoras going?"

"Do you know anything abut the Baja Nueva Company?"

"The one that sent out that bulldozer? That was quite a story. No, but I'll ask around. And you should check with the secretary of state's office. If the company's incorporated in California, they have to file."

"What about Craig LaBerge?"

"I don't think he has anything to do with Baja Nueva."

"No, I meant . . ."

Dorothy glanced sharply at the tape recorder Margo was carrying; Margo switched it off.

"I assume what you're after is the kind of thing he wouldn't talk about publicly? Dirt?" Dorothy's tone was joking, but not friendly.

"I just wanted to know your general impression of him and why his shelter company is so successful . . . if it really *is* successful. Or is that just hype?"

"Craig is successful, that's no hype," Dorothy said. "He saw the potential of the maquiladora business early and he saw that U.S. companies would need help operating in Mexico. I'm sure he's greased a few palms on the Mexican side, if that's what you're looking for. But who hasn't?''

"Did he know Zeke Holroyd?''

Dorothy paused and lit a cigarette. Sean paused, too, a few steps behind them; Margo had almost forgotten he was there.

"Craig and Holroyd wouldn't have run in the same circles,'' Dorothy said. "Craig, in spite of being a capitalist, is . . . I'd hardly say liberal, but he's definitely not ideological the way the fundamentalists are. He gives campaign contributions to whoever he thinks is going to win, Democrat or Republican. Even yours truly. In a close race, he'll donate to both sides. I'd say the fundamentalists put God first, whatever their bizarre idea of God may be. Craig's got his priorities straight—he puts Craig first. What makes you think he would have known Zeke Holroyd? And what does it matter, since Holroyd's dead?''

"Craig made a hundred-dollar donation to Holroyd's mission in Tijuana.''

Dorothy let out a whoop of laughter that echoed in the concrete parking structure. "I've got news for you. A hundred dollars to Craig LaBerge is like you and me handing fifty cents to a bum on the street. Maggie, are you going to tell me the real reason you want to know about this, or are you going to keep farting around? Because I've got to go.'' If there were a Harry Truman Award given to politicians for plain speaking, Dorothy would win it.

Margo waited until they reached Dorothy's car and Sean went around to the driver's side.

She drew close to Dorothy. "I heard Zeke Holroyd was putting pressure on people to donate to his church.'' When Dorothy didn't respond, she took a deep breath and softly used the word she'd heard in the colonia. "I heard he was blackmailing people.''

Dorothy lowered her voice, too. "That's a helluva serious charge to make. Do you have any evidence?''

"I know he was leaning on some of the poor people who went to his prayer meetings.''

"Mexican peasants! Maggie, listen to some advice from an old pol. This minister is dead, he can't do any more harm, at least not according to what the nuns taught me. So let it go. And believe me, you don't want to be spreading shit about someone like Craig LaBerge. There's one thing I will tell you about LaBerge. He's smart, but not like the refined college kids you work with at the public radio station. He's got a kind of animal, survival intelligence. Street smarts. If he feels like he's being pushed into a corner, he'll fight tooth and nail."

"Sounds like you and LaBerge are pretty close."

"Nope. Just takes one to know one." Dorothy stepped into the car, a new burgundy Buick.

"Ever miss the old VW bus?" remarked Margo.

"Sure, but you better drive an American car if you want a future in politics in this country."

"Margo! Margo Simon?"

Where had Harry Rusk come from? Mr. San Diego Labor appeared behind her in the parking lot as she walked away from Dorothy's car.

"Hi, Harry." Sighing inwardly, Margo turned on the tape recorder. "Any comment about Dorothy's candidacy?"

As she could have predicted, Harry offered five minutes of blather, of which perhaps ten seconds were usable.

"Heard that story of yours yesterday," he said when she stopped taping. "About those Mexican women fighting off the bulldozer. Where did you say it happened?" Sweat gleamed on Harry's face. Small wonder. It was hot in the parking structure and Harry had the body of a meat-and-potatoes man.

"Colonia Zapata, it's on the east side of Tijuana."

"Who authorized the bulldozer?"

"No one's taking responsibility, but there's a development company called Baja Nueva that claims it owns the land."

"Well, good story. Good to hear about working women fighting for justice."

"Thanks, Harry." Margo virtually ran from the labor leader. Once he got started on working people fighting for justice, there was no limit to his storehouse of clichés.

The international headquarters of Mexican Assembly Brokers, Craig LaBerge's company, were less sumptuous than Margo would have expected. Located in one of the new industrial parks in Otay Mesa, just north of the border, the firm occupied a nondescript stucco building identical to the dozens of other stucco buildings in the area. Most likely, ninety percent of the other bland complexes also housed U.S. offices of companies operating in Tijuana. Someone trying to sell the maquiladora idea politically had once coined the term "twin plants," as if every Mexican factory would have a corresponding U.S. facility, employing an equal number of workers. The reality was that the U.S. offices housed little more than a handful of administrative personnel.

Inside LaBerge's company, all the furnishings appeared new but utilitarian, with nothing that seemed calculated to impress potential clients. Apart from some colorful Mexican folk art hanging in the reception area, the wall decoration was haphazard, an expression of the employees' personal tastes rather than an interior designer. A photograph of the Grand Canyon hung above one desk, a cluster of Matisse prints by another.

The only truly distinctive feature sat on a perch in LaBerge's private office: a brilliantly colored bird that he identified as a Hyacinth macaw.

"I try to bring in a different bird from the aviary every day," LaBerge said, as he got Margo settled with a bottle of cold sparkling water. Rather than placing himself in the authority seat across the desk, he drew up another chair next to hers. "At least," he added, with a wink at the macaw, "I bring the birds who know how to behave."

Talking to LaBerge, Margo found out the reason for the relatively low-budget surroundings: The company maintained an office downtown, where meetings with clients took place. Often, of course, his clients preferred that he come to them . . . in Milwaukee or Denver or Pittsburgh. That, after all, was the point of using a shelter company, for a business to avoid the day-to-day hassles of managing its Mexican plants.

Obviously accustomed to being interviewed, LaBerge spoke in well-framed sentences that Margo knew she'd only have to edit lightly.

On the cultural differences between Mexican and U.S. workers: "There's a manager at a box factory we operate, a man who was very successful at a similar factory in L.A. In Tijuana, he wasn't getting the kind of cooperation he needed. A consultant spent time at the factory, and we found out the manager routinely asked workers' opinions about how to do things, the way he'd always done with his people in L.A. To the Mexicans, that made them think he was stupid. They expect their managers to give orders, not solicit their ideas."

On problems with Customs: "With the phenomenal growth in the industry, the traffic at the commercial border crossing—which you realize is separate from the two passenger crossing areas—has gotten way out of hand. It's common knowledge that a lot of U.S. managers do a little light smuggling when they use the passenger crossing. For instance, you're supposed to buy your copier paper in Mexico, help out the Mexican economy, but the same box of paper costs twenty dollars in the U.S. and sixty down there. So you throw a box of paper in your trunk when you go down. You'd be crazy not to."

On the subject of Zeke Holroyd, LaBerge was equally articulate . . . and showed no sign of a guilty conscience.

"Poor fellow, I hadn't met him but I knew of him," LaBerge replied, when Margo asked if he'd known the young preacher. "Some of my managers said he was helping their workers."

"Did you donate to his mission?"

LaBerge laughed, a sound echoed briefly, eerily by the macaw. "What don't I donate to! We're on the hit list for every charity operating in Tijuana. I gave a personal check and also one from the corporation to that group Jimmy

Carter's involved with that puts up houses in Tijuana for the poor. I'm not a fundamentalist, but as long as this reverend was doing some good, helping people from small farming villages make the adjustment to life in Tijuana, I'm sure we gave him something. Why do you want to know?''

"You know this industry, you must know a lot of the people involved in it," she said carefully. To paraphrase Dorothy, this wasn't the kind of shit she wanted to spread around.

"Quite a few."

"Did you ever hear any complaints about Reverend Holroyd? About . . . his using unorthodox methods to raise money for his church?"

"Unorthodox? Not a thing. As I said, I believe I donated to his cause, and I wouldn't have if there were some question about him. What have you heard?"

"Nothing specific, just a few hints I'm trying to follow up on, see if there's a story there."

"Did you know Holroyd well?"

"Not really. He took me on a tour of the colonias the week before he died. It was the only time I ever met him."

The macaw, relatively quiet until now, started screeching. Margo jumped. She hadn't realized how tense she'd gotten; had the bird sensed it? David was full of stories of how attuned animals were to human beings: the giant turtle that bore a shipwrecked woman to safety, carrying her for two days on its back; the pig that saved a little boy who'd fallen into a pond.

LaBerge went over to the bird, scolding it affectionately and stroking its feathers until it calmed down. He turned back to Margo.

"By the way," he said, "did your son want to come see the aviary?"

"Thanks for remembering. I'm afraid David's going through an animal rights phase. Not that I don't agree with a lot of what he says. He's just so extreme. At the moment, he doesn't feel any wild animal belongs in captivity. Including your birds."

LaBerge smiled ruefully. "I've decided the real goal of

education is to make kids feel their parents are hypocrites. Either it's the way you make your living or the fact that you drive a car and pollute the air, or you have an occasional glass of wine, or you enjoy a disgusting, violent sport like football. My daughter gets on my case over the sexual harassment of women maquiladora workers. It doesn't matter how many times I tell her the industry record on that is really very good. I'm not saying harassment is never going to happen, it's inevitable when you've got a work force that's predominantly young females and managers who are mostly male. But we've been dealing with issues like that in the States since, when?—the late sixties? It's a lot better for a Mexican woman at a U.S.-owned factory than at a factory owned by Mexicans."

Margo thanked him for the interview and got up to leave.

"In case your son changes his mind, the invitation is still open," said Craig LaBerge, who was stroking the macaw's feathers again.

Having started carrying a hammer with her, Margo whacked the solenoid to get her car started in LaBerge's parking lot; she really had to get that fixed soon. It occurred to her she'd met one Mexican worker who probably could complain of sexual harassment: Rosalia, the young woman who had gotten a black eye from the boss she was dating, and who disappeared from the colonia after hearing Zeke's body was found. What had Anita said about her cousin? That Rosalia was upset about something she'd told the Padre? So much venom continually spewed from Anita's mouth that Margo hadn't paid much attention . . . but at the time, she hadn't known that Zeke engaged in blackmail. Now she experienced a twinge of anxiety. Rosalia had confided a secret to Zeke just four days before he died. Had Rosalia's secret given Zeke the upper hand on someone in the maquiladora industry, whom he then attempted to blackmail? Was that why Rosalia became distraught when she found out about Zeke's death, why she ran away?

If she'd run away. Tijuana had a multitude of canyons

where a body might lie for days. And no one seemed to be looking for Rosalia. Something about the young woman had touched Margo, maybe the fact that Rosalia was so close in age to Jenny, maybe Rosalia's spirited defiance of her jealous cousin Anita. Margo had driven out of the parking lot, but now she pulled over for a moment and checked her notebook. She found a reference to Rosalia's employer—a manufacturer of medical equipment called Sani. She had been headed for the freeway back to the radio station. Instead, she turned south. Mexico was less than half a mile away.

15 / Searching for Rosalia

Driving into the Ciudad Industrial, Margo recognized Diego Torres's brown Volkswagen. She waved, but the union organizer appeared deep in thought and didn't see her.

She remembered roughly the street where she and Zeke had come upon Rosalia and drove there. The operator of a roadside taco stand then directed her to the Sani medical equipment factory. Some of the neighboring maquiladoras had made an effort to spruce up their exteriors with brightly painted stripes or other inexpensive design touches. Sani, however, occupied a blocky gray building to which no such attention had been paid. Margo walked through a steel door into a grim, airless reception area . . . and was greeted by a radiant smile that surely belonged in a gleaming new office with expensive art on the walls.

"Can I help you?" asked the young Mexican receptionist in excellent English.

"I'm looking for someone who works here. Rosalia . . ." Margo realized she had never heard Rosalia's last name.

"Rosalia Nuñez?" the receptionist said helpfully. The name "Silvia Delatorre" was on the placard at the edge of her desk. "About seventeen, very pretty, with long black hair?"

"I think so." Although Rosalia hadn't been pretty with her bruised face. "She lives in the colonia just east of here."

Silvia Delatorre nodded enthusiastically.

"Is she at work today?" asked Margo. It was possible that Rosalia had simply left her cousin's house for more hospitable lodgings, and she was reporting to her job regularly each day: mystery solved.

"I'm very sorry." Silvia sounded as if she meant it. "Señorita Nuñez doesn't work here anymore."

"Did she quit? Did she call to say she wasn't coming in anymore?"

"I'm sorry, I don't know. I think she just stopped coming. Sometimes people do that. They have an illness in the family and they have to go back to their village suddenly, things like that. If someone is not here for more than three days and we hear nothing, their employment is terminated."

"Wouldn't she have tried to collect her pay?"

"I could ask Señor Vega, our bookkeeper. He'll be back soon."

"Thank you. It's very important that I get in touch with her. Is there anyone here who might know where to find her? A friend?" Margo cast her mind's eye over her notes, where she had jotted down the name of Rosalia's manager, the married man with whom Rosalia was carrying on an affair. "Or what about Señor Galván?"

"Maybe." Over the phone, Silvia told the manager that Margo was looking for Rosalia Nuñez. Ten minutes later, Jaime Galván opened his office door and came out to meet her.

It had occurred to Margo that Rosalia might have been dating her boss not to get ahead at work—or not only for that reason—but because he was a real hunk. One look at Jaime Galván changed her mind about that. Squat and fortyish, the manager of Sani had sunken cheekbones and pouchy jowls, as if the flesh had slipped down his face and puddled around his jawline. His body followed a similar pattern, narrow shoulders and chest bulging to a thick waist and hips. Strands of black hair were oiled rigidly across his shiny pate, emphasizing rather than disguising his partial baldness.

Whatever Galván lacked in looks, he didn't make up for in charm. Although he fussed over Margo, insisting that Silvia bring her a soda and taking her on a brief tour of the factory, he showed no real friendliness. He glanced at his watch often—was there some time allotment he was required to give each visitor? Back in his office, Galván took his time clipping the end of a cigar and lighting it before finally addressing the question of Rosalia's whereabouts.

"Silvia say you . . . look one of employees." His English was far inferior to his receptionist's, and Margo would have preferred conducting the conversation in Spanish. But she suspected Galván would be insulted if she shifted to his own language.

"Rosalia Nuñez."

"She come no more." His gaze was fixed on the cigar, which he played with, in fat, nail-bitten fingers, more than he smoked it. It didn't take Sigmund Freud to speculate that the mention of Rosalia had led Jaime Galván to communicate the nature of their relationship unconsciously.

"Did she tell you she wasn't going to work here anymore? Did she say she got another job? Or she had to go home to her family?"

"These girls, they come, they not come."

"But didn't she tell *you*?"

Galván shrugged.

"Wasn't she dating you?" Margo persisted.

"Who tell you that?" Galván spoke slowly. But something in his tone made Margo feel as if he had leaped up and fired the question at her.

"I just heard it. It's not important. I'm just trying to find her. Did she tell you where she was going?"

Had there been a macaw in the room, Margo felt sure it would have shrieked in response to the tension in Galván's body.

The phone rang. Galván grabbed it and twice muttered *sí*. After hanging up the phone, he stood and said to Margo, "Silvia show you out."

"Would you like to use the ladies' room before you go?" offered Silvia Delatorre.

"I don't know, I guess . . ."

"We keep it very nice!"

Obviously, Silvia wanted her to go to the ladies' room for some reason. Margo followed her down the hall.

"I asked Señor Vega," said Silvia. "Rosalia never got her pay. Usually when people have an emergency, they have a friend or relative pick up their pay." She opened the ladies' room door and gestured Margo inside. "Do you speak Spanish?" Margo nodded. "Good. Just wait here. I have to go back to my desk, but I think there's someone who will talk to you. A friend of Rosalia's—Laura."

A moment later, another woman came into the ladies' room; young, like Silvia Delatorre, but with none of Silvia's girlish freshness. Dressed in jeans and one of the light blue smocks Margo had seen on the workers on the factory floor, Laura expressed her individuality via teased dyed-blond hair and eyes raccooned with black liner; it was the kind of look favored by sixties' "girl groups" who sang about their boyfriends' motorcycle wrecks. Not speaking, Laura turned to the mirror, took a comb from a pocket of her smock, and ratted her hair some more. From another pocket came a can of hair spray and a pack of chewing gum. She used about a quarter of the hair spray and shoved a stick of gum into her mouth. Throughout these motions, she stared at Margo.

"*Hola*," said Margo. "Laura?"

"Why do you want to know?" A tough manner to go with the hair.

"I think Rosalia's in trouble. I want to help her."

"Yeah, you and the boss. You gonna tell Galván where she is? He's been asking about her, too."

"No! Absolutely not."

Laura faced Margo directly, staring some more.

"Who pays your salary?" Laura ought to get along well with Diego Torres. "This company? Another American manufacturer?"

"I'm a reporter from San Diego. I met Rosalia while I was doing a story on the maquiladoras."

Laura gave her hair a couple more sprays. "Okay," she said. "I don't trust you, but I'm worried about Rosa and I can't do anything. I have to work all week and I've got kids to take care of when I'm not working. Rosa always said if she was in trouble she'd go to Patricia. Patricia Colón Flores, she used to work here at the factory with us. Then she married a man who has a stand at the Bufadora. You know where that is, south of Ensenada?''

Margo nodded.

Suddenly Laura thrust herself at Margo, pinning her against the bathroom wall. Fight or flee, said Margo's instinct, but she forced herself to remain still as Laura pushed her face forward, the jutting chin grazing Margo's breastbone, the cloud of hair spray making her gag.

Laura's Spanish was rough, country-bred, but her meaning was clear. "If you hurt Rosalia, I swear, *Señora Gringa*, I will find you. And I will kill you."

Laura kept her against the wall for another ten seconds—as if to prove she could—before stepping back. "Remember, *Señora Gringa*," she said. She checked her hair in the mirror again, then left the room.

16 / The Bufadora

By the time Margo had driven as far as Rosarito, some twenty miles south of Tijuana, she could begin to imagine laughing at the incident in the dingy ladies' room of the maquiladora. "Hey, Jenny, David," she'd say to the kids. "Guess what happened to your stepmom when she was doing her boring old job today?" In fact, Laura probably wasn't much older than Jenny, despite her tough, seen-it-all pose. She definitely had Jenny's adolescent flair for drama. *Señora Gringa*, really!

Margo could begin to *imagine* laughing. But she hadn't gotten out any guffaws as yet. Her back ached from being slammed against the wall, and in spite of rolling down all the car windows and filling her lungs with gulps of sea air, she couldn't purge her nostrils of Laura's hair spray or the sick-sweet odor of the cinnamon gum she'd been chewing.

Not that Laura had meant what she'd said, lines she must have heard in the movies—"I will find you and kill you." Laura's threat, like the fact that she had confided Rosalia's location to a stranger, only reflected the depth of her worry about her friend.

Margo stepped on the gas, ignoring the Toyota's squealing tires as she took a sharp curve, heading from Rosarito south toward Ensenada—the route Zeke Holroyd had taken the night he died.

She had always pictured the toll highway as arching directly above the sea. Now she realized that for miles south of Rosarito, the highway was as much as several hundred yards inland, separated from the ocean by a broad mesa. (The old, potholed free highway, still used by locals, was downhill from the toll road much of the way.) If Zeke had gone off the tollway along here, he might still have died, crashing down one of the steeper inclines. But he might have landed in an open area or in one of the settlements that alternated between Third World shacks and modern developments catering to *norteamericano* vacationers and retirees; Zeke might have had a chance. It wasn't until just south of El Mirador, "the viewpoint," that the highway ran so sharply above the ocean that a car going over the side would plummet two hundred feet into the sea. And that, according to Ashley Green, was exactly where Zeke had crashed.

It *could* have happened the way she'd first assumed, thought Margo as she drove along the cliff edge, noting the sign CURVA PELIGROSA—dangerous curve. Zeke, probably speeding, could have swerved to avoid something in the road and lost control of his car. Or, driving late at night, he could have nodded off at the wheel. As to why the accident had happened here and not anywhere else, there was the *curva peligrosa*. But what *had* he been doing, thirty miles south of his prayer meeting? Knowing, as Margo did now, about Zeke's blackmail, it wasn't impossible to imagine him on the way to collect a payoff; nor to imagine that one of his victims had tampered with his car, or more likely, forced him off the road—how else to guarantee he'd go over where he'd be sure to die? Was that why Ashley Green had wanted Zeke's car, to look for evidence that someone had hit him from the side?

She entered Ensenada at the height of rush hour and for the next forty minutes thought of nothing but crawling through the traffic. Finally, south of the city, she reached the turnoff to Punta Banda, the point at the end of which the Bufadora was located. She jounced over a giant speed bump that extended over both lanes, then ascended the two-lane, twisting route with its dramatic drop-offs to Todos Santos Bay. The late afternoon breeze was lovely, the view magnificent, and the memories best of all. When they were first getting together, Barry, the oceanographer, had taken her to see the natural wonder where, when the tide was right, the incoming waves shot up a crevice in the cliff in a breathtaking spray. She and Barry had returned several times, staying at a shabbily elegant (irresistibly romantic) hotel across the bay. Few gringos seemed to know about the spectacular "blowhole," but the Bufadora was a popular spot for Mexicans and a small tourist area had developed there, with stands selling refreshments and trinkets. At the height of the summer tourist season, Margo assumed Patricia or her husband would be tending their stand.

At the end of Punta Banda, the road crossed the high spine of the point and arrived at the Bufadora on the ocean side. Margo parked in the dirt lot, seeing fewer cars than she had expected; past six, the tourists must have left for the day. Most of the stands remained open, however. At one, she bought a mango on a stick. The vendor rapidly peeled the fruit with a sharp knife, making a series of deft slices that turned the mango into an orange flower, and then squeezed lime juice over it. "No chile, *por favor*!" she requested. Eating chile powder on mangoes was one aspect of Mexican culture for which she had yet to develop an appreciation.

The mango vendor pointed out the stand where Patricia and her husband sold jewelry. A very pregnant woman of about twenty stood behind the counter. Chewing her mango, Margo inspected the beaded earrings, rings, and necklaces on display; there were also quite a few crosses.

"*Bonita!*" she said. Pretty. "Do you make them yourself?"

The woman nodded. "*Sí*, my husband and I."

Margo selected a pair of earrings for Jenny and a necklace for herself. She waited until she had paid—fourteen dollars—and the woman was wrapping the purchases, before she asked, "Are you Patricia Colón Flores?"

"*Sí.*" Patricia kept wrapping, unconcerned.

"Laura from the Sani factory gave me your name."

This time Patricia looked up and lowered her voice. "What do you want, señora?"

A man holding a half-finished necklace emerged from behind a curtain at the back of the stand, as if he'd sensed

Patricia's sudden apprehension.

"I just want to know if Rosalia is all right," said Margo. "Just to see if she needs anything."

"Rosalia's not here," Patricia began, but her husband broke in, "Do you have a job for her, señora? Some money? We want to help her, but we can't afford to have her stay with us, we only have enough work for two."

"But, Tomás, she can help after the baby comes . . ." said Patricia.

The curtain swung to the side and Rosalia came out, head high.

"It's all right, Patricia," she said. Margo guessed that both living and jewelry-making took place behind the curtain. In the cramped quarters, Rosalia must have overheard any arguments about her presence that took place between husband and wife.

"Did you come here alone?" said Rosalia. Margo nodded. "And you were a friend of the Padre?"

"I knew him. And I have a message from Beatriz," Margo added, remembering the name of Anita's oldest child.

That brought a smile. "Beatriz, is she okay?"

"She misses her favorite cousin."

"Come with me and we'll talk," said Rosalia, leading Margo outside and down the row of stands.

"Do you want a beer? Or a soda?" Margo offered.

"Beer."

Margo bought two cans of Carta Blanca, then followed Rosalia, who veered in the other direction from the wide, paved walk to the Bufadora. Instead they took a path along the cliffside. At a spot where the path widened slightly, Rosalia motioned her to sit down. The tough dry coastal grass was softer there, matted, as if Rosalia had come there before.

Rosalia opened her beer and took a swallow. "You told Patricia you want to help me. Why?" Although Rosalia seemed resigned to having to talk to Margo, her tone was belligerent. "Are you just a nice *norteamericana* who wants to give me charity? Or are you like the Padre? He wanted to help people but only if they prayed with him.''

''I'm not like the Padre. If you're in trouble, if you're afraid of someone, maybe I can help with that.''

Rosalia gave a harsh, older-than-her-years laugh. ''How about money, señora? I always gave most of my pay to Anita—Anita would never admit it, but I did. I didn't have much money to bring with me, and you can see, it's difficult for Patricia and Tomás to let me stay here.''

''I can give you some money. Rosalia, why did you run away after the Padre died?''

''I just didn't want to stay there anymore.''

''Is there some particular person you're afraid of? You asked if I came alone. Were you afraid that someone came here with me? Jaime Galván?''

Rosalia closed her eyes, tilted the can of beer to her lips. She drank in tiny sips, as if she didn't really like the taste. ''If I were afraid of someone, how could you do anything about that?'' she said after a moment. ''Could you send me to New York and get me a job and a place to live, so he couldn't ever find me?''

''I could find out what happened. I could find out if someone killed the Padre,'' Margo promised.

Rosalia moaned. ''You don't think the Padre died because of what I told him? He just had an accident, didn't he?''

''If that's what you think, then why did you run away?''

''It's just that the Padre had a way of making you tell him things. You were only going to tell him one thing and you felt better after you told him one thing, so then you told him more. Patricia says I never should have talked to him, only to a priest. It's so crazy, I never wanted to pray with the Padre, but now I pray with Patricia all the time. Catholic prayers. Those are the only real prayers, Patricia says.''

''What did you tell the Padre?''

''I didn't think it was important.''

''It probably wasn't. If you just tell me about it, I can prove it wasn't important and then you won't have to be afraid to go back to Tijuana. Did the Padre ask who hit you?'' Margo felt as if she were coaxing information from Jenny, reminding her keenly that Rosalia was only seventeen. As with Jenny, the girl's fear might mean she was in real danger . . . or it might result from nothing more than teenage hormones and the emotional maelstroms they caused, which surely crossed every cultural barrier in the universe. Whether or not Zeke had been killed, Rosalia's connection with his death might exist nowhere outside her own highly colored imagination . . . not to mention her longing to escape a tedious forty-eight-hour workweek, a bedroom shared with three small children, and a cousin who called her a whore, thought Margo, skeptically listening to the story Rosalia had told Zeke.

Several days before Zeke's trip with Margo to the colonia, Rosalia had gone to the Sani factory on a Sunday afternoon. She and *el jefe*—the boss, as she jokingly called her boyfriend—had a date and she was supposed to meet him at Sani. No one should have been at work on a Sunday, but that day *el jefe* was supervising two men unloading barrels, the kind chemicals came in, from a big truck. When *el jefe* saw Rosalia there, he got furious. *What are you doing here?* he shouted at her. He was so mad he even hit her. He'd apologized later for having hit her: a new sweater, an evening at a fancy club in *el norte*.

"How many barrels?" asked Margo.

"Seventy? Eighty? Maybe even a hundred."

"Did it say anything on the sides of the barrels? For instance, *residuos peligrosos*?" Toxic wastes.

Rosalia looked sulky. "I don't know." It occurred to Margo that Rosalia might not know how to read.

"What were the men doing with the barrels? Were they dumping them down the drain?"

"*Por supuesto no!*" Of course not. "We all know that's illegal, that it makes people sick. They were just putting the barrels in an area of the factory where chemicals are stored all the time."

"It doesn't sound like there's anything wrong with that."

"Exactly."

"So why did you run away?"

"I don't know. *El jefe* acted really strange that night he took me to the nightclub, and then I came home and found out the Padre had died the night before."

In a panic, she had fled to Patricia's. She'd walked half-way across Tijuana at night and in the early morning caught a bus to Maneadero, the closest town to the Bufadora. She'd picked up a ride the rest of the way. She had spent the first several days at Patricia's so terrified she couldn't eat or sleep. But it was already a week now. No one had come after her. And Tomás clearly wanted her gone.

"I am just being stupid, no, like Tomás says?" she said. "A tiny little thing happens and I act like it's the end of the world."

Tomás might well have a point. What had Rosalia seen, after all? Jaime Galván was probably just taking a routine shipment and had gotten irritated at Rosalia because he didn't like having to work on Sunday, or because she'd misunderstood their meeting plans, or because of trouble at home . . . or just because he was a bully who enjoyed hitting a woman if he could get away with it.

"If you think you're stupid to be afraid, do you want to go back?" said Margo. "Should I drive you back to the colonia tonight?"

"Oh, no, señora." Even if Rosalia's intellect said that she was overreacting, apparently her gut refused to believe it. Then again, Margo cautioned herself, Rosalia's gut was seventeen years old.

Margo had only two twenty-dollar bills in her wallet. She handed them to Rosalia, who accepted the money with proud thanks, as payment for information given. "The tide's coming in," said Rosalia. "You should go see the Bufadora."

Margo left her sitting, watching the sea.

The sun was just setting when Margo got to the Bufadora, and the tide must have been perfect, because there were dazzling explosions of spume against the backdrop of the flaming sky. The sight was so beautiful it occurred to her she could die immediately and her last moment would be pure bliss.

There is a popular California saying, borrowed from the Chinese: *Be careful what you ask for. You might get it.* Margo drove down the narrow road toward the main highway, able to slow when she needed to by shifting gears. Toward the bottom of the hill, however, several vehicles had come to a full stop before proceeding over the giant speed bump. Directly ahead of her was a rickety old truck loaded with bales of hay. Margo briefly, absurdly thought of the Spanish word for brakes—*frenos*—when she realized she had none.

She pumped on the useless brakes nevertheless, at the same time she frantically downshifted and scanned the roadside. At least this area was flat, no drop-offs, but she saw a group of children standing right next to the road. She laid on the horn and pulled up on the emergency brake, which slowed her only a little. Just past the kids was an open area; it was slightly blocked by the hay truck but the truck was moving forward at last. Margo steered off the road. A *wham!*—to the car and her body—when she nicked the edge of the hay truck. Loose hay spilled across the windshield, blinding her as the car kept going off the road.

17 / A Body Is Found

It was hot work for a man in a suit, crawling over the exposed undercarriage of the Toyota, flipped over on the Mexican mesa. The late morning sun burned mercilessly. Less than a quarter of a mile away, at the bottom of the hill, the sea itself seemed to burn with a deep turquoise flame. If there was a breeze from that burning ocean, it only made things hotter, steamier.

Although Ashley Green had taken off his suit jacket, he couldn't help sweating profusely as he crouched on top of the crashed car.

"Totaled," he said to the mangy yellow Mexican dog that had come to watch what he was doing. Not that the damage to the car was so extensive; the several bales of hay that had burst and covered the car had provided some protection. But no car six or seven years old could take much damage before the repair costs went higher than the Blue Book value of the car.

And already scavengers had removed the two right-side tires, as well as—Green jumped down and looked inside—the car stereo.

Someone had either made off with the rest of the stuff Simon was carrying in the car—her purse or appointment book, whatever—or had gathered the things up for her. Lying on the upside-down ceiling of the car was nothing but junk: advertising fliers she must have removed from under her windshield wiper and tossed in the backseat, a few crumpled tissues, an empty soda bottle. That and half a dozen cassette tapes, apparently not to the taste of whoever had stolen the stereo: Kate Bush, Peter Gabriel, Miles Davis, cello concerti, the Bulgarian Women's Chorus, and some group called the Roches. What weird kind of radio station did this Simon work for, anyway? "What the hell," Green remarked to the dog, pocketing the Miles Davis tape and the cello concerti.

He beckoned to the tow truck driver who was waiting on the road. The man came over, but shook his head no—how could he tow the car when it only had one back tire? Green argued with him in ungrammatical but effective Spanish, pointing out that he could transfer the remaining left front tire to the right rear. Finally he bought the man's cooperation with another twenty-dollar bill. Green made sure the man understood about the garage in Tijuana where he should take Simon's car, because he would have to get authorization to take it back over the border.

He spent the next hour asking questions at the little stands at the end of the road. No one claimed to know anything about a *norteamericana* who had been there the day before, one who'd crashed her car driving back from the Bufadora. *Oh, a señora had a car accident? Qué lástima! How unfortunate.* But each time someone denied any knowledge of Margo Simon, they looked in the same general direction, or else they tried very hard not to look that way. So maybe Margo Simon had talked to someone at the fish taco stand, where Green made himself eat a very greasy taco—thank God he had some antacids in his car. He'd be willing to bet a lifetime supply of Tums, however, that the radio reporter hadn't gone to the taco stand but to its neighbor, a stand overseen by a young, very pregnant jewelry vendor. Green took his time buying a bracelet for his wife, lazily, skillfully lobbing in questions. But he got no answers. He debated offering the woman money for telling him about Simon's visit—she could surely use it, with a baby coming—but he decided to take a walk first. Might as well check out this Bufadora, as long as he had come all the way here.

He got a bottle of mineral water, hoping it might help settle the fish taco, and walked down to the Bufadora. The tide was out so there were no spectacular waterworks, but it was a pretty spot, up high on the cliff. It might be worth bringing the kids to see; he'd check a tide table first to make sure they'd get a good show. At the far side of the parking lot, he found a path along the cliffside and followed it a bit. He wanted to give the pregnant lady some time before he came back, so she wouldn't feel he was rushing her. Ashley Green knew he had discovered a great secret of life when he'd learned not to rush people. Better for his professional purposes and for his own touchy digestion.

He'd walked about a hundred feet down the path when he noticed some broken vegetation with threads of fabric caught on it. Looking all the way down the cliffside, he saw something caught—half-hidden—in the rocks at the water's edge. He ran and scrambled the rest of the way down to the woman's body with the long, sodden black hair.

The rocks had kept her from being pulled out to sea. The rocks had broken her as well.

18 / Zeke's List

"Margo?" The whisper penetrated her consciousness. After the awareness of the voice, came a fresh awareness of pain. "Margo, are you asleep?"

"Just resting," Margo lied. With her fingertips she touched her face around her right eye. The area was swollen and it hurt like hell.

"Look what I made. Tabouleh. Your favorite."

"That's great, Jen." Forcing herself to sit up without groaning, Margo let Jenny place the bed tray over her legs. The Middle Eastern salad—bulgur wheat, tomatoes, cucumbers, parsley, and fresh mint leaves—was attractively arranged on the plate, surrounded by little crackers and even radish rosettes. She took a forkful. "Umm, you put extra lemon in it, didn't you? It's delicious."

Under most circumstances, Margo would have loved the TLC from her stepdaughter; in fact, she would have regarded it as a minor miracle that Jenny had insisted on spending the day nursing her, instead of hanging out at the beach with her friends. (Where *had* Jenny learned to make radish rosettes?) At the moment, however, her head throbbed too much to leave her with any appetite. All she wanted to do was lie in the darkened room, maybe listening to very soft music.

"Turn on the radio?" she asked.

"Sure!" The girl's eager voice boomed in Margo's head.

The radio was tuned to KSDR, where Larry Weil, the fund-raising director, was doing a pledge break. Margo sometimes liked to listen to her colleagues asking for money, to pick up pointers for her own technique; this was not one of those times. She was about to ask Jenny to switch to the jazz station, when she heard Larry say her own name. He was "sending her good wishes while she's at home recovering from the car accident she had in Mexico yesterday." Someone had mentioned the accident on the air earlier and the station had gotten numerous calls, said Larry, from fans concerned about her condition. At least the accident had had one positive outcome: KSDR—and Margo—now knew she had "fans." She would have to appreciate the fact . . . when she regained the ability to think.

"Thanks, Jen, I'll eat more later," she said, closing her eyes. "And I don't need the radio right now. I think I'll sleep a little more."

"Don't you want a radish? I thought you loved radishes."

"They're so beautiful, I just want to admire them." She was making an effort to go along with the girl's ministrations, knowing the accident had shaken up Jenny, too. But the crunch of a radish between her teeth would resound in her head like a jackhammer. "Jenny, if you'll give me some water, I'll take another pill." Tylenol with codeine, that ought to help.

Jenny left her alone at last, after several admonitions to summon her—with two Tibetan cymbals tied together with a string that Jenny had discovered among her dad's old hippie trappings—the second Margo needed her.

Cuts and bruises did, in fact, seem to be the major damage the crash had inflicted on Margo's body. She didn't know how she had gotten hurt in some places, a badly scraped elbow, for instance. Had she thrown up her arm to protect her face? She couldn't remember the actual accident at all.

She had a clear image of driving down the road from the Bufadora, then seeing the hay truck stopped ahead of her and realizing her brakes were gone. She had steered off the road, downshifting frantically. After that came a blank . . . until the memory of hanging upside down from her seat belt, people speaking excited Spanish around her.

Someone mentioned the *Cruz Roja*, the Mexican Red Cross. Someone else insisted they must get her out of the car, in case of leaking gasoline. Hands reached over her then to unfasten her seat belt, at the same time other hands firmly supported her shoulders. She hadn't been feeling any pain at first, probably the result of adrenaline and shock. The pain came when she was being lifted from the car. She blacked out.

The next time she'd regained consciousness, she was lying by the roadside with a rough blanket wrapped around her, hearing the sound of sirens. The Cruz Roja! It was not the Red Cross, however, but the police, and once they saw that she wasn't bleeding to death, they began shouting questions at her about car insurance. Oh, God! She told them to check for a policy in her glove compartment or purse. But her injuries hadn't left her *that* confused. She knew she had crossed the border without buying Mexican auto insurance.

More sirens sounded, this time the Cruz Roja. While the police searched for her nonexistent insurance, two young men gently probed her body, cleaned and dressed several cuts, and shone a light in her eyes. The men helped her stand up; she was able to hobble around. They asked her what day it was and who was the president of the United States. If she'd guessed what was coming, she would have answered, "Mickey Mouse." Anything but the correct response, which got her a nod of okay from the nice Cruz Roja men and delivery back into the hands of the police, who were not nice at all.

"You have no insurance policy," said one of the policemen.

"Did you check the backseat?" she asked. At the time, she thought the accident must have affected her Spanish, because the man's reply made no sense at all.

"Breathe," he said.

"I'm sorry?"

"Breathe out." He leaned toward her mouth.

Margo hadn't thought things could get worse. She'd forgotten about the beer she had drunk with Rosalia.

In the cramped, smelly police station to which she was transported, the police laughed when she asked them to go back and investigate why her car had lost its brakes. To them, she knew, she was just another gringa who'd come to Baja to get loose and was trying to get out of trouble for driving drunk, not to mention the really serious offenses of driving without Mexican insurance and damaging Mexican property—the hay truck driver was complaining about the loss of some of his hay as well as damage to his truck.

After they'd made her sit two hours in a cell, they finally allowed her to telephone Barry. (For twenty dollars, they would have let her use the phone sooner, but she'd given all her money to Rosalia.) After another three hours—and two hundred dollars, cash, a bounty to be shared by the hay truck driver and the cops—Barry was driving her back across the border. They went first to a hospital emergency room, where Margo once again named the president correctly and a doctor extracted her contact lens from her puffy right eye, an experience she would gladly never endure again. The doctor told them signs of concussion to watch out for, although he said her seat belt had probably saved her from hitting her head too hard. Lying in bed now, she indulged in a groan (too soft for Jenny to hear). She hated to think how much more her head might be throbbing if she had hit it any harder.

Although Jenny had moved the fan close to the bed, it was having little effect against the sweltering day. A breeze from the canyon usually cooled the old house, but there was no breeze today. Worse, the cat had curled up beside Margo. She pushed it away, but it returned, its body like a damp hot water bottle against her side. (Grimalkin, having witnessed the murder of its former mistress, seemed to need reassurance that Margo was alive.) Finally, uncomfortably, she fell asleep.

It was a dream she used to have as a child.

She'd be riding on the school bus. The bus made a stop and the driver had to get out for a moment. While the driver was away, the bus started moving—slowly at first, but then faster and faster. Little Margo on the bus experienced pure terror. She didn't try to call out to the driver, she knew he couldn't do anything. Could she stop the bus by herself? What were you supposed to do? Even though she wasn't aware of standing or moving up the aisle, the driver's seat got closer and the steering wheel grew bigger in her field of vision. But she still didn't know what to do next!

She always used to wake up while the bus was still hurtling forward. This time she felt the impact as it crashed into the fence around the school playground.

Another childhood nightmare. She'd be riding her bike down the steepest hill in the Connecticut suburb where she grew up. It felt exciting, but she couldn't make the bike stop! She was coming to an intersection at the bottom of the hill, a street with lots of traffic. The bike was going faster, the wind rushing past her. She heard a pounding noise, then the sound of voices yelling.

She woke up sweaty and panting. That hadn't been in the dream before—pounding and yelling. Or was she still dreaming, since the yelling continued? Groggily she sat up. She recognized Jenny's voice.

"She can't see anybody. She's sleeping," Jenny said loudly.

The other voice was softer but insistent. "I'll wait until she wakes up. Please!"

Margo reached for the Tibetan cymbals. *Ding-ng-ng-ng! Ding-ng-ng-ng!* They sounded as if they were ringing right inside her skull. Yow, those things would definitely get your attention if you were trying to meditate and your thoughts wandered.

"See, you woke her up!" Jenny's footsteps thundered toward the bedroom at the back of the house. "Margo," she called out, entering the bedroom, "there's this woman here and she really looks weird."

The feet that followed Jenny knew how to move lightly—all those years of dance. And "weird" was right.

"Oh, Margo, I'm so sorry!" Lael Holroyd burst after Jenny into the room. Then, "Oh! Oh, they said on the radio you had an accident, but I didn't . . .'' Taking a good look at Margo, Lael turned white.

Margo felt shocked, as well. She knew how bad *she* looked; she had taken a peek in a mirror earlier. What she wasn't prepared for was Lael's appearance.

''What did you do?'' she gasped, at the sight of Lael's raggedly shorn hair.

Formerly her prettiest feature, now none of Lael's hair was more than an inch long. In some places it was cut to her scalp.

Lael ignored the question. ''Please, I've got to talk to you. . . . It's all my fault,'' she said, once Margo had convinced Jenny to leave the intruder alone with her. Lael sat on a chair next to the bed.

''What's your fault?''

A glazed look came into Lael's eyes. '''The wrath of God is being revealed from heaven against all the godlessness and wickedness of men who by their wickedness suppress the truth.''

''Lael. . . . Lael!'' Margo got her attention. ''Are you saying you've been suppressing the truth?''

Lael nodded. She looked like a twelve-year-old urchin, maybe a victim of some vitamin deficiency that had ravaged her hair.

''Do you want to tell me the truth now?''

Lael handed her a piece of paper. Margo put on her glasses—ouch! that hurt!—and looked at the list. It was organized in three columns: dates, initials, and dollar figures.

''Zeke's private file,'' Lael explained. ''I always knew how to access it, but I never would have. But then I heard about your accident. I kept thinking about that man who said he was from the insurance company. Ashley Green.'' Her eyes glazed again. '' 'Your enemy the devil prowls around like a roaring lion, looking for someone to devour.' Ashley Green is the Antichrist, he's the devil!''

Did the people in Lael and Zeke's church often bounce back and forth between rationality and the lunatic fringe? Or was this mode of discourse unique to Lael? Seeing her butchered hair, it was impossible not to speculate that she was seriously disturbed, whether as a consequence of her grief or because she had been unbalanced to start with.

At least the list in Margo's hand was real. There were twenty-five entries on it, dating back two years, roughly to the time Zeke had started the Tijuana mission. Margo assumed the first entry, "R.K.," stood for Robert Kohler, the maquiladora operator who had employed women to sew in their homes and hadn't filed the proper papers. Finding out about Kohler's illegal operation must have been the golden egg that made Zeke think of blackmailing not just the struggling colonia dwellers, but far wealthier participants in the maquiladora industry. And R.K.'s first payment—five thousand dollars—had demonstrated how handsomely crime could pay. Kohler's initials appeared quarterly after that, with payments of twenty-five hundred dollars each time. Most of the other amounts on the list were smaller, five hundred to one thousand dollars, and the initials weren't repeated, as if Zeke had caught people in relatively minor infractions . . . or the people had proved tougher marks than Kohler had been.

There *was* one other person, however, who'd paid as consistently and as richly as Kohler: "D.T." D.T.—Diego Torres?—had started off with a bang a year ago, handing over eight thousand dollars, and had kept paying a thousand dollars a month. It added up to a bigger annual "contribution" to Zeke's church than even Bob Kohler was making; and the monthly payment schedule meant that D.T. was reminded even more frequently of Reverend Ezekiel Holroyd's unwelcome intrusion into his life.

"Lael, do you know what this list means?"

"Not really. I just know Zeke kept it secret." She smiled. "He had to ask me how to set up a secret file. But he knew I wouldn't look. I wouldn't have, either, if the Antichrist hadn't come."

She was slipping back into the ozone. Margo reached for her hand. "He put down initials and amounts of money. Don't you have a guess about what it is?"

"Sure. Donations to the church. If you total them up, it's

about a thousand less than all the money he got at speaking engagements. Those people must have wanted to donate anonymously.''

"Okay, but do you know who any of these people are?'' Margo spoke patiently. She didn't know whether she was going to be answered by the religious zealot, the pathetic little widow, or the bright business major who had figured out that the secret donations entered the pot through Zeke's speaking gigs.

Lael shook her head.

"Did Zeke ever mention Diego Torres, a union organizer working in the colonia?"

Lael moved her chair closer. "I really don't know anything about the list. I'm just giving it to you because you need it.''

"What do you mean, I need the list?" Even if Lael, for all her innocent air, had figured out what Zeke was up to, wouldn't she want to keep his blackmail a secret?

"You need to protect yourself. Zeke crashed his car in Mexico and now the same thing happened to you. Don't you see, the Antichrist Ashley Green is after you, too!" Lael stood up, smiling, as if she hadn't just taken a wide detour into la-la land. "I've got to go now. I'll pray for you.''

She turned, with that dancer's grace, and scurried out of the room.

Margo—hearing Jenny escorting their visitor out the door—felt awake for the first time since the accident. Too bewildered by shock, pain, and pills, she had ignored the evidence right in front of her, until Lael had stated it so clearly. *Zeke crashed in Mexico and so did you.* It was exactly what Margo had been looking for, proof that Zeke Holroyd had not died by accident but had been killed . . . because the same person who killed Zeke had tried to kill her. What if she had needed her brakes not at the foot of the hill, where the road leveled off, but on one of the curves higher up the road, where she would have encountered a sheer drop?

It occurred to Margo that she still must not be thinking

properly because, realizing someone had tried to kill her, shouldn't she feel terror? Instead, she felt excited . . . and suddenly, extremely hungry. She went to the kitchen, where she loaded a plate with tabouleh and wolfed it down.

19 / Throwing Pots

Black Mountain is the mushiest of clays, the most sensual. With a sigh of happiness, Margo got her hands around a damp chunk of the chocolate-brown clay she had cut from a twenty-five-pound block. Only two days after her accident, she still had to stay home from work and rest. To the doctor, that might mean lying in bed. But Margo couldn't imagine anything more healing than throwing pots.

Carefully she wedged the clay, pushing it forward on a slate board to remove any air bubbles. She had already assembled a bowl of water, a sponge, and various tools on the semicircular metal tray at the front of the wheel. Although the patio was getting a breeze this afternoon, the weather remained brutally hot and humid, and her head still throbbed. The discomforts of heat and headache faded, however, when she sat down, flicked the switch that made the wheel turn, and began to work the clay—pushing it up into a cone, flattening it with the heel of her hand, and pushing it up again. Plasticizing, the step was called. The term always struck her as strange, since the dense clay was so much the opposite of plastic and the artificial.

Margo had tried meditation, but she had never found the experience as quieting to her mind as working with clay. Sitting in a half-lotus and mumbling a mantra, she tended to think of everything from a recent conversation to world politics to what she wanted to eat for dinner. At the pottery wheel, she dropped almost instantly into clay-mind, a state in which her intelligence shifted into her fingers. After a while, her thoughts took on words again, but it was as if she had gotten—not smarter but wiser, her inner voice more resonant.

By the time she had completed two large bowls and was starting a third, she felt ready to return to the questions she'd been mulling over since the day before . . . beginning with her conviction that the ''D.T.'' on Zeke's list must be the Mexican union organizer, Diego Torres.

Torres seemed to exist in a state of chronic anger, and he hated Zeke, an antipathy not the least softened by Zeke's death, Margo reflected, cupping her hands behind the rotating mound of clay to center it. And Torres was rumored to have planted caustic chemicals in at least one of the colonia water barrels as a ploy to drum up support for his union. Had Zeke acquired proof of that? Margo didn't know how Diego Torres could have paid Zeke almost twenty thousand dollars during the past year, but Torres was an educated man; maybe he came from a wealthy family, like any number of social reformers who dedicated themselves to helping the poor. And whether he was desperately scraping together the money each month or withdrawing it from a fat trust fund, it would have galled him to give Zeke Holroyd a single dollar. How much must it have galled him to hand over thousands? Enough that he'd killed his tormentor?

Margo opened a hole in the center of the clay and began to push up the bowl's sides.

Torres spoke passionately of the injustices suffered by the maquiladora workers, but he was a planner as well. Wouldn't it take both a planner and a passionate man to set up a meeting with Zeke in Ensenada, follow him from his prayer meeting in Rosarito, and at just that point where the highway curved dangerously close to the cliff edge, force Zeke's car off the road?

Torres must have overhead Carmen telling her about Zeke's blackmail and feared what Margo would discover next. As for opportunity, on the afternoon of her ''accident,'' he had probably only pretended not to see her in the Ciudad Industrial; all he had to do was follow her, then wait in the Sani parking lot until she left. And he knew enough about cars to cut her brake line, she thought, picturing him starting her car by hitting the solenoid. . . .

"Shit!" She had been opening the bowl, the finishing touch, and she had pushed the clay too far so it collapsed outward. She excised the ruined top of the piece with a wire tool—a length of wire stretched between two wooden handles—and commenced a salvage job; this bowl would just be short and squat.

Margo could see Torres running Zeke off the road, but not trying to murder her. Why not? she challenged herself. Was she soft toward Diego Torres because he reminded her of a flamenco dancer? Or because she liked his politics, even if she found the man himself prickly and argumentative?

Cutting the finished bowl off the wheel with the wire tool, she slid it onto a batt, a flat square of plywood that wouldn't stick to the clay later, and set the bowl to dry in the sun. She decided to do a vase next, which meant she needed to throw onto a batt directly. She secured the batt to the wheel, then sliced another hunk of Black Mountain. She kept wanting to work big today, as if to assert her strength after the vulnerability of the accident.

If Diego Torres could have followed her from Sani, she reflected, plasticizing the clay, so could Jaime Galván. The factory manager only had to slip out to his car and wait until she came out from her talk with Rosalia's friend. That brought Margo back to Rosalia's story, of seeing Galván unloading barrels that might have contained toxic chemicals. Damn! What could the story have revealed to Zeke that Margo remained unable to perceive? On what grounds would Zeke have attempted to blackmail Galván? Rosalia had sworn *el jefe* wasn't dumping the toxins. And although Mexico legally placed limits on how long toxins could be stored, was that regulation even enforced? How serious could breaking it be? Even if Zeke went ahead and reported Galván for illegally storing toxins, so what? Galván could have gotten rid of them before any inspector came.

Unless Rosalia hadn't told her the whole story that day at the Bufadora. Margo wouldn't be surprised if Rosalia had held something back—though whether it had any actual relevance or only played some part in Rosalia's dramatic imagination was anyone's guess.

Margo centered the vase and began forming the walls, paying more attention this time.

Of course, there was another explanation, much simpler than the toxins mystery, for what Zeke might have had on Galván; say he threatened to tell Galván's wife about the affair with Rosalia. Señora Galván might have a well-off family to whom she could flee, or brothers who believed in revenge. Or, what if Zeke had threatened to tell *el jefe del jefe*, the boss's boss? What would the U.S. owner of Sani think of his manager dating a seventeen-year-old worker? As Craig LaBerge had said, U.S. businesses had been grappling with the issue of sexual harassment for decades. Say that Galván had previously been reprimanded for going after his employees. If he was reported for the affair with Rosalia, could he have lost his job?

Margo had to admit that she preferred Galván in the villain role . . . and that she had not a single piece of evidence that Zeke had ever approached him. There was, in fact, only one blackmailee, among the maquiladora management, whose identity she felt sure of. And he seemed the most unlikely suspect of all.

Robert Kohler owned a maquiladora and tooled around in a Porsche, so maybe the bite Zeke was putting on him—over twenty-two thousand dollars in two years—barely left any teeth marks. Further, Kohler hadn't shown up at the church until the day *after* Zeke died, after his body was found and the news broadcast on a Mexican radio station. If Kohler had killed Zeke, he wouldn't have needed the radio to tell him about it. Wouldn't he have searched Zeke's office the same night he forced the preacher off the road? And what about the attempt on Margo? How would Kohler have known she was going to the Bufadora?

Then again, Kohler would have heard she had visited his factory. If he was as rich as he appeared, he could have paid someone to follow her, even hired a killer, keeping his own hands clean.

Margo finished the vase and carefully cut the batt off the wheel, feeling a great sense of accomplishment. It was the largest vase she'd ever made.

Diego Torres. Jaime Galván. Robert Kohler. That left only one more person whom she considered highly suspicious, although that person's connection to Ezekiel Holroyd eluded her.

As if on cue, Mr. Ashley Green walked around the side of the house and onto the patio. "Howdy." He smiled.

Margo didn't give him a chance to get any closer. She was holding the batt with the new vase, seven pounds of thick, wet Black Mountain clay. She flung it as hard as she could at Ashley Green.

20 / Ashley Green Comes Clean

Margo ran inside the house and locked the back door.

"Hey, wait a second!" Ashley Green yelled after her.

She didn't know if she should shut all the windows next or call the police. She compromised by slamming shut the big, low window in the dining room that could be easily climbed through. Then she snatched up the cordless phone that was sitting on the dining room table. One of the automatic dial buttons was programmed for the 911 emergency number.

"Don't you want to find out more about that accident you had?" said Green.

Margo moved to where she could see and hear him easily through the screened window above the kitchen sink. Green was wiping blobs of clay off his face. He didn't look happy about the clay, but he hadn't pulled out any weapons of his own to retaliate.

"Who are you?" she called out the window.

"Like I told you, Ashley Green, from the insurance company."

She waved the phone so he could see it. "The insurance company has never heard of you. I'm calling the police."

"Hey, okay." He held up his hands, an I-give-up gesture. "You're right, I'm not from the insurance company. I'm a private detective."

"Sure, and your name is really Ashley, like the plantation owner in *Gone With the Wind*."

"Frankly, ma'am," he said, exaggerating his Southern

drawl, "it is. My mamma didn't go to the movies much and she sure didn't have the time or the education to read novels. She heard the name Ashley and thought it sounded real elegant; she didn't have any idea who Ashley Wilkes was. By the time I thought of changing it, all the good African names were already taken by basketball stars. You know, Kareem Abdul-Jabbar, Hakeem Olajawon, Dr. J."

Margo found herself smiling.

"What about the detective part?" she said. "Is that true?"

"I swear."

There ought to be something else to ask him. "Do you have a license?"

"Sure do, if you don't mind my reaching into my pocket to get it." He moved with exaggerated slowness—no gun, see?—as if he'd seen plenty of movies himself, to make up for all the ones his mamma missed, or as if he genuinely did things like this in real life. He advanced toward the kitchen window carefully, holding up a state of California private investigator license for her to see. Not that Margo knew what a bona fide PI license would look like. Couldn't Green have had his "license" printed at the same place where he got the business card identifying him as an insurance agent?

"If you want to, call up Werth Investigations, that's the firm I work for," he said. "They'll confirm it. The number's—"

"That's okay." Margo kept an eye on him as she got out the telephone book. If Green were bogus, he could give her a bogus phone number, with an accomplice primed to corroborate his story.

"It's spelled W-E-R-T-H," he said. "God, this clay gets itchy when it dries."

She found the listing, called, and was told that Ashley Green was indeed one of the agency's "operatives."

"Can I come in?" pleaded Green. "I'd sure like to use your washroom to get this stuff off. Then we can talk."

"There's a hose on the patio."

Margo wasn't going to let Green in the house, but she

was tempted to go out and talk to him. First, however, she wanted to alert someone. Not Barry, who had worried several dozen new gray hairs into his sandy thatch since her car crash. She needed an ally with good nerves and not a tremendous amount of concern for her safety. She waited until Green had turned off the hose, then punched the button for one of the numbers programmed into the phone. Loudly, so that Green could hear, she told Claire De Jong at KSDR who Green was and that she was going out to the patio to talk to him. Claire promised to call back in fifteen minutes. If Margo didn't answer, Claire would call the police. Eventually, Claire was going to demand a detailed explanation and Margo knew she would have to provide one, but she'd think about that tomorrow. Tomorrow was another day.

"Good for you," said Ashley Green, when she came out the back door. "I'm always telling my wife to be more careful about who she opens the door to. Thanks." He caught the towel she tossed him and dried his face. "You wouldn't believe the people she invites in. Folks selling magazine subscriptions, these aggressive guys who ask you to vote for them but it's really a sales pitch, Jehovah's Witnesses. She talks to all of them. Leaves them alone in the living room and gets them a big glass of lemonade. She buys something from all of them, too, or gives a donation. You'd think, married to a PI for twenty years, she'd be more suspicious, but it has the opposite effect. She figures I've got all the suspiciousness the family needs. She'd rather trust everyone." He was using the towel to dab water on his shirt. "Hey, this clay doesn't stain, does it?"

"It always comes out of my clothes. Wash the shirt in cold water." Although the peach-colored shirt Green had on might prove an exception. Margo tended to do pottery in old jeans and T-shirts that could take plenty of abuse.

Green's disarming chat partly reassured her he was what he said he was; she assumed that a private detective would use the same techniques she did to relax an interviewee. But a con man, too, was surely expert at putting his victims at ease. Look how skillfully Zeke had elicited people's confidences. Margo kept the cordless phone in her hand and stood between Ashley Green and the back door. Green himself leaned back in the wicker chair.

"If you're a private detective, someone must be paying you to look into Zeke Holroyd's death," she said.

"Let's just say I'm helping someone who wants to know a little more about how Reverend Holroyd died."

"Not good enough." She waved the phone. For all she knew, he could be working for Zeke's murderer.

Ashley Green sighed. "This can't go on the radio. And for God's sake, don't tell Ms. Holroyd, I don't want to give her any ideas. Okay?"

"Okay."

"I'm working for Suzuki."

"The car maker?"

"Well, not the violin teachers. Because of the bad publicity the Samurai got, about flipping over, they're worried Ms. Holroyd will sue. The U.S. government tests came down on the company's side, so they'd have a good chance of winning in court, but going to court at all would cost a fortune. A lot cheaper to hire me to find out the real cause of Reverend Holroyd's accident.

"So," he continued, "I meet you at Holroyd's house and find out you're a reporter. Then you go off the road in Mexico, just like Holroyd did. Probably just a coincidence, hundreds of gringos have car accidents in Mexico every day. Hey, hundreds of Mexicans have accidents in Mexico. But that's a big part of my job, figuring out what's a coincidence and what isn't. Why don't you tell me how your accident happened?"

Green's explanation sounded plausible. A good con man would sound plausible, too, Margo cautioned herself. Still, she saw no reason not to answer him.

"I lost my brakes."

"Your car was a few years old? Maybe more than a few years?"

"Six."

"Maybe you haven't had it in the shop recently for a diagnostic, or you put off getting something fixed?"

"I wasn't aware of any major problems." It occurred to her that he was asking all the questions. Her turn. "From what you said to Lael, you initially figured Zeke went off the road because he was drunk or he was on drugs. It sounds like you don't believe that anymore. How do *you* think Zeke died? Do you think someone cut his brakes, and also cut mine?"

"Uh-uh. Someone might've cut Zeke's brakes, but I think he had to be forced off the road for him to crash exactly where he did. Have you seen the place?"

She nodded. Green's theory jibed with her own.

"If someone forced Zeke off the road, could you find dent marks on the side of his car?" she asked.

"I wish. The car bounced off the cliff a few times on the way down and then spent about twelve hours in the ocean. It's hard to tell anything. What I think is, the rev was up to something, or say he knew something he shouldn't have known, and it made someone feel real threatened. Say you found out about it and the person felt threatened by you. So this person engineered an auto accident for him and tried to do it for you, too, they just used a different method. And, lucky for you, they weren't as successful."

The phone rang—Claire De Jong, checking to make sure Margo was all right. Claire offered to call back in another fifteen minutes and Margo agreed. She still didn't trust Ashley Green.

"You said something earlier about helping me find out more about my accident?" she said.

"Right. Would you let me have the lab take a look at your car? As I said, I don't think your accident happened the same way Holroyd's did, but if we have evidence someone engineered your accident, it would help us make a case that someone engineered Holroyd's."

He showed her the same type of release form he'd given Lael. She couldn't see any reason not to sign.

"We'll pay for a rental for you, too," he offered, "until you get yourself a new car."

"A new car?" Bleakly, she pictured her trusty old Toy-

ota. She had always envisioned herself in one of those com-
mercials, bragging about how her car had made it over two
hundred thousand miles. "Do you really think it's so badly
damaged it can't be repaired?"

Green scratched at his chin, where he had missed a blob
of clay. "I don't know. The lab would have to tell you."
He leaned forward and spoke with an intensity she hadn't
heard before. "Look, Ms. Simon, I'm going to say
something. I want you to listen. I don't think this is the
kind of story you usually do for that radio station you work
for. And this all happened in Mexican jurisdiction. If you
raise questions about your accident or try to link your accident to Holroyd's, believe me, the Mexican police won't
lift a finger to help you. They'll assume you're just trying
to get out of your own insurance problem. What I'm saying
is, this is a bigger, meaner pond than you're used to swim-
ming in. So if you know something that would give anyone
a motive to kill Reverend Holroyd, do yourself a favor. Tell
me what it is."

Did Green really not know about Zeke's blackmail? Or
was he only fishing to see how much *she* knew? And why
were warning bells going off in her head?

"I wish I knew," she lied.

Green gave her a very long look, but simply said, "Tell
me about the Holroyds, then. How do you know them? You
don't go to their church, do you?"

She explained how she had met Zeke and Lael.

"What did you think of him?" asked Ashley Green.

"Not just smart, but savvy. I expected the stereotypical
fundamentalist, very rigid and moralistic. Zeke knew exactly what I expected, and he played against the stereotype.
He came across as a nice guy who just happened to be a
fundamentalist missionary."

"What about her? Ms. Holroyd?"

"She acts like she's under everybody's thumb—Zeke's
and the church's. But she isn't stupid. She's majoring in
business at San Diego State. She's only been in the church
a couple of years and I think some of the teachings contra-
dict her common sense."

"Would you say she's unstable?"

"I've mostly seen her since Zeke died and she's been grieving."

"Think she could force her husband off a cliff?"

"Lael? You've got to be kidding!"

"No, ma'am, I'm not. The way I see it, you have this impressionable young woman who's gotten her head filled with all these 'thou shalt not's—and believe me, growing up in the South I heard plenty of them. Say her husband does something to violate one of the commandments. There he is in Mexico with a lot of pretty señoritas doing his prayer meetings and counseling late at night. Let's face it, some of those holier-than-thou types preach so hard against lust because they have such a hard time controlling their own. Look at all the big evangelists involved in sex scandals. So say the reverend's having a little fun on the side and his wife finds out about it."

"No way," she said. Ashley Green clearly read too many supermarket tabloids. Nevertheless, the memory of Lael as Margo had last seen her came to mind. Was there some biblical injunction that a widow should chop off her hair? Somehow Margo thought she would have heard if fundamentalist widows were all looking like punk performance artists.

"I've got a friend with U.S. Customs at the border," Green said. "Did you know they record the license number of everyone who comes through from Mexico? I asked my friend to find out if Ms. Holroyd was in Mexico on the days you and her husband had your accidents. Is there anyone else you'd like me to have my friend check on? Anyone you know of who had it in for Holroyd?"

Margo shook her head. Neither Diego Torres nor Jaime Galván would have crossed back into the U.S.; as far as she knew, both men lived in Mexico. As for Robert Kohler, she'd be curious to know if he had come back later than usual on either of the nights in question. But she had no intention of being the first one to mention Zeke's blackmail.

"Here." Ashley Green wrote in pencil on a business card, this time from Werth Investigations. "My office," he said, indicating a printed telephone number. "And these are my home and my car phone. I think you're going to be needing some help. When you do, call me. I mean it, day or night."

Distractedly, Margo took the card. She was thinking of her own plan for dealing with Robert Kohler.

21 / Hey, Big Spender

It was the kind of reasoning the kids would have used, the same semantic nit-picking that drove her and Barry nuts, acknowledged Margo, strapping her bike helmet under her chin. *Stay close to home for a few days,* the doctor had advised. *Don't drive.*

He hadn't said a word about not bicycling, had he?

By Saturday morning—three days after the accident— she didn't feel too bad; just a touch of headache remained. And Barry, who might have insisted the doctor was referring to all forms of transportation, was away for another hour, playing his weekly soccer game.

Margo put a small cassette recorder into her fanny pack and clipped the pack around her waist. She felt a little dizzy when she swung her leg over to mount her bicycle, but once she got going she was all right.

She *was*, at any rate, staying "close to home," she continued her semantic argument, pedaling down Washington Street. Only a mile and a half separated Mission Hills from University Heights, where she and Barry lived. A mile and a half . . . but it was a significant leap up the socioeconomic ladder. And up the socioeconomic ladder was exactly where she would expect Robert Kohler to park his Porsche. In the telephone book, she'd found four "Robert" and "R." Kohlers, three of them in lower rent districts. She was betting on the Mission Hills address.

She turned right onto Goldfinch, down a block of cute little restaurants and shops. A couple of jogs took her into the heart of the Mission Hills residential area. Almost all of the houses were large and gracious, many of them older

California Mission and Craftsman styles. The yards were beautifully kept, the winding streets broad. Situated on a bluff that caught an ocean breeze, Mission Hills even seemed cooler than the rest of town, a phenomenon for which Margo felt grateful. The bike ride was proving more strenuous than she had anticipated, the sun already wicked at ten A.M.

She stopped to consult the small map she'd drawn, then turned down the next side street for a block and a half. The black Porsche with the CALTI license stood in the driveway of a pretty, blue-painted wooden house. The house was modest by Mission Hills standards. But Margo doubted anything in this neighborhood cost under three hundred thousand dollars.

Her heart started pounding when she saw a pair of long legs in jeans and Reeboks extending out from under the Porsche. As sure as she had been that Kohler was one of Zeke's blackmail victims, she'd felt almost as certain that he wasn't Zeke's murderer. In part, she realized now, it was because she hadn't been able to picture Bob Kohler working on a car.

She walked forward, straddling the bike in case she needed to make a quick getaway.

"Hi," she called out.

Robert Kohler inched his body out from under the car. His dark curly hair was tousled and there was a smear of grease on one cheek. He really did look like the kind of nice Jewish boy her mother used to love for her to go out with. Her mother wouldn't have had to push, either. Kohler was cute. Bugsy Siegel was probably cute, too, she told herself, noting that Kohler had one hand around a large wrench.

"What is it?" He sounded perfectly calm, as if he hadn't bolted at the sight of her at the maquiladora conference a week before.

"I wanted to ask you a few questions."

"Sorry, I don't have time for a survey."

No wonder he was acting so blasé! He didn't recognize

her, with her bike helmet and big sunglasses. Margo removed the sunglasses.

"My God!" He stared at her face, where the bruises had reached the angry purple stage. "What happened to you?"

"Car accident." Was he acting shocked because he really hadn't known about her accident . . . or because he was confronting the results of his own actions?

"How did it happen?"

"I went off the road in Mexico a few days ago. The same thing that happened to Zeke Holroyd. Only I was lucky, it wasn't serious."

Bob Kohler glanced toward the house, as if he wanted to run inside, but hesitated. Did he expect to find no refuge in his own home?

As if in response to Margo's mental question, a young woman came out on the porch, shoving the screen door so violently it banged against the house. "Dammit, Bobby, can't you give it a rest already?" she said. "Oh!" Noticing Margo, she paused, embarrassed, then came down the steps, her hand extended. "Hi. I'm Judy." She was twenty-something, with a wiry, athletic body clad in shorts, a skinny crop top, and running shoes.

"Margo Simon." Judy seemed to be waiting for more, so Margo went on, "From KSDR, the public radio station. I'm doing a story on the maquiladoras and I wanted to ask Bob a few questions."

"I've heard you on the radio! Come sit on the porch," invited Judy. "Some iced tea?" Margo could swear she knew that Kohler was squirming.

"I'd love some." As a matter of fact, Margo was feeling a bit light-headed. Maybe the doctor had been right about not going anywhere.

Kohler's, like many of the Craftsman homes built in Southern California in the early 1900s, had a broad, deep front porch shaded by an overhanging roof. On the porch was an attractive set of wicker furniture—two chairs, a love seat, and a small table. Margo sat in one of the chairs.

Outmaneuvered, Kohler grumpily offered to get the iced tea himself and went into the house. Judy kicked her long, tan left leg up on the porch railing and started doing hamstring stretches.

"You must be Bob's wife," said Margo.

"We just live together." From the way Judy said it, it sounded as if she'd been reconsidering the arrangement. "We share the housework, except of course I do most of it. We fight over him working too many hours and whose parents to spend the holidays with. All the same things as married couples, only no ring." She flopped into the love seat. Margo nodded encouragingly. She'd been in the kind of mood Judy was, where she would have poured out her tale of woe to the first sympathetic soul who came along.

"I don't want to give you the wrong idea," Judy said. "Bobby's a great guy. It's just we had this stupid fight this morning, the one we always have, about the way he spends money. Everything he gets has to be the best, the newest, the most expensive." She indicated the wicker furniture, a matching set that was a lot more comfortable to sit in than the motley garage sale collection on Margo and Barry's patio. "We keep our money separate, so I guess I shouldn't care. But I hate to see him . . ." She sighed. "Anyway, now he's demonstrating how thrifty he really is, by changing his own oil for the first time in his life. I didn't think he even knew how to pop the hood of the Porsche."

"So he doesn't usually work on his car?"

"Bobby, a mechanic?" A great sense of relief flooded over Margo—Kohler *didn't* know how to work on cars!— as Judy continued, "He can fix electric things like lamps, he's good at that. And of course sewing machines. But cars? What's gonna happen is he'll screw up the Porsche in some expensive way or whack his thumb, and guess whose fault that'll be?"

Bob Kohler came back with a pitcher of tea and two ice-filled glasses. "Judy, Margo and I need to get started," he said tensely, sitting down on the love seat.

"Oh, sure. I was about to do the NordicTrack, anyway." Judy's abdominal muscles, exposed by the crop top, looked like an advertisement for the exercise machine. "Nice meeting you, Margo." She reentered the house and Margo heard her running up the stairs.

Bob Kohler—blackmailee, possible murderer—handed Margo a glass of iced tea, poured one for himself, and spoke.

"You visited my factory a few days ago. You told my staff we had an appointment." Intelligent brown eyes regarded her warily—angrily—dispelling any illusions Margo might have had that she could just pull out her cassette recorder and get permission to tape him.

She considered easing into her real questions, but the keen brown eyes changed her mind. "I want to know about Zeke Holroyd," she said.

"You mean, what was I doing at his church that day?"

"Yeah."

"Not that it's any of your business, but I met Holroyd through some of my employees. Believe it or not, I liked a lot of what he had to say. You start having spiritual questions around thirty, I think. He and I got to talking a little when we'd run into each other down in Tijuana. Occasionally I'd stop by the church and we'd have a longer talk. About God." There was a loud clink: the ice in Kohler's glass. His hand was shaking.

"You must have felt he had a lot of answers," said Margo. "To give him twenty thousand dollars over the past two years."

"I don't know where you get your information, but . . . Hey, who are you really? What do you want?"

Kohler half-stood and Margo mentally plotted her escape route. A jump from the porch would get her to her bike.

"Margo Simon, from KSDR. Really."

"Do you have an ID?"

"Not with me." Who brought a press pass or even a driver's license on a bike ride?

"What's in the pack?"

Margo unzipped it and took out the cassette recorder, which Kohler grabbed.

"Look at the tape," she said. "You can see it's at the beginning. I wouldn't record without your permission." She waited while Kohler examined the tape and put it in his jeans pocket, then said, "Bob, I don't care if you didn't file all the right papers when you first started doing business in Mexico. I want to know about Zeke Holroyd. How did he approach you and ask you for money?"

"Come on. You say you don't care about any mistakes I might have made in my business. But you can't be asking about this because you want to go after Holroyd—he's dead, so what difference does it make? Jesus. Wait a second." The ice in Kohler's glass was doing a percussion riff. "You're asking about Holroyd and he's dead. Are you saying someone killed him?"

"I think it's possible."

"You think someone forced him off the road, something like that?" He gestured at her bruised face. "And then tried to do the same thing to you? Oh, God. You can't believe I had anything to do with that? Hey, I may have inadvertently broken a few rules when I first set up in business in Mexico, but I don't kill people. Look, I'll tell you what I can. That ought to prove I'm innocent."

"Why don't you start by telling me how you met Zeke?"

"We met in Colonia Zapata, about two years ago. I'd been going there for a year or so, hiring women to do sewing in their homes. As far as I knew, I was operating legally." Margo didn't believe it but didn't bother to challenge him. "If you've ever looked at the laws governing the establishment of a maquiladora, they're incredibly complex. You've got to deal with both U.S. and Mexican regulations. I just didn't understand all the fine points. And besides, I was helping the people who worked for me, women who needed work but couldn't leave their children to go to the factories every day. It may sound self-serving, but I really do care about the people who work for me."

That she believed. She'd seen the photographs he took.

"Zeke Holroyd," she prompted.

"When Holroyd started working in the colonia, I ran into him once or twice. Two gringos, you both stand out, you know. We just talked the first couple times, shot the breeze. He seemed nice enough. Then one day, maybe a month after I met him, he talked to me about the laws governing a U.S. business operating a maquiladora and the penalties for breaking the laws. He didn't say a word about my business, he was too smooth for that. I got a lawyer to check it out and everything Holroyd said was right."

"Did he threaten to report you? And the alternative was to give money to his church?"

"Like I said, he was really smooth. He just talked about how he and I had the same basic goal, we were both trying to help people in the colonia, only I made a profit whereas he needed help to bring his mission to people. It didn't take a rocket scientist to figure out what he meant."

"So you gave him a . . . donation?"

Kohler nodded.

"And after that, did you file the papers right away?"

"It takes time for all the paperwork to be processed. The first thing I did was hook up with a shelter company."

"Like Craig LaBerge's company?"

"Similar, but LaBerge generally likes to operate the companies he shelters. I went with a shelter that provided the legal umbrella I needed but let me run my company. I only stayed with the shelter until all my permits came through."

"So once you made arrangements with the shelter company, you were perfectly legal, right?"

"Right."

"Then why did you keep paying Zeke?"

Kohler turned for a moment, apparently fascinated by two boys skateboarding down the sidewalk. "He still could have turned me in, they could have fined me retroactively."

"But you gave Zeke twenty-five hundred dollars, four times a year for two years. Even if you got fined, wouldn't it have cost you less, in the long run, than you ended up giving him?"

"Your source is wrong. I'm sure I didn't pay him that much." He reached into his pocket and tossed her cassette tape back to her. She missed it; baseball had never been her game. While she was bending down for the tape, Bob Kohler escaped into the house, slamming the door.

• • • •

Margo had bicycled several blocks from Kohler's when she heard feet pounding behind her and someone calling her name. Judy, Kohler's girlfriend, was running after her. Margo stopped, walked the bike over to the curb, and let Judy catch up with her.

"I had the window open upstairs and I could hear you talking to Bobby." Judy was scarcely out of breath. Margo vowed to start exercising more herself. "I heard the idiotic thing he did, not telling you why he kept paying that guy."

"Did you know about it?"

They moved out of the street into the shade of a eucalyptus tree.

"Not the details," said Judy, "but I had a feeling he was paying out money he didn't want to. I figured bribes. That's what everyone says about Mexico, isn't it, that bribery's a way of life? The thing is, Bobby was so evasive I thought you might get the idea he was hiding something terrible. He can be such a dope! I just wanted to tell you there's no big mystery about why he kept paying this minister. See, if you knew Bobby, you'd know there's something he's a lot more scared of than being fined by the Mexican government . . . or even doing time in a Mexican jail."

Having just "visited" a Mexican jail, Margo couldn't imagine a lot that would be more frightening.

"What Bobby's really scared of," said Judy, "is his father. His daddy bankrolled the company initially, even though he didn't want Bob to start the business in Tijuana, he never thought Bob could pull it off. But Bobby kept insisting, and Daddy put up the money finally. Still, he didn't believe in Bobby. Shitty, isn't it? If his dad was going to come through with the money, would it have hurt him to give Bobby a little moral support? Anyway, that's why Bobby spends so much money now, to prove to Daddy that he's a success. Only he never feels like he's really proved it, that's how this sick game works between them. It doesn't matter if he doubles the company's sales every year, he's got to show up for family visits in the Porsche.

That's why our arguments about money are so intense, he's got so much emotional baggage around it.'' She was silent a moment, playing with a eucalyptus pod she'd picked up from the ground.

"Anyway," Judy said, "I don't know if Bobby would have told this minister about his dad, but he might have."

We just shot the breeze at first, Kohler had said. And Zeke was so good at getting people to confide in him.

"The point is," said Judy, "all this minister had to do was threaten to tell Bob's father. So you see, Bobby wasn't trying to cover up anything, he was just embarrassed to talk about his relationship with his father. You do see that, don't you?" she pleaded, the picture of a devoted young woman desperate to remove the clouds of suspicion from the man she loved.

Could she really not know she had given Bob Kohler a stronger motive than before?

22 / People Always Argue When They Shop for a Car

"The danger of being reported to the Mexican authorities would've decreased as soon as Bob Kohler made his business legal," Margo explained to Barry, on their way from looking at the second used car on her list; the car's advertised "mint condition" had included an engine suffering from emphysema and a dented driver's side door. "But the threat of being exposed to his critical father wouldn't have ended until Bob's father—or Zeke—died."

Margo thought her reasoning was impeccable. Barry just grunted. He had been angry for the past three hours, ever since she had bicycled into the yard and told him where she had gone.

Don't you realize this man may have tried to kill you three days ago? he'd said; he had actually shouted at her.

I really didn't think it was him, she'd replied.

You had no evidence he didn't do it!

He wasn't going to do anything to me at his house. How would he explain a body in his front yard?

A phone call from Ashley Green had interrupted their argument. The lab had declared Margo's car totaled, he said. The call had thrown her into a flurry of activity: running out to a convenience store to get a weekly magazine offering used cars for sale, making phone calls, and now going to see the cars.

"You've got to go to the police," said Barry . . . as he had said several times already—on the freeway to Del Mar to see the first car, on Torrey Pines Road in La Jolla, and now on Mission Boulevard in bumper-to-bumper Saturday afternoon Mission Beach traffic. Every car except theirs contained half a dozen teenagers and had at least one surfboard strapped to the top. And every car radio was turned up full blast, as were the boom boxes of kids passing on the sidewalk.

"The Mexican police who put me in jail?" said Margo, for the third or fourth time as well.

"Say there's as much as a fifty percent probability that your accident and Zeke's were completely unrelated."

"Can't we turn up the air conditioner?" Margo usually enjoyed her husband's capacity to be logical. At the moment she wanted to scream. Probability! Did he think this was a scientific experiment?

"The air conditioner's not putting out much because we're not moving."

Margo leaned forward, plucked her sticky shirt from her back.

"You and Zeke both had old cars, you were both driving after dusk," Barry said. "So say there's a fifty percent chance you both had pure accidents. That still leaves a fifty percent chance that someone killed him and tried to kill you, too."

"I know that."

"Then go to the police."

"The Mexican cops will say Zeke and I were just two dumb gringos who didn't have the sense to slow down on their roads."

"Those were just country cops, the ones who gave you trouble after your accident. Mexico does have homicide investigators."

"Not to mention I didn't have Mexican insurance *and* I was drinking." It was the same line of argument Ashley Green had taken. Funny, Margo couldn't actually remember telling Green about her difficulties with the Mexican police. But she had still been a bit groggy from the accident when she talked to him—who knew what she'd said?

"Where's the address we're looking for?" said Barry.

She told him.

"I might just let you out, I don't know if I'm going to be able to park."

She felt perversely satisfied that Barry sounded as cross as she felt.

The next car she looked at was a silver Mazda Miata convertible that must have appealed to some younger image she'd had of herself—Margo speeding along the French Riviera, the wind doing sexy things to her hair. She took the car on a three-minute test drive, which was as long as she could tolerate hearing the twenty-year-old owner in the passenger seat extolling the virtues of the gear ratio, and rejoined Barry in his car.

"You ought to be taking some precautions," said Barry, as they drove back toward the freeway.

"Isn't that what we're supposed to say to the kids when we think they're starting to have sex?"

"Come off it, Margo! You didn't have to go see this Kohler guy by yourself. I would have come with you."

"Great! A bodyguard."

"Jesus! Even cops use backups when they go into a dangerous situation. Also," said Barry, accelerating onto the freeway, "you shouldn't go into Mexico alone."

"Great! Next thing, you'll be saying I shouldn't leave the house. Or maybe I should just get out of Southern California and hide?"

He didn't respond.

"What?" she said.

"My gut feeling? Yeah, I'd like you to leave town, go stay with Audrey for a month."

"My sister the Yuppie? Audrey would kill me for sure, if I didn't kill her first."

"Look, I know."

"And the murderer would still be here when I got back. Am I supposed to stay in hiding for the rest of my life?"

"I know, dammit!"

"What are you . . . ?"

Barry pulled the car to the shoulder of the freeway and stopped. Cars zoomed by.

"Let's not fight about this," he said. "I'm just worried

about you. God, especially after what happened at that gallery a few months ago,'' he added, reminding Margo of her rather close brush with a murderer.

She reached for his hand. ''Okay. I'm scared, too. In fact, I blew up when you suggested I go to Audrey's because I'd actually thought of it myself. But I can't.''

A horn blared at them—someone had been trying to pass by driving on the shoulder. The driver honked again as he waited to get around them.

''Couldn't you call the San Diego homicide lieutenant you know?'' said Barry.

''Lieutenant Obayashi? It isn't his jurisdiction. Not even his country.''

''Okay, but there have to be homicide investigators in Mexico that the San Diego police cooperate with. Maybe he could put you in touch with the right person in Mexico, someone who'd listen to you.''

''You're right. I'll call him first thing Monday.''

''Call him today. Those guys work all kinds of crazy hours, he might be on this weekend and off Monday.''

''Okay.''

Barry started up the car.

''Would you mind stopping at KSDR?'' she asked as they neared the Old Town freeway exit. ''I'd like to pick up my maquiladora file.''

Later that afternoon—after a much-needed nap—Margo sat, puzzled, with two documents in front of her. She kept looking from one to the other, and they kept making no sense. On one side of the desk was the list Lael Holroyd had given her, showing Zeke's blackmail victims and when they had paid. The other document came from the file she'd collected from her office, a newspaper article Ray Fernandez had clipped during his initial research. The article concerned a suspected occurrence of toxic poisoning in Colonia Zapata, surely the incident in which Diego Torres was rumored to be involved, and the reason, Margo had assumed, that Zeke was blackmailing Torres. There was one problem, however. The toxic poisoning scare had taken place only six months ago. But "D.T." had been paying blackmail for a full year.

Margo picked up the phone and push-buttoned Lael's number. Lael sounded calm, though Margo realized Lael's calm could be deceptive; she hoped the young widow had been eating and that she hadn't taken a scissors to anything beyond her hair.

"Lael, do you remember anything special happening about a year or thirteen months ago? Just before the first donation from D.T.?"

"No, but I can check in my diary. Not right now, I've got someone here." Her voice brightened. "But I could tell you about it tomorrow, at church. Come, won't you? Please?"

A thousand excuses raced through Margo's mind, but Lael sounded so sweet and so needy. "What time does church start?" she said.

"Nine-thirty. Promise you'll be there!"

"Promise." Margo regretted it already.

23 / The Sacred and the Bagel

"Sinners! All of us! Yes, you, you, and you!" Reverend Paul van den Moeller gestured dramatically at his congregation. "But Jesus Christ still loves you. Open your hearts to Jesus' love. Confess your sins to Jesus, repent and your soul will be washed clean."

Van den Moeller seemed to be hitting his stride. The faces around Margo lifted raptly toward the minister of Revelation of God Church. The sermon was more or less what Margo had heard before, watching television evangelists. But the congregation surprised her. Of the one hundred and fifty or so people attending the Sunday morning service, most of them looked more affluent, as well as younger, than she would have thought. And more *hip*! Well, what had she expected? Weathered, toothless visages and threadbare clothing, straight out of *The Grapes of Wrath*? In their California casual attire of bright summer dresses and knit polo shirts, the Revelation of God crowd would have fit right in on Margo's patio, where Barry and their friends were blasphemously spending the morning munching on bagels, lox, and cream cheese. That thought gave Margo a twinge. When she'd promised Lael that she would go to church, she'd completely forgotten it was the last Sunday of the month, when she and Barry hosted their monthly Bagel Salon. Barry hadn't minded holding down the fort alone, but sitting in the church, Margo felt a surge of guilt.

"I've sinned terribly myself," the reverend rolled on

mellifluously. "When I was a young man, I didn't know
Jesus Christ, I closed my heart to Him. Closed my heart. I
tell you, I was such a hell-raiser in my hometown, back in
Clarksville, Missouri, my daddy came to me one day and
said, 'Son, you've got two choices. You can be a man and
join the U.S. Army. Or you're heading straight to jail.' "

It was the same story Margo had heard a few days ago,
and she doubted it was new to most of the people in church
this morning. But no one looked bored. Tears were trickling
down several faces, including that of Lael Holroyd, who
sat beside her. Like a parody of a Victorian lady, Lael had
worn her mourning, the too-big black dress that fell tentlike
around her, emphasizing her fragility. With her thin neck
and shorn head, Lael Holroyd resembled a scrawny bird. A
very pale scrawny bird. Margo eyed her closely. Had Lael
brought a paper bag to breathe into if she hyperventilated?

"I want you to come on up here," said Paul van den
Moeller. "I want you to come and ask Jesus to cleanse you
of your sins. Let the force of His love flow through you.
The Son of God came to earth to redeem us. All He asks
is that we speak from our hearts, that we ask His forgiveness. 'Create in me a pure heart, O God; and renew a stead-
fast spirit within me.' Psalm fifty-one, verse ten."

In spite of herself, Margo felt the energy building in the
congregation—the quickened heartbeats, the impulse to
stand, as a woman did in the front row, and exclaim, "Forgive me, Jesus!" Van den Moeller came over to her, holding out his microphone.

"I hit my little Denny yesterday," the woman said. "I
promised I'd never do it again, but he got me so mad."

"We love you, Sister Alice, and Jesus loves you, too,"
said van den Moeller, laying his hand on her head. "Jesus
loves you," echoed the congregation. "Let's pray for Sister
Alice," the minister said. Prayer couldn't hurt, but Margo
figured Sister Alice should also be referred for professional
counseling. There was no child sitting beside her, and
Margo wondered if little Denny had sustained too many
bruises to appear in church today.

During the next ten minutes, half a dozen people owned

up to various forms of wrongdoing, everything from cheating on a contracting bid to devoting only five hours of the previous week to Bible study.

"I've sinned!"

Margo jumped at the young female voice so close to her. A teenage girl in the row behind her was pushing her way to the aisle.

"I killed my mother!" The young woman ran to the front of the church and fainted.

Van den Moeller knelt beside her and took her hand. "Pray for our sister!" he said. There were murmurs through the church.

She sat up in a moment, supported by the minister, who held the microphone before her lips. "Tell Jesus," Paul van den Moeller crooned. "Tell it to Jesus. He loves you."

"God had to punish me." Her whisper was amplified by the church's excellent sound system. "He had to teach me a lesson by taking my mother."

"Tell Jesus."

"I used to be really bad. Disobedient. I hated my mother and argued with her all the time. I kept thinking of ways, I kept thinking, oh . . ." Tears filled her voice.

"Jesus loves you," urged van den Moeller. "Tell it all to Jesus."

"I thought of all the ways she could die. She could have a car accident or she could get cancer or some crazy person could come into Kmart while she was there and start shooting. And then she did get cancer."

" 'If a man digs a pit, he will fall into it,' " quoted van den Moeller. " 'If a man rolls a stone, it will roll back on him.' Proverbs twenty-six, verse twenty-seven." Hardly words of comfort, but the girl's sobs quieted. The minister stood, leaving her to the care of the woman in the front row who had confessed to beating her child.

"The Ten Commandments given by God at Mount Sinai tell us to honor thy father and thy mother," intoned van den Moeller. "Our young sister may be right, that God punished her for breaking the commandment by taking her mother's life."

Margo nearly cried out in protest. How could anyone be so cruel as to foster the young woman's delusion that her mother's death was a punishment she deserved? It occurred to Margo that although she had heard the melodramatic tale of van den Moeller's wayward youth twice in the past week, neither time had the minister mentioned the particular sins that had led to his choice between the Army and jail. Was he speaking figuratively, that is, if he continued down the path he was on, he would have most likely wound up in jail? Or had there been something specific, a theft or an assault, and the prospect of criminal charges? She pictured van den Moeller in a scene from *The Wild One*, a young, secular version of the spiritual bully he'd become, terrorizing the good citizens of his small Missouri town.

" 'A broken and contrite heart, O God, you will not despise,' " van den Moeller said. "Lord, look on the true repentance of this child and forgive her."

From throughout the church came calls of, "Jesus loves you."

"Jesus loves you." Lael added her trembling voice to the chorus.

Standing with Margo in the parking lot after church, Lael acted edgy, a bird feeling the cat's breath. She had, however, checked her diary and related what she had found, speaking so softly that Margo had to lean close to hear her.

"Just before the first donation he got from D.T. last summer, Zeke went to a big dinner in Tijuana, for people involved in the maquiladora industry. He got home real late that night and stayed up praying until two or three in the morning. I know because I could never sleep if he wasn't in bed." A tear welled, but Lael took a deep breath and went on. "The next three or four nights, it was the same thing. Zeke stayed up praying until one or two, and the next morning he'd be up at five."

"Did he seem upset? Did he say if something was bothering him?"

"Not upset, happy. Excited. He'd come to bed and . . ." Lael blushed. Margo had heard of one fundamentalist leader, a woman, who promoted Christian sexual ecstasy, but that philosophy might not be part of the canon at Revelation of God.

"Did you ask him why he was so excited?" said Margo.

"He would have said, if he wanted to. Sometimes a spiritual experience is really personal."

Spiritual experience? Margo tried not to wince. "What about the dinner he went to? Who put it on? Do you know anything about it?"

Lael shook her head.

"Lael, can I ask one more thing?"

"Sure."

"Why did you cut your hair?"

"To atone."

"For smoking?"

Lael's eyes rolled back in their sockets. For a moment Margo thought she was fainting, but she whispered, "Just to atone."

Bagel Salons, she and Barry had laughingly dubbed the monthly gatherings, when they'd had the first such party two years ago. They would go out and buy several dozen fresh bagels and some cream cheese, make the first of multiple pots of coffee, and be ready for guests by ten; the parties usually lasted until two or three. When Margo got home, some two dozen people were spread through the living room, kitchen, and patio. The fruit salad she'd made before she left had been consumed, but plenty of bagels remained, thank goodness.

"Margo, you're here!" David was bouncing with excitement.

"Give me a minute!" She poured a cup of coffee and put an apple-cinnamon bagel in the toaster. "Okay, what is it?"

"You know that aviary you saw a few weeks ago? With all the parrots? What kinds were they?"

"The parrots? I'm not sure."

"You don't remember? Don't you even know what countries they were from?"

"I think there were Eclectus parrots." Defense attorneys should rehearse their clients with squads of eleven year olds. "And some kind of macaw. Most of them were from Mexico or Central America."

"What about Indonesia? Australia? New Guinea?"

"I think you're right, a few were from the South Pacific." The toaster popped up. Margo snatched the hot bagel halves with her fingertips, dropped them onto a plate, and reached for the cream cheese. Barry had bought "lite" cream cheese. At least David hadn't put the kibosh on getting any dairy products at all.

"I talked to Pam this morning." David referred to a professional puppeteer, one of the kids' favorites among their parents' friends. Pam was also an avid bird-watcher. "She says a lot of exotic birds like that are endangered species. Exporting them is prohibited by an international wildlife treaty, unless the birds are going to zoos. Usually the way people get them in the U.S. is by smuggling."

"Do people smuggle in the birds themselves?"

"Bird dealers do and then sell them. Pam says some of the birds sell commercially for fifty thousand dollars!"

"Fifty thousand for one bird? Davey, are you sure?"

"Come talk to Pam, she'll tell you."

David led her onto the patio, where Pam confirmed that the smuggling of rare birds was a serious problem. There had been a big local case several years ago, where the birds were flown into Mexico City, transported to Tijuana, and smuggled by car at the San Ysidro border crossing.

"Do they really sell for fifty thousand dollars?" asked Margo.

"I've never heard of one going for that much," said Pam. "But the rarest birds, like Black Palm cockatoos from Australia and New Guinea, can cost as much as ten thousand dollars each. Hyacinth macaws, from South America, go for eight thousand." Margo realized it was a Hyacinth macaw she'd seen perched in LaBerge's office a few days ago.

"It's a big business," Pam continued. "Anyone who could figure out a way to get birds across the border in quantity, without too many of them dying on the way, could make a small fortune."

24 / A Bird in the Hand

SEE ME! commanded the note from Claire De Jong that Margo found on her desk Monday morning. She almost tossed the note in the trash, but everyone at KSDR was trying to be more environmentally conscious; she turned the note over and wrote on the back, *Jaime Galván, D.T. (Diego Torres?), Bob Kohler.* Then she added two new names: *Paul van den Moeller* and David's favorite villain, *Craig LaBerge*.

Most likely, LaBerge was guilty of nothing more than purchasing some exotic birds that had been smuggled into the U.S. Still, with forty maquiladoras under its wing, so to speak, LaBerge's shelter business must generate hundreds of cross-border shipments a year. How difficult would it be to conceal a dozen boxes of birds—tranquilized, Pam had said yesterday, and often with their beaks taped and tails cruelly clipped so they would fit in the boxes—in some of the huge semis that carried commercial shipments? How difficult . . . and how tempting, if a small fortune could be made by anyone who could bring in the birds in quantity? Margo placed a call to Pete Demetrides, the maquiladora attorney she was scheduled to see that afternoon; he said he'd try to pull the firm's resident Customs expert into the meeting.

As for Paul van den Moeller, whatever the minister had done in his sinful youth, Margo was sure Zeke had gotten the story. Zeke wouldn't have coerced van den Moeller to give money to his own church, but the minister had other things his young assistant coveted—influence and, ultimately, his job. How serious *were* van den Moeller's past offenses?

"Do you have an atlas?" Margo asked her office mate, Dan Lewis. Dan's side of the small office was a model of chaos, the lair of a man who'd spent all of his formative years fiddling with his ham radio and never having to clean up his room. Fortunately, Dan didn't let the mess spread beyond an invisible dividing line, and he had an amazing amount of useful material squirreled away. Sure enough, he produced an atlas from a three-foot-deep pile of books and papers.

Margo located Clarksville, Missouri, the small town van den Moeller had said he'd come from, and then checked a national directory of public radio stations. She called a colleague in Columbia, Missouri. Clarksville was part of his beat, said the reporter. A forty-year-old trail would be pretty cold, but he'd find out what he could about the preacher as a young man.

She tried Lieutenant Obayashi for the third time in three days. This time she reached him and briefly told her story.

"Is there anything you can do . . ." She hesitated a moment, then added, "Donny?"

"I don't know, Margo," he said, evidently comfortable being on a first-name basis with her. What he had to say was not comforting at all, however. "All this happened in Mexico?"

"That's right."

His sigh was audible over the phone. "I can call a colleague there, but frankly, you shouldn't expect much. Sounds like as far as they're concerned, this minister was just another bad driver. I don't suppose it'd do any good to advise you to stay on this side of the border?"

"I've got a story to do. But I'll be careful."

"Look, be more than careful. How about, if you have to go into Mexico, you don't go alone?"

"Okay," she said, and meant it. She had figured Obayashi would dismiss her suspicions. Having him take her seriously gave her a sinking feeling in her stomach, pure fear. She said goodbye to him, hung up, took a deep breath.

Margo had one more call to make before facing Claire De Jong. She was hoping that Silvia, the cooperative receptionist at Sani, could tell her when Jaime Galván had left work the previous Wednesday. If Galván had slipped out at about the same time she'd left, she'd bet he was the one who had followed her to the Bufadora.

When Margo identified herself to Silvia, however, the young woman dropped her voice to a nervous-sounding whisper. "Where are you calling from? You're not here in Tijuana, are you?"

"No, San Diego."

"Thank goodness. I have something to tell you. But please don't come here. You know the McDonald's at the shopping center just north of the Otay Mesa crossing? You turn down the road like you're going to cross the border, but you go to the shopping center?"

"I can find it."

They agreed to meet at six.

"Can't you give me an idea of what's going on?" asked Margo, but Silvia hung up.

"My sentiments exactly," said Claire De Jong. "Give me a little idea of what's going on. Specifically, why you thought I might need to call the police the other day." Standing in the doorway of Margo's office, the news director smelled of chlorine from her pre-work swim.

Margo had known, when she called Claire for protection while she spoke to Ashley Green, that she'd have to explain a few things. The hour of reckoning had clearly arrived.

It was worse than she'd feared. She assumed, following her supervisor through the radio station, that they were going to Claire's office. Instead, "I mentioned this to Alex," said Claire, continuing down the hall to the station manager's door. "We don't usually get reporters afraid for their safety. He wanted to sit in on our meeting." Was Claire apologizing for dragging her before "the big boss"? Margo realized she didn't really know how Claire felt about Alex, who'd brought Claire to KSDR just six months ago, having worked with her at National Public Radio. Alex had only recently made Claire news director, after firing the job's previous inhabitant.

Margo's own feelings toward Alex Silva were firmly established. She grudgingly respected the increased professionalism Alex had instilled during his eight months as station manager. But she detested the way he motivated everyone to excel, not by appealing to their own professionalism but by making them fearful of losing their jobs. As for Alex's opinion of Margo, he'd promoted her to a full-time reporting position, which ought to indicate some confidence in her abilities. Nevertheless, he retained an East Coast disdain for all of the San Diego reporters he'd inherited, as if he secretly believed they researched stories by consulting the Tarot deck or communing with spirits at psychic fairs.

Certainly that seemed to be his attitude toward Margo's theory that Zeke had been killed and the same murderer had tried to kill her.

"He drove a Samurai and you said he was a rotten driver," said Alex. "And on those lousy Mexican roads! Have you talked to the police? Are they looking into it?"

Margo repeated her conversation with Lieutenant Obayashi.

"See!" Alex often sounded as if he were pouncing on a smaller, more vulnerable creature. "Now the blackmail angle's something else, you've convinced me this minister was blackmailing people. But didn't you get *anything* on tape? Not even the guy you talked to Saturday, who admitted he was being blackmailed?"

"Especially not him. He would barely talk to me at all, much less agree to be recorded."

"What about the widow? How could she not know what was going on? I bet if you pushed her—"

Margo imagined "pushing" Lael, imagined Lael toppling over.

Alex said, "It's a great story. Religion, scandal. NPR would love it. But you can't do it unless you get someone willing to go on tape. And besides . . ."

It turned out Alex had another reason for taking an interest in Margo's work. He had his own plans for her: with the special election coming up in a month, he wanted her to do a profile on Dorothy Troupe.

"You know that Dorothy and I are old friends, don't you?"

"Right! That will help you get close to her!" exulted Alex.

Margo considered mentioning that the former station management had exercised care in assigning her to do stories on her friend. It was one thing to cover a routine news conference as she had last week, another to do something in depth. But Alex had already picked up the phone and was gesturing her and Claire out of the office. And why couldn't she benefit from her and Dorothy's friendship without sacrificing objectivity? Margo demanded of herself, although the thought made her squirm a bit inside.

She ignored the squirming feeling and turned to Claire De Jong, who was whispering to her in the hall.

"What about asking that private detective to help you?" said Claire, outside the door to her office.

"Are you saying you think I should keep looking into this?"

Claire had sat back while Alex dismissed the story. Margo had assumed that meant Claire agreed with him.

"Come on in. Sit down." In her office, Claire took a swig from a big bottle of mineral water and leaned against her desk. "You said the Mexican police won't take this seriously. I'm thinking there are some things you'd want to know that cops—or a private detective—can find out. What if you talk to this man, tell him what you know, and ask him to check some things out for you?"

"Maybe." Ashley Green had entered Margo's life lying. It was still hard to trust him. And when it came to trust: "Claire, if you believe me, why didn't you say something to Alex?"

Claire grinned. "I've worked with Alex for four years, between NPR and here. Sometimes it's best to agree with him, then go ahead and do what you want. As long as you get a great story, he forgets he told you not to do it. Especially if you didn't give him a big argument in the first place." Margo tried not to let her mouth hang open, as

Claire went on, "You heard what he said about the bad Mexican roads? He doesn't know what he's talking about. I happen to know that the whole time he's been in San Diego, Alex has never once crossed the border. I have. I love the lobster at Puerto Nuevo and I went to Ensenada to run a half-marathon last month. That main highway, the one Zeke went off of, is fine. And look, Margo, if you want some company the next time you go to Mexico, let me know."

Margo would have taken a moment to marvel over finding an ally in Claire De Jong, but she had to start scrambling—going through files and making phone calls—to do the story on Dorothy Troupe. Lunch was a blueberry yogurt from the supply she kept in the station refrigerator, and she didn't eat that until three, when she was getting a lift to the garage that had completed the pre-buy check on the Mazda Miata. (All right, she'd succumbed to the youthful fantasy of driving along the Riviera. Could menopause be far behind?)

She put the Mazda's convertible top down, then drove downtown to her appointment with Pete Demetrides, the attorney for the Baja Nueva Development Company.

A certain type of man looks smashing in a business suit. Tall but not too tall, distance-runner thin, with hair the tiniest bit long, so if you saw him striding briskly down the street, the breeze would just slightly ruffle his hair.

Pete Demetrides was not that type. Demetrides, thought Margo, seated on the client side of his desk, was a man who, if you saw him striding down the street toward you, you might cross over to the other side. Squat and muscular, the attorney had a wrestler's neck and a bald pate. There was nothing smooth about Pete Demetrides' appearance. All of the man's considerable smoothness went into deflecting Margo's questions about Baja Nueva.

"Who are the primary investors?"

"Baja Nueva is a consortium. The way something like that works, there are a number of investor entities, on both sides of the border."

"Can you give me any names? Someone must be the owner."

"I didn't make myself clear. The investors aren't primarily individuals, but investor groups. If you've ever bought shares in a mutual stock fund, it's similar to that. I haven't offered you any coffee. Our office has its own espresso machine."

"No, thanks. But someone has to make decisions. For instance, someone decided to hire a bulldozer last week and raze the homes of people who lived on that land. Was that your call?"

"The company would never authorize anything like that." Demetrides sighed. "If there's one thing I've learned from being involved in the maquiladora industry for ten years, it's that you can never predict what the Mexican government is going to do next. And no one will ever take responsibility for it. Speaking of the government, I understand you wanted to talk to our Customs expert. He's based in Otay Mesa and he made a special trip downtown to talk to you. But he can't stay long. Let me bring him in now."

Before he finished speaking, Demetrides picked up his phone and summoned Ron Alvarez, a former U.S. Customs agent who now worked for the law firm.

Ron Alvarez delivered a barrage of facts and figures. Over 150,000 trucks a year crossed from Mexico into the U.S. at the Otay Mesa commercial crossing, and almost 200,000 went the other way, into Mexico. Companies shipping products did all of their paperwork in advance, but no matter how meticulous a company's paperwork, U.S. Customs officials regularly—arbitrarily—declared a "red light" and pulled over a truck to search it.

"Don't people sometimes offer bribes?" said Margo. "Not necessarily because they're doing anything wrong, but say they got pulled over and they've got a shipment due in Los Angeles in three hours."

"That's when they call their Customs consultant. We try to help in a situation like that."

"Still, some corruption must go on. Smuggling, for instance."

"Sure, there's always some. But the Feds are getting a lot more sophisticated at catching it. For instance, one guy used to bring through a truck with a two-foot hiding place built in; the hiding place was filled with pot. Now they shoot these laser beams to measure any difference between the inside and outside of the truck, and they only allow a one-inch discrepancy."

"What about birds? I heard a lot of exotic birds were smuggled over the border."

"Whoo! Not in commercial shipments. You've got dogs at the commercial crossing. They're all over the trucks; the smell of birds would drive them wild. You're right that there's bird smuggling, I saw it when I was an agent. But we're talking small-time. Someone'll pay an illegal to bring across a bird in a backpack, or a smuggler brings over maybe half a dozen birds at the tourist vehicle crossing." He chuckled. "Once I was on duty at the tourist crossing and there was a guy with a bird tucked down inside his pants. We got him out of his car and asked about the bird, the damn thing was flapping around by this time. 'What bird?' he said. Just then it flew up out of his pants and took off.''

If Margo wasn't building a case against Craig LaBerge as a smuggler, at least she was getting some entertaining comments on tape.

Alvarez left, offering an invitation to show her around the commercial customs station. Margo was packing up her equipment, having decided she surely wasn't going to get Pete Demetrides to say anything about Baja Nueva, when it occurred to her that Demetrides might have attended the dinner a year ago . . . after which Zeke had started to blackmail D.T.

"You must mean the San Diego-Tijuana Friendship Dinner," said Demetrides when she asked. The big man had turned pale.

"What's wrong? Did something happen there?"

"Oh, man. It's just that on the way back, just a little north of the border, there was an accident. A whole Mexican family got hit crossing the freeway. Papa, mama, two *niños.* I must have driven up right after it happened. I pulled over and helped. It was bad. The mother and one kid died, and the father and another kid were seriously hurt. The driver of the car that hit them didn't even have the decency to stop, it was hit-and-run. Man, I'll never get those sights completely out of my mind." He shook his head. "Well, you asked about the dinner. What can I tell you?"

"Who put it on?"

"The San Diego Chamber of Commerce and the maquiladora association in Tijuana."

"Remember who was there?"

"Everybody who was anybody involved in the maquiladora industry."

"Diego Torres?"

"The union leader? Sure. Like I said, everybody who was anybody."

Driving to her meeting with Silvia Delatorre, Margo scanned the hills beside the freeway, looking for any movement that might signal a person about to dash in front of her. How difficult—how impossible—it would be to avoid running into someone, if you were zipping along at sixty miles an hour and they suddenly ran into the road. Is that what had happened to Diego Torres last year? Had he driven across the border, hit the Mexican family, and fled? And could Zeke have been driving right behind him?

25 / Help from an Unexpected Quarter

Silvia Delatorre was already at the McDonald's when Margo arrived. The young woman had an untouched hamburger in front of her. She was tearing a napkin into shreds.

"Thank goodness you're all right," Silvia said when Margo sat down in the booth with her.

"Thanks, the accident wasn't that bad."

"I don't mean that." Silvia was surprisingly brusque. "You shouldn't come into Tijuana, at least not into the Ciudad Industrial. You remember Laura?"

"Rosalia's friend."

"She wants to kill you."

"No, it's all right. Laura was just acting tough. She said she'd kill me if anything happened to Rosalia." Margo heard her own words. "Oh, no. Oh, no. Is Rosalia hurt?"

"She's dead."

"How?" Margo's throat felt so tight she thought she might never swallow again.

"She fell off a cliff by the Bufadora. They found her last Thursday. They think it happened Wednesday night."

"But no one contacted me. Wouldn't Patricia and Tomás have told the police I was there? Wouldn't someone have questioned me?"

Silvia didn't look cynical or angry, only resigned. "The police just say Rosalia was unhappy and she jumped off the cliff, or maybe she was drunk and she fell—there were beer cans around. But Laura keeps saying it's your fault. I said she was crazy, that you just wanted to talk to Rosalia, you wanted to help her.''

''Rosalia was fine when I left her.'' Margo answered the question Silvia was too polite to ask. Some help she had given. She had probably led Rosalia's killer to her.

''Don't worry,'' said Silvia, ''I don't think Laura can find you. She knows you're a reporter from San Diego, but she doesn't even know you work for a radio station. Still, if you go near the factory and she sees you . . .''

''Silvia, what time did Señor Galván leave the factory the day I was there?''

''Señor Galván?'' Surprised. ''Around six, I guess, maybe a little later.''

''Are you sure? Did you see him at the factory after I left?''

''Yes. He called me into his office around five, he had some work he wanted me to do. We both stayed late to finish. It was almost six when I left and he was still there.''

It made no sense, thought Margo, sitting at the table after Silvia had left. Assuming someone had followed her to the Bufadora and engineered her car accident, presumably the same person went to see Rosalia and either pushed her or else frightened her so much that she slipped and fell, running from him on the cliff path. Who could it be except Jaime Galván? But if Galván had stayed at work until six, he couldn't have followed Margo. Maybe he had already found out where Rosalia was and driven straight to the Bufadora the minute he left the factory. Still, how could he have had time to get through Tijuana traffic, sabotage Margo's car, and then find Rosalia?

Still, the question remained: Why would Galván kill Rosalia? . . . Which brought Margo back to Rosalia's story, of seeing *el jefe* unloading barrels that might have contained toxic chemicals. Every maquiladora that used chemical processes—in other words, most factories—kept some toxins on site, there was nothing criminal in that. So what was different about the toxins Rosalia had seen?

Another question: Were the barrels still at Sani?

Margo went to the counter and ordered a Big Mac, fries, and a chocolate shake—not her typical fare, but having put up with David's self-righteous vegetarianism, she felt wild and defiant chewing on the greasy meat. Wild and defiant, she decided, was precisely the attitude a woman required as she contemplated trespassing at a factory after hours, especially at a factory where a worker wanted to kill her.

At a convenience store in the small shopping center, she bought a flashlight and batteries. Then she sat at the wheel of her tiny, exposed Miata and felt a shiver go through her body at the thought of crossing the border. What had possessed her to buy a car that offered virtually no protection? Had she needed to pretend she was invulnerable, in the wake of her accident? Compared to the Miata, even Zeke's Samurai was a tank. Margo sat in the car for fifteen minutes, then turned the key in the ignition and drove home.

Barry was at a meeting and the kids at their mother's, so she had the house to herself. She put on a compact disc—Talking Heads—and danced until she'd sweated out the fear, not to mention the toxins from the hamburger. Then she took a shower, poured a large glass of wine, and telephoned a number written in pencil on a business card.

She said, "This is Margo Simon. I could use some help."

"No kidding," said Ashley Green. "A mechanic went over your car today. Somebody cut your brake line. It was just nicked, so the fluid would drain out slow. If we hadn't been looking for the cut, we might not have found it. Somebody likes car accidents."

Green arrived at Margo's house within half an hour. Over another glass of wine for her, club soda—and a swig of Mylanta—for him, she told him what she had learned about Zeke's blackmail and the latest development, Rosalia's death.

"Tell me everything you remember from your talk with Jaime Galván," Green said.

Margo went over her interview with the manager of Sani

five days earlier: the grudging tour he had given her of the factory, his pretending not to know who Rosalia was, his anger when Margo revealed that she knew he was dating Rosalia.

"Describe his actions, his gestures," said the detective. "You must have to do that for the radio."

"Okay. He kept looking at his watch, an expensive watch. He took out a cigar and played with it. And he got a phone call. After the phone call, he ended the interview."

"What was the phone call about?"

"No idea. All Galván said was yes, maybe twice. The other person did all the talking."

"Could be he had an accomplice. Say he called this person when he first heard you were there—did he see you right away or did you have to wait?"

"I had to wait, about ten minutes."

"So he called his buddy and then waited for him to do something, probably to show up at the factory," speculated Green. "The phone call let him know the accomplice was ready. That way Galván didn't have to follow you himself, the other guy could do it and then call, maybe from a car phone, and let him know where you were going. The buddy could have even doctored your brakes, if Galván was paying him enough. Or say the guy was Galván's brother, something like that. *If* Galván is our man."

"Who else but Galván would have wanted to kill Rosalia?"

"Whoa! You can't just assume Rosalia was killed. Somebody might have pushed her, but she might have started to run and then fell. Or it could be what the police say, she had a few beers and lost her footing. Think about it. She was unhappy and scared. She couldn't hide out with her friends forever, she didn't know what to do next. Maybe she wasn't trying real hard to keep her balance. I'm not saying I won't check out this story she told you, about the barrels she saw at her factory. And I'll ask around about Galván. But we've also got to check the other people on your list. And that dinner with the hit-and-run afterward, who put it on?"

She repeated the information she'd gotten from Pete Demetrides.

"I'll get you the guest list. That's a piece of cake. One more thing. You need to start carrying some protection."

"I can't . . ."

"Hey, I'm not asking you to pack a gun. There are already too many guns in the hands of people who don't know how to use them."

Thank goodness. Target practice was one of the local diversions when she'd lived in Santa Fe, a Wild West ritual that had never appealed to her.

"Have you ever used this stuff?" Green opened his briefcase and pulled out a can of Mace.

A brisk young woman at the "Dorothy Troupe for Congress" office had promised Margo a set of position papers over the phone the day before. Margo went to the office the next morning and, as directed, asked for Dorothy's media assistant—her son, Sean. Sean, however, not only didn't know *where* the position papers were, he appeared not to know *what* such things were, either.

"Hey, Kelly, do we have some papers for Margo Simon?" Sean called out, after fumbling through a few boxes. "She's from . . . sorry, Margo, what TV station are you with?"

"She's radio, KSDR," said a young woman, actually a teenager, who quickly assembled a packet. "Sean, I told you about this yesterday," she chided.

Sean seemed to notice neither the irritation in the girl's voice nor the disgusted look she gave him. In fact, in the room with half a dozen hyped-up campaign workers, Sean provided a slow-moving counterpoint—as if, while the rest of the crew was downing their first six cups of coffee, Sean had slipped out and smoked a joint. Which was probably just what he'd done, Margo realized, taking in Sean's vagueness and red-rimmed eyes. Good grief, didn't Dorothy understand that a druggie son could be a major liability? If she wanted to give the kid a job folding envelopes, okay, but he shouldn't be dealing with the media. Eventually, someone would raise questions about Sean's drug use; maybe Margo ought to bring it up herself, in the interview she had scheduled with Dorothy in an hour.

But was it really "news"? she debated with herself, as she reviewed the position papers in a nearby coffee shop. Who the hell didn't have problems with their kids? Would it in any way aid the public debate—or get the community the best Congressional representative—if people knew Dorothy's son did drugs?

Margo walked in to see Dorothy, having decided not to mention it. Nevertheless, at the end of the interview, she switched off the tape recorder.

"Just as a friend," she said.

"Go ahead." Dorothy was wearing a better-fitting suit than usual, but in the poorly air-conditioned campaign office, she had taken off the jacket and still looked like her slightly blowsy self.

"Dorothy, I'm worried about Sean. It looks to me like he's doing drugs. Please, keep him away from the front line of your campaign. I won't go after this story, but someone's bound to notice him."

"There's nothing wrong with Sean."

"Dorothy! What about that fall he took in the parking structure at the convention center? You think he was straight when that happened?"

"Probably not. They were serving drinks at the lunch, it was a hot day, and the kid can't hold it as well as his mom used to. Look, Sean used to have some trouble with drugs, I'll admit that to anyone who asks. And maybe he does a little pot now. But where did you get so moralistic, Maggie, condemning someone for smoking an occasional joint?"

As in the past, Dorothy had the ability to make Margo feel she was being small-minded. She still feared Sean might be a drag on his mother's campaign, but what had happened to her own judgment, jumping so quickly to the conclusion that Sean was heavily into drugs? What had she seen this morning, really? An easygoing—what she would once have called "laid-back"—young man relaxed amid the frenzy of Dorothy's campaign office, his red eyes as easily a sign of allergies as of anything else. Maybe Sean was the only sane one, the hyped-up campaign workers the ones who needed help.

"I'm sorry," she apologized. "Good luck with the campaign."

"No hard feelings." Dorothy gave her a hug. "When this circus is over, let's go down to Baja. Barbecue some fish, bitch about men, just like the old times. I told you, didn't I, that I got a little weekend place, close to where we used to go camping?"

Not until late the next afternoon did Margo complete the report on Dorothy and have time to see Ashley Green. They met at a coffeehouse downtown, near the studio where Margo had her weekly dance class.

"To get the easy ones out of the way first," Green said, "I checked the license numbers for Bob Kohler and Paul van den Moeller. Neither of them came up from Tijuana at the right time, either the night Zeke died or when you had your accident. Van den Moeller didn't cross the border from Mexico at all, not then or for the next two days. And Kohler came back too early to have been south of Ensenada, and too late to have used another car and gone back down there."

A waiter brought the cappuccino and pasta salad Margo had ordered and Green's peppermint tea (soothing to the stomach).

"Then Jaime Galván," he continued. "If he was storing dozens of barrels of toxins at that factory, then they aren't there now. I looked myself and I am not a man who leaves stones unturned. True, he could have moved the barrels. But another thing. I couldn't find a shred of proof that Galván was dating this girl, Rosalia, or that he dated any of the girls from the factory. According to the folks I talked to, he's a real toucher, he can't keep his hands off the girls. But they all say that's as far as it goes. They say he's a good family man, goes home to the wife and kids every night."

"I know he was dating Rosalia. Her cousin said so, and so did Rosalia."

"Maybe she said she was dating the boss so she'd feel important, or because she was dating someone her cousin would object to even more. The point is, there's someone else who turns out to be a better suspect than Galván or any of the others. I think I found Zeke's 'D.T.' "

"Diego Torres?"

"I don't think so. Torres lives in Tijuana, why would he have come into the States after that dinner? And I've got someone with a hell of a motive to cover up a hit-and-run." Green took a folded piece of paper from his pocket. "This is a list of the people who attended that dinner. Eight D.T.'s and guess what? One of them *did* cross back from Tijuana the night Zeke died. I didn't find the same license number the night of your accident, but maybe she was getting nervous by then and she borrowed or rented a car."

"She?"

Green handed Margo the list, with a name circled in red. "I've heard of this lady, she's a politician. You better believe if a politician was involved in a hit-and-run, killing a Mexican woman and child, she'd pay to cover it up."

Margo's stomach turned so sour she could have used some of Green's peppermint tea.

"Any chance," he said, "that this lady would have known you were asking questions about Holroyd's death?"

Growing up, Margo had studied ballet and modern dance—standing at the barre, dutifully following the instructor in pliés, tendus, and arabesques. The class she attended now, however, focused not on technique but on using dance as a conduit for feelings. That evening, because of the heat, the teacher put on soft music and invited the class to do gentle movements. Margo spent the first half of the two-hour class curled up in a miserable ball, thinking:

That dinner was a year ago and it was a year ago that Dorothy Troupe stopped drinking.

Dorothy was considering running for Congress and she declared her candidacy shortly after Zeke's death.

Worst of all . . . Margo had told Dorothy she suspected Zeke of blackmail and Dorothy warned her to back off. Later that same day, someone cut Margo's brake line. And Dorothy knew how to work on cars.

After lying motionless for an hour, an imperative for action surged through Margo's body. Jumping to her feet, she scooped up her clothes, slipped bare feet into her pumps, waved goodbye to the dance teacher, and dashed to her car. Driving to the freeway, she considered going to confront Dorothy. But there was someone else she wanted to see first, someone with whom she'd been far too gentle up to now.

26 / Moondance

Margo, urgent and angry, pounded on Lael's door. *Could you really not know what Zeke was doing?* she intended to demand the minute she saw Zeke's widow. *You don't expect me to believe you bought his story about the ultragenerous people at his speaking engagements?*

The person who answered the door, however, was not Lael but a fiftyish woman in whom Margo recognized Zeke's lanky build. Quickly—and imperfectly—Margo put on her social face, conveyed her sympathies to Zeke's mother, and let herself be invited in to meet Zeke's father. Lael sat on the couch, her arms and legs pulled in close as if for protection. She stared at Margo in apparent amazement, as if Margo had waltzed in with circus plumes bobbing in her hair. No shit—Margo realized she was still wearing her colorful geometric print leotard and turquoise tights from dance class, and she had slipped her bare feet into her businesslike red pumps.

The elder Holroyds seemed unfazed by either her attire or her manner. They probably assumed that all Southern Californians dressed oddly and spoke in abrupt phrases as if they were about to explode. Lael, however, clearly understood that Margo hadn't just stopped by to say hello.

"I've got to get milk, just up at the corner," she mumbled. "Margo, want to come?"

"Nonfat, dear," called Mrs. Holroyd after her. "We have to watch our cholesterol."

"They're really good people," said Lael, as she and Margo walked down the apartment building stairs. "Most people talk a lot of Christianity but only live it a little. They live it all the time.'' Nevertheless, getting away from Zeke's parents, Lael seemed like a prisoner escaping.

Once on the street, they proceeded by wordless agreement toward the beach, both stopping to remove their shoes when they reached the sand and then continuing toward the water's edge.

"Were you dancing tonight?" Lael asked eagerly.

"I was at my class. Actually, I was too upset to dance." Margo tried to summon back the anger with which she had driven to Lael's, but felt only pity for the young woman, having to play host to Zeke's saintly progenitors. She walked a few steps into the water, which was warmer than usual, a benefit of the hot summer. "Feels great," she said. Lael took a tentative step into the ocean as well.

The moon was waxing, in its third quarter, and into Margo's head came "Moondance" by Van Morrison. Into her head and then out of her mouth, substituting "la la" wherever she forgot the words.

"I love that song!" said Lael, la-la-ing along. As if a dam had broken, Lael started dancing and turning at the water's edge. She really did dance beautifully, her carriage erect but fluid, her slender legs lifting with superb control that had slackened little during her self-imposed exile from the art she loved.

Margo joined her, swirling and singing the light, jazzy song. She grabbed Lael's hand and the two of them improvised a duet. At the end of the song, Lael started sobbing. Margo had seen it in her dance class, the way emotions held inside the body were released when the body moved. She sat quietly on the sand, Lael's head in her lap, until the young woman's sobs subsided.

What now? Grill her on Zeke's "fund-raising," as Margo had planned to do? Lael seemed so fragile, Margo was uncertain how she would respond even if simply encouraged to talk about why she was crying.

Lael herself broke the silence. Her head still in Margo's lap, she said, "Remember at church the other day, the girl who said she killed her mother because she wished for her mother to have cancer?"

"Yes, but I don't believe she killed her mother. You don't believe that, do you?"

"Just from hating her mother? No, of course not." It was the practical business major suddenly speaking . . . and as suddenly giving way to a trembling child. "But I really am responsible for Zeke's death. I couldn't say it in church—Reverend Paul always likes it when people confess big sins, but it's different when you're the minister's wife, you have to set an example. But I can tell you, you don't count." Lael paused a second, barely registering the insult she'd delivered. She was right, however; Margo didn't count the way her fellow parishioners did. "And I have to tell someone," she said.

Margo virtually held her breath, afraid the slightest interruption would scare Lael into silence. What could she have done that she considered so sinful?

"My first year and a half in college, before I was called of God . . ." Lael spoke even lower and Margo leaned forward to hear. "To support myself, I . . . I started out working as a waitress, but the hours were long and it was hard to study, and the pay wasn't that great. This girl in my dorm told me about a place she worked for, an escort service. You just had to dress up nice and, you know, go out for the evening with someone. Only one night a week, and she made more than I did waitressing." She hesitated, then continued, "Sometimes, if you thought the man was okay—it was completely up to you—you'd offer to go to bed with him. You got a lot more money that way. The men were all right. They screened them real carefully, there was no one disgusting. I . . . I wasn't a virgin or anything, I slept with my boyfriend in high school. It didn't seem so bad, till I met Zeke and got involved in the church. Then I realized what a terrible sin I had committed."

"Did Zeke know?" What a hold he would have had over her then.

Margo felt the head in her lap shake no. "I should have told him, he would have helped me atone. But I was scared he'd hate me. I didn't believe enough in Zeke's love, or in Jesus' love and forgiveness, to tell the truth. That's why

Jesus took Zeke. He did it to show me I had to believe in Him.''

For just a moment, Margo thought of Ashley Green's theory that Lael was the murderer, her head stuffed so full of church dogma she had used it to justify her crime. If she were convinced she deserved to be widowed for her past sins, had she brought it about herself? But Lael wasn't a person who took action, she was a person acted upon.

Margo lifted Lael up to look her in the eye, albeit a shadowy proposition in the moonlight.

"I don't believe that," said Margo.

"You don't believe what I did? The escort service?"

"I don't believe Zeke died because of that. Look, Lael." At last, the question she'd come to ask. "You must have wondered about the people on that list of Zeke's. Since when do so many people make substantial contributions anonymously, so they can't deduct it from their taxes? And why did Zeke keep the list a secret?"

"Maybe they weren't itemizing," mused Lael, but she wasn't arguing; rather, the business part of her mind was engaged.

"R.K., for instance, gave over twenty thousand dollars," said Margo. "Didn't you wonder about that?"

"He gave that much? I didn't really pay attention to the list, I was so upset."

"D.T. gave that much, too. The totals on that list were nearly as much as the amounts Zeke said he collected at his speaking engagements."

"Oh." The business major was rapidly putting two and two together. "There must be an explanation. Maybe those people sinned and didn't want anyone to know about it. That was their way of atoning."

"I think," Margo said carefully, "Zeke probably told himself that he was helping them atone. And I think he threatened to report them if they didn't give him money." Lael half-stood, as if about to run. Margo caught her hands. "Listen to me. Zeke didn't die because of anything you did. It was because of what *he* did. One of those people killed him. You have to tell me more about what you know.''

''But I didn't know. I swear it.''

''Did Zeke ever say anything about seeing a hit-and-run accident? About a year ago?''

''No. . . . Well, actually, I guess it must have been a year ago, he started talking about being super careful every time he crossed back from Mexico, he said how easy it would be to run into someone. But he didn't say anything about seeing an accident himself.''

''What about Dorothy Troupe? Did he ever mention her?''

''The county supervisor, the one who's running for Congress? He mentioned her sometimes. Even though they disagreed on a lot of issues, Zeke always felt there were areas where they could work together. Is she the D.T. on the list?'' Lael's business mind had thoroughly clicked into gear.

''Probably not.'' Margo experienced a sharp sense of what Lael might have felt, the refusal to believe anything bad about someone you cared for. ''What about after he took me to the colonia?'' she said. ''Did he say anything that would make you think he had found someone else to ask for money?''

Lael thought for a moment, shook her head. ''But he didn't talk about the others, either. I should get back, Mother and Father Holroyd will worry. And I'd better stop for the milk.'' She started walking toward the convenience store. ''Zeke and I both had such secrets from each other, didn't we?''

Lael was laughing and crying at the same time, but she seemed real at last, an image on a screen that had finally come into focus.

Lael was going to be okay, thought Margo, lying in bed that night. Rather than destroying her, hearing that her self-righteous husband had feet of clay had given Lael back some faith in herself.

If Lael's well-being were all Margo had to think about,

she would have been asleep, instead of lying awake at two A.M. She kicked off the sheet and padded through the house, out onto the patio. The odor of sage from the canyon became more intense at night. The cat, nocturnal beast, followed her. She and Grimalkin sat on the wicker couch. Grimalkin no doubt thought about the likelihood of mice in the canyon. Margo thought about Dorothy Troupe. If D.T.'s crime was the hit-and-run that occurred after the dinner in Mexico, how could Dorothy be D.T.? She might have run into someone—it would be nearly impossible to stop in time if people dashed across the freeway. But Dorothy Troupe never would have run away.

Returning to bed, Margo dropped off finally at five and let herself sleep in until nine-thirty. She arrived at work an hour later. First she telephoned the California Highway Patrol and Ashley Green, and asked some questions. Then she invited Claire De Jong out for lunch.

27 / Doesn't It Ever Rain Here?

"The highway patrol confirmed there was a hit-and-run half a mile north of the border at around eleven-twenty on the night of that dinner." Margo lifted the damp hair off her neck. The day being too hot and oppressive to encourage alfresco dining, the other outdoor tables at the deli near KSDR were unoccupied . . . which made it a perfect place to talk to Claire privately.

"Did they have any leads?" Claire looked disgustingly fresh despite the heat. Was her secret simply her youth, or was it that she was training for a triathlon and her body was accustomed to sweating?

"No. They need at least a partial license plate number or a good description or some kind of physical evidence— for instance, if a headlight got ripped off in the accident and it was a type of headlight used only in certain models of Fords."

Margo closed her tired, scratchy eyes for a moment. She still didn't trust Claire, but she distrusted her own judgment as well, when it came to evaluating whether Dorothy Troupe was D.T.

"You said the Customs people record the license numbers of everyone crossing the border into the U.S., right?" Claire had a sharp, incisive way of posing questions—not the kind of interviewer, like Margo, who gradually established rapport, but someone who zeroed in on an interviewee. "Didn't the highway patrol check on people who came across during the five or ten minutes before the accident?''

''I asked. Too many cars, for one thing.''

''That late at night?''

''Sailors down in Tijuana for the evening, vacationers. Especially in the summer. And the accident took place half a mile north of the border. So the hit-and-run driver might not have come across the border. They might have gotten on the freeway on the U.S. side, somewhere in San Ysidro. There was no way the CHP could narrow it down.''

Claire picked up her egg salad sandwich, then put it down. ''Hard to have an appetite in this weather,'' she murmured. ''I wish it would rain.'' Margo felt mildly ashamed of the inner gloat she experienced; Claire might be human after all.

''What about your friend Ashley Green?'' said Claire. ''Did he find out when Dorothy came back into the U.S. that night?''

''Not yet. Dorothy has a new car, so first he has to get her old license plate number and then run it by his friend at Customs.'' Dorothy had decided to buy American, she'd said. Was that the only reason she had gotten the shiny new Buick? Or did her old car bear traces of blood from the Mexican mother and child she had killed and then left? Margo recoiled at the thought, just as she had in the middle of the night, and her reasons seemed just as valid in the light of day.

''I've known Dorothy for almost ten years. She isn't the kind of person who'd plow her car into a Mexican family and *not* stop to help them. And why run? She wouldn't have been charged. They don't hold someone at fault for hitting people who run across the freeway, especially not at night. No one would have been able to stop. Sure, there would have been bad publicity. But Dorothy's tough, she can handle bad press.''

''Margo,'' Claire said firmly. Margo steeled herself for the speech on objectivity, but Claire said, ''You told me that Dorothy stopped drinking a year ago. I'm not one hundred percent up on the law, but isn't it a felony to cause an injury accident when you're drunk? If Dorothy had been drinking at that dinner—and let's assume she was—we're not just talking bad press. She could have gone to jail."

Margo poked at her salad with her plastic fork. Between the heat and too much Italian dressing, the lettuce leaves had almost liquefied. She pushed the sodden mass away.

"She still wouldn't leave those people. If she were going to be charged, she'd face it. Of course, she'd fight it in court. She'd argue that anyone, drunk or sober, traveling at freeway speeds couldn't have avoided hitting those people. But she'd go to prison if she had to. Dorothy wouldn't run away from anything."

As she spoke, however, Margo recalled Dorothy's defensiveness regarding Sean's drug use. That was one area where Dorothy did exhibit a marked aversion to reality— her son. *Her accident-prone son.*

"Oh, my God. Claire, I bet Dorothy wasn't driving the car," said Margo. "I bet she was just a passenger."

Margo described the scene unrolling vividly in her mind: Sean, probably high on something, at the wheel, the horrible instant when he must have seen the Mexicans but couldn't stop—or did he even realize that people were on the freeway until he felt the impact? The panicked young man must have stepped on the gas and fled.

"Dorothy probably tried to get him to go back to help the people and face the police," Margo said. "But if he wouldn't go back, she'd have been willing to let him run away."

"Would she be willing to pay blackmail, to keep him out of prison?"

"Absolutely."

Zeke Holroyd must have been right there when the accident happened, thought Margo, as Claire scribbled something on a piece of paper. Either Zeke recognized Dorothy's car or he followed her and found out who she was . . . and then hit her up for money. He would have known Dorothy was considering running for Congress this summer, it was all over the news. Had he demanded bigger payments, since she would have had more at stake? Or maybe he hadn't been after money. Zeke's politics must have been one hundred and eighty degrees different from Dorothy's. What if he'd tried to keep her from running for office, threatened that if she announced her candidacy he'd go to the police? Who knew how Zeke would have explained keeping silent about the hit-and-run for a year, but he was sharp . . . and Dorothy would hardly accuse him of blackmailing her, since that would mean admitting she had paid the blackmail.

Still, could Dorothy have forced Zeke off the road? Could she have cut *Margo's* brakes? How far would she go to protect her son? Of course, Sean was the one who had committed the hit-and-run. Could he also be the murderer? Sean seemed too ineffectual to do anything more aggressive than a heavy breathing phone call. But he was as loyal in his way to Dorothy as she was to him. And his drug use must have thrown him in with some rough friends. Did he know his mama was paying blackmail to keep his ass out of jail?

Claire, who had covered a page with notes, looked up, hectic with excitement. "You just got a convertible, didn't you?" she said.

"What?"

"A convertible. I heard you got one."

Margo nodded, perplexed. She had assumed the top item on Claire's agenda would be to request Dorothy's appointment calendar and check on the candidate's whereabouts the nights of Zeke's and Margo's accidents.

"Here's what I was thinking," said Claire. "There's still a big piece of the puzzle missing. Why would Dorothy kill this maquiladora worker, Rosalia?"

Margo found herself repeating Ashley Green: "The police say Rosalia was depressed. She had a few beers, she lost her footing on the path. It might be a coincidence."

"Some coincidence, that you go to see Rosalia and while you're there your brakes are sabotaged and the same night Rosalia gets so depressed she falls off a cliff." Claire's smile reminded Margo of one of the kids trying to talk her and Barry into a slightly wacky plan. "I don't have any deadlines this afternoon and I'd love a ride in a convertible," Claire said. "How about going to Mexico?"

"Doesn't it ever rain here?" said Claire.

They were ten miles south of Tijuana on the toll highway. To the west, the sky above the ocean hung heavy and gray.

"Rarely in the summer," replied Margo. "I've never really gotten used to it."

"Did you grow up back East, too?"

"Connecticut. You?"

"Ohio. A summer day like this at home, you'd get rain for sure. God, I'd love a good storm."

"A thunderstorm!" agreed Margo. "The best thunderstorm I ever saw was when I was at the University of Wisconsin. I was sitting in the student union, drinking tea and just watching the storm come in over Lake Mendota."

"Awesome." Claire giggled. Her small face was half-covered by movie star sunglasses, her short blond hair whipped straight up by the breeze created by the car's speed; however, the air, when they stopped at the toll stations, was still.

Strange, thought Margo, that in the six months Claire had worked at KSDR, they had never had such a simple, friendly conversation. Margo realized she had regarded Claire—whom Alex originally hired for a reporting job she'd wanted—as an extension of the hated station manager. She had been wrong.

They chatted a bit more, then settled into a comfortable silence, Claire scanning Margo's file on the maquiladora industry and making occasional comments as Margo drove.

"This is interesting, Margo, this study where the women workers made innovations in the manufacturing process but didn't share them with anyone because they didn't want the production schedule speeded up. . . . Can it really cost as much as six hundred dollars to dispose of one fifty-five-gallon drum of toxic waste? . . . Are you talking to any of the Japanese maquiladoras? Says here they're only five percent of the maquiladoras in Tijuana, but they account for ten percent of the maquiladora employment . . . Yecch! This river that flows north from Mexicali—that's on the east side of the Baja peninsula, isn't it?—contained one hundred different industrial chemicals and viruses that can cause polio, dysentery, cholera, typhoid, meningitis, and hepatitis. Make sure you put that in your report, try to get an actuality from one of the scientists who did the study."

Margo responded perfunctorily. She had started the expedition feeling, as Claire appeared to, that it was almost a lark. But as she drove deeper into Baja, her mood darkened. Past Ensenada, when she turned onto the road to the Bufadora, her bruises began to throb, as if her skin had become hypersensitive.

Twenty minutes later, she parked in the dirt lot by the tourist attraction. She found a boy about David's age and engaged in a quick exchange in Spanish. The kid nodded and Margo handed him a dollar.

"What was that about?" asked Claire.

"I gave him a dollar to watch the car for us and promised him another dollar if he's still here when we get back. Just like in the movies." Margo tried for a light tone but couldn't achieve it.

She led Claire to the path she had taken a week ago with Rosalia.

"It *is* narrow," remarked Claire.

"So you think maybe Rosalia really did just slip and fall?"

"You don't believe that, do you?"

"Only if she was running away from someone."

They reached the spot where Margo and Rosalia had sat talking.

"What was she like?" said Claire.

"Very, very young. Romantic. Foolish. Feisty. Her seven-year-old cousin adored her." At the memory of little Beatriz, who wouldn't see her favorite cousin again, tears filled Margo's eyes. She hated crying! They turned to go back and she blinked the tears away.

When they neared the jewelry stand, the tears returned, this time not just welling up but running messily down her cheeks. Damn! It was going to be hard enough to approach Patricia and Tomás—who might even suspect that Margo had killed Rosalia—and now she was bawling.

"Ai, señora!" Patricia, who was tending the stand, started crying, too. "Please, come." She gestured for Margo and Claire to join her behind the counter.

"I was so sorry to hear about Rosalia," Margo got out. It occurred to her that her tears were proving the perfect icebreaker, a technique she'd never learned in journalism school. She took Patricia's hand and they wept together for several minutes. Claire handed out tissues and turned on the tape recorder.

"The police, they say she killed herself." Patricia clutched at the large cross she wore around her neck.

"But you don't think so?"

"Rosalia was so upset when she was staying with us, she cried all the time. 'What am I going to do?' she kept saying. She was scared to go back to Tijuana, but she couldn't go home to her parents' village, there was no work for her. She talked a lot about dying—she was afraid of dying, so because of that, I don't think she killed herself. But Rosalia was a little crazy, too. That's why I didn't worry when she didn't come back that day, after she went to talk to you. Of course, I asked Tomás to go look for her, but when he didn't find her we decided she probably went with you. She would do things without telling people, without thinking. So I think the police must be right." Patricia started crying again. "If she killed herself, she will go to hell."

"Patricia, I don't think Rosalia killed herself."

"You don't?" Patricia smiled. The prospect of Rosalia's eternal damnation evidently grieved her as much as Rosalia's death.

"I want to find out what happened to her," said Margo. "You can help me. When Rosalia and I talked, she said she was scared of her boyfriend, *el jefe* at the factory. She told me about seeing him unloading some barrels that contained toxic chemicals. Did she say anything to you about that?''

"Yes." Patricia sighed. "I told her she shouldn't have dated him. He always made her keep it a secret. She couldn't even call him by his name, only *el jefe*. What kind of man makes you keep him a secret? But Rosalia liked secrets.''

"Did *el jefe* ever come here looking for Rosalia?"

"No one came here for Rosalia except you. The man who came the next day asked about her, but that was only after he found her. First he wanted to know about you, señora.''

"What man?"

Patricia looked alarmed and Margo realized she had spoken sharply. "Tell me about the man who asked about me," she repeated, forcing herself to sound calm.

"I don't know for sure it was you he was asking about," said Patricia. "He wanted to know if a *norteamericana* came here the day before. He said she had a car accident on the road back to the highway and he was asking questions for the insurance company. He asked at all the stands, not just here. Don't worry, I didn't tell him anything. I didn't trust him, he was a *negro*.''

"You said he was the one who found Rosalia?"

"Yes. He went walking on the path and looked down, and he saw her on the rocks. Señora, can I ask you something?''

Margo nodded, but she was barely listening.

"When you came here before, you said you knew Rosalia's little cousin, Beatriz. Rosalia had some special things, her treasures, she called them. She would want her treasures to go to Beatriz. Could you take them to her?''

"Of course." Margo automatically took the small bundle tied in a scarf that Patricia handed her. Her thoughts were miles away.

Ashley Green had found Rosalia's body last Thursday. He had come to see Margo the next day. But he'd mentioned nothing about Rosalia's death, nothing to indicate he had even gone to the Bufadora.

"Hey, Margo!" said Claire, who'd understood none of the revelations Patricia had made in Spanish. "Look, isn't it wonderful? It's raining!"

28 / Rosalia's Treasures

"The car!" Margo cried.

Thank heaven it was only drizzling, since she discovered she had paid less than perfect attention when the convertible's previous owner had instructed her about putting up the top. The task took ten minutes of trial and error, and the assistance of both Claire and the boy who had watched the car for her.

"Ready to roll," said Claire.

"A minute." Margo couldn't help herself. She got on her knees in the dirt and shone a flashlight under the car. There were no signs of dripping brake fluid. "Okay."

"What did Patricia say?" demanded Claire, once Margo had steered through the small crush of people around the outdoor stalls.

Margo repeated the conversation, ending with Patricia's revelation about Ashley Green.

"Why shouldn't Green come here and ask questions?" said Claire. "He heard about your accident. He must have assumed you were coming from the Bufadora. So he wanted to investigate."

"He came here on Thursday. The next day, he came to talk to me. He didn't say a word about being here, or about finding Rosalia's body."

"But how would he know there was any connection between you and this woman he found, a woman the police said committed suicide? He'd just figure it was a coincidence."

"I don't think coincidences happen around Ashley

Green." Ally or not, Claire could be as argumentative as Margo's stepson.

"What is it? Are you stopping?"

"Just testing the brakes." They were fine. But as Margo approached the speed bumps, she broke into a sweat.

"Wow!" exclaimed Claire. "Was that thunder?"

"Sounded like it, out over the ocean."

The rain was falling intermittently, enough to snarl the traffic, by the time they were driving through Ensenada. Conversation stopped as Margo concentrated on driving, with Claire helping her find the haphazardly marked route to the highway.

"The thing is," said Margo, when they had gotten out of Ensenada and were heading north, "Green lied about being at the Bufadora. Now, I don't know if anything he told me is true."

"For instance?"

"He said Jaime Galván doesn't date his workers. Hell, Galván could be Green's client. That whole story he told me about working for Suzuki is plausible, but so what? Think if I called Suzuki, anyone would admit hiring a private eye because they wanted to avert a potential lawsuit?"

Claire appeared to consider the question for a moment, then said, "What about using your own sources to find out about Galván? Is there anyone you could ask who'd know for sure if he was dating Rosalia?"

"Anita, Rosalia's cousin, said they were dating."

"Okay, but how did Anita know? Would Rosalia have told her the truth?"

El jefe had made Rosalia keep their relationship a secret, Patricia said. Rosalia and Anita were hardly on giggling, secret-sharing terms. In fact, hadn't someone pointed out Anita's tendency to cling to erroneous assumptions despite evidence to the contrary . . . the way Anita couldn't get it out of her head that Margo belonged to Zeke's church? And hadn't someone—the same person—raised a skeptical eyebrow when Anita referred to Rosalia's affair with Jaime Galván?

"Carmen!" Margo said out loud.

Claire started singing "The March of the Toreadors" from the Bizet opera, accompanied by the patter of rain on the canvas top.

"Carmen's the shopkeeper where Rosalia lived," laughed Margo, when Claire reached the end of a phrase. "She knows everything going on in the colonia. I think she even works at Sani when they need extra help."

"Let's go! Or maybe we should call her first." Claire eyed the sky. The storm was gradually overtaking them. Although the rain remained a drizzle, the clouds had turned the color of lead and the rumbles of thunder sounded closer.

"No phone. No electricity. No running water. Besides, if we go to the colonia, we can take that thing to Beatriz."

"What thing?"

"Tied up in the scarf, behind the seat. Some special things of Rosalia's that Patricia asked me to give her little cousin." Margo had neglected to report that part of the conversation to Claire. In fact, in her distress at hearing about Ashley Green, she had paid little attention to the parcel Patricia had handed her. Rosalia's treasures. What would a seventeen-year-old Mexican factory worker prize? Probably the same kinds of things Margo had cherished at seventeen: jewelry, mementos of a special occasion . . . *a gift from her boyfriend*! Not that Jaime Galván would have put his name on anything. Still, there might be something linking him to Rosalia.

Claire was already untying the scarf.

"A lipstick," Claire inventoried as Margo drove. "Avon's 'Luscious Plum.' "

"I've heard that Avon's big among the maquiladora workers," commented Margo. "One woman starts selling it and all her friends feel obligated to buy. It isn't just politeness, it's a vital aspect of the social network."

"Two feathers, they're beautiful," Claire continued. "A photograph, this must be her family. There are about a dozen kids younger than she is, no wonder she felt she couldn't go back. Hmm, would you believe a drinks menu from the Cowboy Club in Chula Vista? D'you think Jaime

Galván likes country music? And two, no, one and a half, pairs of earrings.''

"Tell me again?"

Claire repeated the list of the items Rosalia had saved.

There was little traffic on the highway. Margo pulled over to the shoulder and reached for the two feathers lying on the scarf on Claire's lap. Both brilliantly colored, the feathers appeared to be from two different birds, one with more red in its plumage and the other with deep blues.

"Are they important?" said Claire.

"Probably not." She gave the feathers back to Claire and restarted the car. "One of the U.S. muckety-mucks in the maquiladora industry keeps tropical birds, but I don't see how he would have known Rosalia. And you always see birds in Tijuana, they're offered for sale in the tourist areas. Someone Rosalia knew was probably a bird vendor. Or she could have found the feathers in the street."

"Tell me about the muckety-muck."

Margo gave a brief bio of Craig LaBerge.

The first streaks of lightning came when they were entering Tijuana. The traffic was much worse than in Ensenada, congested not only by the storm but by the rush hour. It took another forty-five minutes to get across town to the Ciudad Industrial. The lightning flashed every few minutes now and the rain was falling harder.

"Jesus!" said Claire, as Margo turned down the dirt road to the colonia, now slick with rain. People were scurrying along the road, heads bent. "Have you got front-wheel drive?"

"I don't know." That was the kind of question men asked when they bought cars, a question she should have asked.

When they got to the gully, the road was not just wet but muddy, the mud an inch deep. Margo felt the tires slip. She downshifted into first gear.

"Whoops! Close call!" Claire giggled, as the tires gripped and the car moved forward again. "Lucky this car's so small. We can ask a couple of men to help push us if we have to, on the way back."

Hearing the excitement in Claire's voice, Margo reflected that her colleague was new to San Diego . . . and therefore unlikely to realize that the gully was an ideal location for one of the flash floods that occurred in Baja during severe rains. The Miata would be swept up like a child's plastic boat and would provide about as much protection. For a panicky moment, Margo pictured it intensely, the little car caught in a maelstrom and then smashing into a hillside or a tree. She took a deep breath and continued up the hill. They would spend only a few minutes talking to Carmen, then leave. She was certain floods didn't happen until after days—at the very least, hours—of heavy rain. The colonia residents were used to coping with the rain and none of them were fleeing.

People were, however, behaving with an urgency Margo hadn't seen before, running, calling to one another. She drove by a group of men nailing black plastic—torn trash bags?—over the roof of a house, and then a second group doing the same. Carmen's roof already had the black covering. Stopping the car and entering the store, Margo walked through half a dozen men on the porch, apparently a new work party forming.

"Ms. Simon, are you crazy?" someone yelled at her in English. It was Diego Torres, at the center of the group on Carmen's porch. "Coming here in the rain, in a car like that?"

Ignoring him, she went inside.

"None of us can help you, people are trying to save their own houses," Torres called after her.

Carmen looked no happier to see her. The storekeeper glanced up, frowning, from the counter, where she was selling trash bags and a box of Pampers to one customer. An assistant waited on another and a dozen more people crowded behind them. Margo pushed through the crowd, hearing loud complaints and receiving a jab in the ribs from a more energetic soul.

"Carmen, I've got to talk to you," she said. "Just two minutes, then I'll go."

The storekeeper finished her transaction.

"*Por favor!*" pleaded Margo.

"Paco," Carmen alerted her assistant. "Two minutes only," she said, as much to her waiting customers as to Margo. She went through a curtain into a back room. Margo rushed after her, gesturing to Claire to stay behind. This was clearly no time for introductions, nor for convincing Carmen to trust another gringa.

With no lamp and the black trash bags covering the roof, the back of Carmen's store was pitch-dark. Margo half-fell against the Mexican woman, who caught her with strong hands; Carmen had probably nailed all the plastic on her roof by herself.

"What is it, señora?" A quick, no-nonsense voice: Ask your questions and get out of here.

"Was Rosalia dating Jaime Galván?"

"Everyone wants to know that."

"What do you mean, everyone? Who else asked?"

"A man who came this afternoon. A black man, a detective. I'll tell you the same thing I told him. Rosalia wasn't dating Jaime. She just wanted Anita to think that."

"Then who was she dating?"

"*El gran jefe.*" The big boss.

"Someone above Galván?"

"Yes. I don't remember his name, he didn't come to Sani often. He has a kind of company that runs a lot of maquiladoras. Sani was one of them."

"Would he have given Rosalia bird feathers?"

"Bird feathers? Sure, why not? One thing everyone knows about *el gran jefe* is that he keeps birds."

"One more thing." Margo thrust the package of Rosalia's treasures at Carmen. "Can you give this to Beatriz? From Rosalia?"

"Yes." Carmen moved as if to return to the store, but suddenly she grasped Margo's arm. "Do you have children, señora?"

"Two stepchildren, yes."

"*Tenga cuidado.*" Be careful.

29 / Riders on the Storm

Margo found Claire on the porch of the store, sticking a microphone in Diego Torres's face. Torres was smiling.

"Thanks, Diego." Claire turned off the tape recorder. "And good luck."

"Look, you might need help on the road," the union organizer said in English—to Claire, not Margo. "Martín, Beto!" Two young men looked up. In Spanish, Torres told them to accompany the señoras, and not to let them cross the gully if it looked too dangerous. Margo thought of protesting, but Torres was right.

"Ready?" he said, in English again. He took off his jacket and ran alongside Claire, holding the jacket over her as she and Margo dashed to the car.

"How did you do that?" Margo drove slowly, their two helpers trotting alongside. "How'd you get Diego Torres eating out of your hand?"

"One word. Blond." Claire sounded giddy with excitement. "What did Carmen say? Did she confirm Rosalia was dating Jaime Galván?"

"Nope. Rosalia was dating Galván's boss—Craig La-Berge, the man with the birds. LaBerge's shelter company operates Sani. That's not all. Guess who else was here this afternoon, also wanting to know about Rosalia's boyfriend? Ashley Green."

Margo felt giddy herself. Rosalia hadn't precisely lied about the identity of her lover. True, she hadn't objected when Margo had brought up Galván's name, but neither had she herself referred to him by name. It was *el jefe* she'd seen moving barrels of toxins, *el jefe* who had gotten so angry he hit her. Zeke, a master at ferreting out secrets, must have known all along that Rosalia meant *el gran jefe*, Craig LaBerge.

Margo turned down the hill, her hands tightening on the steering wheel.

"Wow!" Claire turned on the tape recorder and began to narrate into the microphone. "In the ten minutes we spent in the colonia, it looks like the heart of the storm has moved directly overhead. There are only instants between each lightning flash and the crash of thunder that follows. And even though it's only six-thirty, the storm has brought on a premature dusk. In the car's headlights, we can see the fat, heavy raindrops pounding the dirt road into Mexican mud." She held up the microphone to get the drumbeat of the rain on the Miata's canvas top.

Margo had an impulse to rip the mike from her hand, but realized that her annoyance at Claire's gee-whiz attitude was tinged with jealousy. The younger reporter had turned on the tape recorder as a reflex action; Claire had the kind of instinct for radio that Margo had to consciously work to develop.

Claire continued her narration, "One of the men helping us, I think Beto, is walking just ahead of us. He's using a stick to gauge the depth of puddles, then he signals us either to go through them or drive around. The other man, Martín, has gone further down the road. There he is, right ahead of us. He's holding up his hand for us to stop."

Margo squeezed on the brakes. They didn't catch. The terror of her accident flooded back over her. She tried the brakes again, no luck. Martín was standing directly ahead of them as the car kept sliding, gaining speed. Honking the horn, she tried steering to one side. Her wheels were locked into the skid. Martín was no more than four feet away. Claire rolled down the window and yelled, "Move!" Tears ran down Margo's face. Through them, she saw Martín leap to the side.

The car stopped just above the gully—just past where Martín had been standing. He came running back now, anxiously asking if she and Claire were okay.

"Fine," she lied. "Martín, are you all right?"

"Sure, no problem." He smiled. He was covered with mud.

He explained that someone had laid two boards across the gully, a makeshift bridge. But the boards—placed for the pickup trucks and twenty-year-old Buicks common in the colonia—were much farther apart than the wheels of Margo's small sports car. He'd been signaling her to stop so that he and Beto could move the boards.

"Margo?" said Claire, as the two men adjusted the "bridge." "Do you want me to drive?"

"I can..." Margo realized she was shaking. "Yeah, thanks."

"Did you ever tell Craig LaBerge you were looking for Rosalia?" Claire had pulled over at the higher end of the Ciudad Industrial. Even though the streets were paved, there was no drainage, and water standing in low-lying areas looked half a foot deep or more. No other cars were in sight; the Industrial City was shuttered, crippled by the rain.

"No, I didn't know LaBerge had anything to do with Rosalia." She offered Claire the bottle of mineral water she carried in the car.

"Thanks." Claire took a drink. "Hungry?"

"Famished."

Claire produced a granola bar from her purse and divided it in half.

"Thanks. I did ask him about Zeke Holroyd. I think the way I put it was, had he heard of Zeke using unorthodox methods to raise money for his church?" Was that when LaBerge's macaw had shrieked? Margo had figured the bird was responding to her own nervousness; it must have been picking up on the tension from LaBerge.

"From LaBerge's office," she continued, "I went to Sani and then to the Bufadora. What I think happened is my question about Zeke made him suspicious, and then, while I was waiting at Sani, Galván called him and said I was there asking about Rosalia. I think that was when he decided to follow me. He must have thought I was making the connection between him and Rosalia and that worried him.''

''But why?'' Even through a mouthful of granola bar, Claire's remark was incisive, challenging . . . and absolutely on the mark.

''Afraid of his affair with Rosalia coming out?'' said Margo, but questioned her own question. ''So afraid that he killed Zeke and Rosalia and tried killing me? Zeke never asked for millions, it would have been more like five or ten thousand. Why not just pay him off? So it couldn't have been the affair.''

''What about the birds?'' mused Claire. ''Say he figured out some way to get them past Customs?''

''He'd have to be caught in the act. If Zeke threatened to turn him in, he could just stop. Damn! What was it about those barrels Rosalia saw?''

She tensed at the hum of tires on the wet street. She and Claire weren't completely alone in the Ciudad, after all. The car passed by.

''Putting aside motive for the time being,'' Margo continued, ''let's say LaBerge got the call from Galván and drove to Sani—it wouldn't take more than fifteen minutes and I was there for half an hour. Once he got there, he called Galván from his car phone. That's when Galván ended our interview. LaBerge just had to wait for me to come out, and follow me to the Bufadora.'' It was Ashley Green's theory, that Galván had alerted an accomplice. (If Green could be trusted. Why had he kept silent about Rosalia's death? And what had he been doing, asking about Rosalia's boyfriend at the colonia that afternoon?)

''About those barrels,'' Claire said. ''I keep thinking of what I saw in your notes earlier. Do you have a flashlight?''

Margo handed it to her, along with the maquiladora folder. While Claire perused the folder, Margo watched the weakening storm. The rain was still falling steadily, but the lightning and thunder had shifted north, over San Diego.

''Got it!'' Claire cried. ''It says here that disposing of toxins costs as much as six hundred dollars per barrel.'' Claire handed over the flashlight and the paper she'd been looking at. ''If Craig LaBerge was storing the toxins instead of disposing of them, he wouldn't just be fined by the Mexican government, he'd also be required to dispose of the toxins properly. Rosalia said she saw as many as a hundred barrels, right? At six hundred per barrel, that's fifty or sixty thousand . . .''

''Ohmigod,'' Margo breathed, staring at the list Claire had given her, printed on the embossed letterhead of ''Diggs Fine Footwear'' of Scranton, Pennsylvania. ''LaBerge wasn't just breaking Mexican environmental regulations. He was committing fraud. This list is from one of the speakers at the conference I covered—Lawrence Diggs, he owns a shoe company back East and has a maquiladora that LaBerge operates. See all these costs?'' The list itemized the major expenses involved in operating Zapatas Finas (''fine shoes''), Diggs's maquiladora. ''Diggs doesn't pay any of these directly. He just writes one big check . . . to Craig LaBerge. LaBerge handles all the individual payments—wages, the lease on the factory, government permits . . .''

''Disposal of toxic waste.''

''Bingo.''

Claire whistled. ''So LaBerge was billing Diggs six hundred dollars a barrel to dispose of waste. But he didn't dispose of it, he stored it. And pocketed the money.''

''Lawrence Diggs came here for the conference two weeks ago and of course he was going to visit his Mexican factory, something he probably didn't do more than once a year. So LaBerge had to hide the barrels of toxins. Easy enough, he just moved them to another factory he operates nearby, Sani. There was only one problem. Zeke Holroyd found out about it, and tried to blackmail him . . . Do you want to bet Zeke didn't have a clue what deep shit he was getting into? He heard Rosalia's story and figured LaBerge was doing *something* illegal, so he threatened to turn him in. But he thought all LaBerge had at risk was a fine—not much more than a slap on the hand—from Mexico.''

''And if LaBerge was defrauding one client that way, he was probably doing it to others.''

"Anyone far enough away—or nervous enough about crossing the border, and most of them are—that they wouldn't make a lot of visits to their Tijuana plant."

A bright light shone through the windshield. Margo grabbed her purse and reached for her can of Mace. Claire was yelling.

"Hey, ladies, it's all right!" The speaker turned the light toward himself, revealing a fortyish Anglo on the driver's side of the car, holding up a hand in a conciliatory gesture. Claire cracked open her window. "Sorry, ladies. Didn't mean to scare you. I just wanted to check if you were okay. Did your car break down?"

"Thanks. No, we're all right," said Margo.

"You ladies shouldn't be down in Tijuana in this rain. Radio says there's another thunderstorm coming right on the heels of the last one. Believe me, you're gonna have a heck of a time getting back to the border."

"All the roads between here and the border are paved, aren't they?" asked Claire.

"That's a good one. Sure, the roads are paved. And all the potholes are repaired *mañana*. Or the day after *mañana*. Look, I'm heading back to the old *Estados Unidos* and I've got a pickup, it's the only kind of vehicle you ought to drive down here. I'd be glad to give you a lift home. You're welcome to keep your car in the lot at my company. It's right here and I'm on pretty high ground."

"Thanks, it's okay," Margo said.

"Well, I mean it, ladies, don't wait for the flooding to get worse. Because I guaran-damn-tee you, it will. Pick up a cute little car like that and carry it right down to the Tijuana River."

"He had a point," said Margo, after the man left. "I guess there's no reason to stick around. And I'm hungry."

"Mind if I keep driving? This is a great car."

"Go ahead."

"What do we need to go ahead with this story?" said Claire, starting the Miata.

"First thing tomorrow, I'll call Lawrence Diggs and find out how much he's paid LaBerge for disposing of toxins.

No, but that's dumb,'' she thought out loud. ''Why would Diggs tell me something like that if I don't have some kind of proof?''

''How about . . .'' said Claire, ''there's got to be a paper trail if someone disposes of toxins properly—Customs forms saying the stuff came back across the border, documents the company files with the Mexican and U.S. environmental agencies. Either LaBerge doesn't have the documentation or else his forms were falsified, and that could be proved. You could track down the paper, then contact Diggs.''

''Great,'' groaned Margo. ''That'll only take three months.''

Claire was driving ten miles per hour, peering ahead for flooded areas. ''What about going after LaBerge for the murders instead of the fraud? Don't we have enough to convince the Mexican police to ask if LaBerge was seen around Rosarito the night Zeke was killed or at the Bufadora the night Rosalia died and you had your accident?''

Margo quailed at the thought of the Mexican police. ''I think we have to establish LaBerge's motive first. . . . You know, Ashley Green—if we can believe him—said he didn't see any barrels at Sani. Diggs was here just two weeks ago, I bet he's not planning to come back anytime soon. What if those barrels got moved back to Diggs's factory? If I could call Diggs and say I saw a hundred barrels of toxins there . . .''

Claire stopped the car. ''How do we get there?''

30 / A Run for the Border

Please, no guard dogs! Margo jammed the toe of her shoe into an interstice in the chain link fence enclosing the Zapatas Finas factory yard. Luckily, her own *zapatas* were flat Mexican sandals with closed toes. Claire, climbing next to her, had on running shoes. And both of them were wearing slacks. How to Dress for Trespass. They only lacked hooded rain ponchos, thought Margo, shaking her damp hair out of her face. The rain had diminished but continued to fall in a steady drizzle . . . and the second storm they'd been warned about was on its way, lightning showing in the southwestern sky.

Carefully placing her hands to avoid the sharp metal points at the top of the fence, Margo swung one leg over, found a fresh toehold, and dropped down. "Ai!" She slipped on the muddy ground and crashed into the fence, setting up a metallic clangor. *No dogs!* She grabbed for her Mace, her old phobia like a huge hand encircling her lungs and starting to squeeze. But there was no frenzied barking, no sign that anyone, man or beast, was guarding the shoe factory.

"Claire, are you okay?" she whispered. Five inches shorter than she, Claire was poised at the top of the fence, trying to get her legs over without scraping the hell out of them.

"Yeah. Oops." Claire half-fell to the ground. "Can you see? I've got rotten night vision."

"I can see all right. I don't want to use the flashlight unless we absolutely have to. The Ciudad Industrial might have some kind of security patrol."

To their right, Margo saw the outline of a low-lying building, no doubt Zapatas Finas's administrative offices. She was more interested in the large, blocky structure straight ahead—the guts of the factory. She and Claire started across the dirt yard, mud pulling at their shoes.

"Shit!" whispered Claire. "Margo, I just kicked something and it moved. Can't we turn on the flashlight for a second? I'm going nuts."

Margo reached into her shoulder bag. Worn bandolier-style, she'd emptied the bag of all but the necessities: car keys, flashlight, a mini cassette recorder, and the Mace, tucked into a front pocket where she could grab it instantly. She turned on the flashlight, blocking most of the beam with her fingers. A few feet ahead of them, a black and white volleyball Claire must have kicked wobbled slightly. Maquiladoras were big on providing recreation for their workers; volleyball supplies were cheap, compared to paying a living wage.

Beyond the volleyball, the flashlight illuminated a loading dock . . . and on the dock, several large, shadowy figures, shapes so weird that as Margo crept closer, she stifled a scream. The things were moving! She took the risk of shining the light full on them, and extinguished it immediately when she saw that she'd let herself get spooked by three forklifts. The forklifts must have been hastily covered with big sheets of plastic against the storm; wherever the plastic was unsecured, it billowed out in the wind.

Past the loading dock, toward the back of the factory, they found a padlocked wooden door. Margo remembered someone saying that padlocks at maquiladoras were rarely fastened. Sure enough, the shackle wasn't engaged. Slowly Margo opened the door, and almost recoiled at the stench. She switched on the flashlight just long enough to confirm that this was a part of the shoe factory where leather was treated. She closed the door and replaced the padlock. The next door, similarly unlocked, opened to a room containing machines of various kinds.

There was a crash of thunder and the rain picked up suddenly, pelting down. The new storm had arrived.

Around the rear of the building, they found a padlock that was indeed locked. It secured the gate to a sort of outbuilding. Although the building was roofed, a wink of the flashlight revealed a gap of a foot or two separating the corrugated roof and the seven-foot-high wall. Margo cupped her hands into a stirrup and boosted Claire up. Able to lie on her stomach across the top of the thick stucco wall, Claire shone the flashlight inside.

"Recorder?" she asked. Margo handed it up and Claire spoke into the machine. "Rosalia wasn't exaggerating. There've got to be at least a hundred barrels in here."

"Do they say anything on them?"

"*Residuos peligrosos*. Does that mean what I think?"

"Toxic wastes. You know, I don't have to convince Lawrence Diggs that his toxins are being stored. I can just contact the Mexican environmental people and tell them to get out here before . . ."

"Oh, God," said Claire. "You know what else is here? A big old Cadillac, with major dent marks in the right front fender. What do you bet there's paint that matches Zeke's car?"

"Shh! Did you hear something?"

"No." But Claire cut the light and dropped down.

They listened silently for a moment, but any other sounds were lost in the pounding storm.

"I thought I heard a car door open," said Margo. "Let's get out of here."

As they half-sprinted, slipping in the mud, toward the chain link fence, a brilliant display of lightning seemed to linger a full ten seconds in the sky. Margo glanced back over her shoulder. Another person was in the factory yard, a figure standing at the edge of the low-lying administration building. In an instant, her mind interpreted the image she had glimpsed in the lightning flash and she understood why no one was chasing them.

"Claire, a gun!"

She heard a shot, but their assailant had fired in total darkness.

"Over here, I'll help you over!" came a voice from the

other side of the fence—Ashley Green.

Margo half-turned back, but heard another shot from behind her in the yard and an exclamation as if someone had been hit. No time to worry whose side Green was on. She leaped onto the fence and threw herself over, barely feeling the metal points ripping into her hands. Beside her, Green was helping Claire over. Clumsily, he pulled them into a shallow, water-filled culvert at the base of the fence.

"Can either of you shoot?" he said, and Margo realized why Green had moved awkwardly. He'd been shot. "It's a semiautomatic, you just point and shoot like a camera." Urgency filled his voice in spite of the joking words.

"No," said both women. And Margo added, "Where were you hit?"

"My right arm."

She didn't have to ask whether Green was right-handed. "Who's shooting at us?"

"Craig LaBerge," said Green, as another shot came, fired in the dark, wild. "I guess he's not gonna just go away. Damn, I was never any good left-handed."

Nevertheless, he took aim and fired two shots that ricocheted off something metal. He hissed at them to flatten themselves into the culvert as LaBerge—now alerted to their position—fired again. His shot ripped a hole in the fence a few feet above them.

"Margo!" Claire's voice was small and terrified. "He's passed out."

Margo reached across Green's limp body and found his gun. "Try to wake him up," she told Claire. "Get to his car phone and call the Mexican police."

Staying low, she ran half a dozen yards along the fence, toward the street. If she couldn't hit Craig LaBerge, at least she could confuse him about their location. She lifted the gun, two-handed and straight-armed in front of her as she'd seen on television—although neither Cagney nor Lacey had ever been shaking. She pointed the barrel through the fence, aimed below the outline of the administrative building where she had seen LaBerge, and pulled the trigger; and nearly dropped the damn gun as it kicked back. She hit the ground and rolled along the fence as a shot answered hers. Holding the gun tighter this time, she aimed and fired again, and again neatly rolled—all her years of dance were coming in handy.

LaBerge didn't shoot back. Instead, a moment later, she heard a car start.

"Margo, what the hell are you doing?" Apparently Ashley Green had regained consciousness.

She should have gone back to Green and Claire and helped them call the police. But she was feeling an adrenaline rush, as if she'd drunk six cups of espresso . . . adrenaline and rage. She raced to her own car.

LaBerge had a head start, but there were only a few roads out of the Ciudad Industrial and he couldn't drive completely lightless in the storm. The lights of LaBerge's pickup went on ahead of her for a few seconds, then were switched off, flashed back on a moment later and off again. Margo kept her own lights on, figuring LaBerge cared a lot more about escaping than about turning around and shooting at her. He was going forty miles per hour, desperately fast for the conditions.

Ahead of her, LaBerge's truck plunged through a flooded area. Oh, God. It looked like one small step for a pickup, and a pole vault for a tiny sports car. She kept her foot on the gas pedal, held her breath. The Miata leaped like a trout through the small pond.

He turned the next corner. She followed. Ahead, at the end of a long block of factories, she saw lights and movement: Avenida Tijuana, the main road that led to the border crossing. LaBerge wouldn't go to the crossing, where he'd get stuck in line and she could ask the authorities to apprehend him. But then, why the hell not? What made her think that anyone would take her word against one of the pillars of the maquiladora community? Yes, he had taken a few shots at her, LaBerge would freely admit it. How could he have known she was a radio reporter? All he'd seen were furtive figures, trespassers at his factory . . . and they'd shot back! Just look at the powder burns on her hands!

Halfway to Avenida Tijuana, however, LaBerge turned down a side road. Margo followed. Instead of making a run for the border, he seemed to be leading her to a remote corner of the Ciudad Industrial. Did he plan to shoot her? He must realize she knew he'd killed Zeke and Rosalia—why take a chance on whether she had any proof? Still, how was he going to explain a dead radio reporter with one of his bullets in a vital part of her anatomy, not to mention Claire and Ashley Green testifying that she had taken off after him? But he'd only seen Margo and Claire at the factory, she told herself; he might not have spotted Ashley. What if he figured he had killed Claire and Margo was the only witness left?

But to shoot her point-blank? LaBerge favored accidents, didn't he?

The road he had taken led toward lower ground. The dips were getting deeper and wetter. Not slowing down, he darted straight into a dip that had become a turbulent river. When he was some dozen feet into it, the water rose over the hood and the truck stopped. Margo had managed to brake at the water's edge, her headlights illuminating the pickup, in which LaBerge appeared to be screaming. So this was the accident he'd planned for her. Knowing the Ciudad Industrial intimately, he had deliberately driven to where the worst flooding would occur. He had bet his pickup could make it through . . . and that she would follow and be swept away in the flood.

She backed several feet from the dip in case the deluge crept higher. Now what? Wait for the Mexican police to show up? A log carried by the current whacked against LaBerge's truck, which teetered but righted itself. He rolled down his window. Margo could hear him even through her own closed window and the storm.

''Help me!'' he bellowed.

31 / The Tijuana Jail

"Help!" LaBerge shouted again from his half-submerged truck.

Sure thing, thought Margo. The man had just tried to kill her. Why not bring him out of the water so he could try again?

The pickup teetered again, hit by some submerged debris. LaBerge screamed.

The thing was, how could she be sure Green and Claire had reached the Mexican police, or that the police would respond quickly? They must have their hands full with rain-caused accidents; why bother with a couple of hysterical gringos?

She rolled down her window and pointed her gun at him. "Throw out your gun," she yelled. "Throw it far away."

LaBerge complied. The gun plopped into the water at least ten feet from him and sank.

Leaving her headlights on, Margo got out of the car, still holding the gun on him.

"Can you wade out?" she called.

"The current's too strong. I've got a rope. If you get closer, I think I can throw it to you."

Margo waded in up to her knees but felt unsafe going any further. Invisible flotsam was hitting her legs, some of it soft things like clothing or small plants but others hard and bruising.

LaBerge tied the rope somewhere inside the pickup, then dragged himself through the window onto the roof. His left thigh looked torn and bloody. One of Margo's or Green's shots must have hit him. Standing on top of the pickup,

LaBerge weighted the other end of the rope by tying a large flashlight to it, and turned the flashlight on—good idea, it would be easier to spot if it landed in the water. LaBerge possessed animal intelligence, Dorothy had said. He was using it now. Margo resolved to get back in her car before LaBerge made it to dry land. He flung the rope, but it landed too far to the side and floated away.

"Can you come a little closer?" he pleaded, reeling the rope back in.

Margo gulped. She had just felt something soft against her leg that she was sure was a small dead animal. Why was she risking her own life for this murderer? The answer came too easily: Because she was Alice Simon's daughter. She walked another two feet into the water; it came midway up her thighs.

LaBerge threw the rope again. This time she caught it and waded out. The rope was long enough to tie to the fence of a factory above the flood line.

"Okay," she called, moving back to her car and opening the door.

Grasping the rope, LaBerge lowered himself into the water, which came up to his chest. Margo kept the gun on him as he began to walk out. He moved slowly because of his wounded left leg.

Hoping that saving his life might make him feel he owed her, she said, "I understand why you killed Zeke. But why Rosalia? You cared for her, didn't you?"

LaBerge, now standing in water a few inches above his waist, didn't answer.

"Did she ask for money?"

He laughed. "No, she asked me to divorce my wife and marry her. The little fool."

Poor Rosalia.

Something big in the current must have hit LaBerge. Thrust sideways, he lost his grip on the rope and went under. Margo waited for five seconds . . . ten seconds. She could see him tumbling, a hand stretching for the rope but missing it, his head jerking up for air.

Fifteen seconds. Finally, taking the rope with one hand—

and still grasping the gun in the other—she ran out to him.

He grabbed instantly for her gun hand, twisting her wrist. She dropped the gun, letting the current take it, rather than chancing it getting into LaBerge's hands. He seized her shoulders and pushed her underwater. She grabbed at his wounded leg. Howling, he released her. She kicked away from him and came up for air, coughing on the slime, which also covered her face. He reached for her again. She hadn't taken the time to remove her purse from across her chest. She got her hands on the can of Mace and sprayed the entire contents into LaBerge's face. As he staggered, blinded, she ran out of the water, jumped into her car, and drove away. Let the flood take him, she had no more ways to protect herself. And she didn't believe any piddling flood was a match for Craig LaBerge's instinct for survival.

Two blocks over, she met Claire and Ashley Green, along with a squad car containing two Tijuana homicide detectives. She led them to LaBerge, who had made it out of the water and now tried to convince the police that she, Claire, and Green had attempted to rob his business and then to kill him. Fortunately, one of the cops happened to be an old buddy of Green's. Despite LaBerge's boasts of all the high-up people in Tijuana whom he knew personally and who would be furious to learn how he was being treated, LaBerge was taken into custody at the Tijuana jail.

Margo, Claire, and Green went to the jail as well. A police surgeon attended to Green's wound and, thanks to Green's friend, they were given scratchy, no doubt jail issue, blankets to wrap up in, instead of their wet clothes. They spent the next two hours being questioned, separately, by detectives. Then came another hour's wait, during which Margo took the opportunity to ask a few questions of her own . . . such as, how did Ashley Green just happen to be across the fence when she and Claire came hightailing it across the factory yard?

Like Margo, Green hadn't been able to dismiss Rosalia's death, he said as they sat, blanket-clad, drinking the jail's strong coffee. He saw no reason for Dorothy Troupe to have killed the young Mexican woman, nor could he convince himself that there was no link between Rosalia falling off the cliff and Margo's accident the same night. That got him thinking, if Rosalia hadn't been going out with Jaime Galván, was she dating someone else? The trail had led, that afternoon, to Carmen and the news that Rosalia's *jefe* wasn't Galván but Craig LaBerge. Green had tried calling Margo at KSDR and found out she'd gone to Mexico.

"There's a feeling I get when a case is about to break," Green said. "I got it then. No way could I track you down in Mexico, so I staked out LaBerge's office. By seven, when he hadn't left work, I was thinking what a fool I was. This workaholic's catching up on his balance sheets and I'm sitting in my car in a thunderstorm, eating Doritos for dinner. Man, those things are greasy." There was a crinkle of paper, Green opening a pack of Tums. "All of a sudden, he came tearing outta there and got in his truck. Somebody must have seen you and called him, or else you triggered an alarm. I tailed LaBerge to his factory. You know what happened from there."

True enough, but that wasn't all Margo wanted to hear from Ashley Green. "Why didn't you say you went to the Bufadora the day after my accident? And why didn't you say anything about finding Rosalia's body?"

"Ah." Green smiled. "It'd go against my nature to give away all the information I've got."

A short, grumpy-looking man entered the room. "Senõra Simon? I'm Virgil Gonzalez, state prosecutor. I'd like to ask you some questions."

It was one A.M. and the prosecutor had pillow lines on his cheek. Obviously dragged from bed into the rainy night, he seemed half-asleep during their interview.

Craig LaBerge was still in jail when she, Claire, and Green were allowed to leave. But Margo had her doubts about how long LaBerge would stay there. He was insisting on calling a local attorney, whose name had made Prosecutor Gonzalez look awake for the first time. Margo made a bet with herself: If the Mexican justice system turned out to be more interested in learning the truth than in taking the bribes LaBerge would offer them, she could buy a rose silk jacket she'd had her eye on. Hell, she'd even treat herself to a new skirt.

"Great jacket, Margo," said Claire, outside the station manager's office on Monday morning. Alex hadn't yet arrived for the eight A.M. meeting to which he had summoned them.

"Thanks." It had been nearly a week before Margo had had time to get to the mall and make good on her promise to herself. With the rose jacket, she'd bought a flowing, flower-print skirt.

In spite of the prosecutor's apparent lack of interest when he had questioned them, wheels had started turning the next day: Mexican environmental officers had staged a virtual raid on the maquiladoras operated by Craig LaBerge's shelter company, discovering sixteen hundred barrels of stored toxic waste. At the same time, the Mexican police had seized the dented Cadillac at the shoe factory and started forensic testing, and had begun showing LaBerge's photo around Rosarito and the Bufadora, trying to find someone who had seen him on the nights Zeke or Rosalia died. And in *el norte*, Federal investigators were checking LaBerge's books and talking to his clients. If LaBerge had billed for disposing of all sixteen hundred barrels of toxins he was storing, at six hundred dollars each, he had cheated his clients of almost a million dollars. No other charges, besides the environmental ones, had yet been filed. But Craig LaBerge was definitely going to be serving time on one side of the border or the other.

For the present, LaBerge continued to reside in the Tijuana jail. A crusading Tijuana magazine had jumped on the story of the rich Yankee maquiladora owner who'd seduced and then killed a seventeen-year-old worker (killing Zeke Holroyd was definitely considered a secondary offense). No Mexican official who cared about his political future was going to let LaBerge bribe his way out of jail.

The one lighter moment, as Margo reported on the rapidly breaking story, occurred when she heard from the Missouri colleague whom she'd asked to check on Paul van den Moeller. The head of Zeke's church did harbor a secret: He had invented the wicked past with which he inspired his followers to turn from their own lives of sin. Far from being a former juvenile delinquent, the young van den Moeller had regularly made the pages of the local newspaper for his prizewinning 4-H projects and his prowess on the football field. He had served as student body president his senior year and even won his high school citizenship award. Everyone old enough to remember him did so with pride.

"How're my star reporters? Can I get you some coffee?" Alex, bounding into his office, sounded as if he'd already had a few double espressos himself.

"Sure, black." Margo trusted Alex in a fawning mood even less than she trusted him ordinarily, but the phenomenon of the station manager fetching her coffee was too good to pass up.

Alex returned in a moment, handing coffee cups to Margo and Claire. "I just came from breakfast with the station attorney. He says to go ahead with the blackmailing minister angle, *if* we can get that clothing manufacturer on tape. Kohler, right, Margo? Tell him we don't have to identify him by name, just get him saying Holroyd blackmailed him and giving some details. Then we've got the list from Holroyd's wife. And Margo's private eye friend got the license of Dorothy Troupe's previous car and verified that she crossed the border two minutes before that hit-and-run occurred."

The coffee in Margo's stomach soured. She had told the Mexican prosecutor about Zeke's blackmail, but he'd felt it would muddy the waters; he preferred just to say that Zeke had threatened to report LaBerge for storing toxins. The prosecutor only had LaBerge in his sights, whereas KSDR had a golden opportunity to skewer the religious right (not a bad outcome, in Margo's opinion) . . . and also to destroy a popular politician who was making a congressional bid.

Alex dropped his last piece of news—"the latest Troupe

scuttlebutt,'' he called it, grinning. "She dropped out of sight over the weekend. Didn't show at a fund-raiser Saturday night. Now, no politician bails on a fund-raiser. Her staff is saying Troupe just needs a rest. But I heard they don't even know where to reach her. I don't suppose you do, Margo? Being old friends and all?''

"Not a clue," Margo lied.

32 / Tequila Sunset

Playas de Tijuana. San Lucas. Rosarito.

Last week's storm had done no damage to the toll highway going south from Tijuana. In fact, the storm had been a blessing, breaking the muggy heat that had gripped the area all summer. This afternoon, the sun shone in a brilliant sky over a jewel-blue sea. The breeze felt fabulous in Margo's face and hair as she zipped down the Baja coast in her silver convertible.

Las Gaviotas—the gulls. Cantamar—song of the sea.

She left the highway at La Fonda.

"It's close to where we all used to go camping," Dorothy had said of her Baja retreat.

There was a lot more development than when she and Dorothy had come here seven or eight years ago. Neat rows of white stucco houses and condominiums, featuring modern plumbing and an ocean view—in that order of importance—for the *norteamericanos* who could afford them. It was a far cry from spreading out sleeping bags on the beach.

Margo cruised up and down the streets of the first development. She had taken a long shot, thinking she could just come here and, as if by instinct, find Dorothy. The long shot paid off, however, when she checked the second development down the road. She spotted Dorothy's burgundy Buick parked outside a modest condo.

Margo knocked on the door. "Anybody home?"

No answer. Dorothy was probably out walking on the beach, on such a splendid day. Margo knocked one more time, then, what the hell, tried the door. It was unlocked.

"Dorothy?"

Past a kitchenette to her right, Margo entered a living/dining room where Dorothy Troupe sat smoking on a couch, slouching, her bare feet on the coffee table in front of her. Dorothy was wearing a red and black San Diego State Aztecs sweatshirt and black leggings. On the coffee table sat an ashtray full of butts and the requisite ingredients for tequila shooters—a bottle of Cuervo Gold tequila, a salt shaker, a sectioned lime.

Dorothy looked up.

"If it isn't fucking Brenda Starr."

"Come on, Dorothy, it's me."

"And you tracked me down purely out of friendship, right?"

"As a matter of fact, yes."

Margo's eyes having adjusted from the brightness outside, she saw that Dorothy's face was mapped with red veins, tequila rivers, as if this wasn't her first bottle of Cuervo Gold since she had disappeared two days ago. The current bottle was three-quarters empty.

"Well, *amiga*, help yourself," Dorothy said. "There are glasses in the kitchen."

"Thanks." Margo got herself a glass, poured a shot of tequila, and sat cross-legged on the floor.

"Salt. Lime," offered Dorothy.

Margo licked the webbing between her thumb and first finger and sprinkled some salt there, then licked the salt, downed the tequila, and sucked on a slice of lime.

"Like old times," she said, although she hadn't drunk a shooter in years; it had burned going down.

Dorothy gave several barks of laughter, which faded to a weary sigh. "Nothing's like old times. Definitely not me. And not you, either. Haven't you heard, Maggie, we're post-feminist women. We've given up on trying to transform the world. We've settled for becoming men with vaginas, only we're harder and colder than the men, since we've got a lot more to prove. Look at you. In the old days, you never would have come after a scoop and tried to call it friendship."

"I didn't come here to get a story," Margo protested.

"At least not like that." She squirmed as she followed Dorothy's gaze . . . at the tape recorder she'd brought in with her. "This thing about you being in the hit-and-run and paying blackmail to Zeke Holroyd, you know I can't sit on that. And when it comes out, there'll be a media feeding frenzy. I wanted to give you a chance to tell the story privately first, the way you'd like people to hear it. Besides, I understand how much you love Sean, how you'd do anything to protect him."

Her own words sounded so self-serving that Margo couldn't look Dorothy in the eye. Still, friendship was the larger part of why she had come here this afternoon, and why she'd told no one at the radio station that she knew where Dorothy Troupe might be hiding. Wasn't it? Or had she changed as much as Dorothy believed?

"Margo!"

Lost in her thoughts (and light-headed from the tequila), Margo hadn't been aware Dorothy was speaking. She looked up.

"Say that again," said Dorothy. "About Sean."

"I was just saying I understand how you could pay blackmail to protect Sean."

"What the fuck are you talking about?"

Dorothy was still standing between her son and trouble. Margo poured fresh shooters for both of them, although she sipped hers this time.

"Dorothy, it's obvious to anyone who knows you. Sean's the one who has accidents. He must have been driving your car that night. He was the one who hit the Mexican family and then drove off."

Dorothy downed her tequila in one swallow, forgoing the salt and lime. A year's abstinence evidently hadn't dampened her ability to hold her booze.

"Did Zeke Holroyd tell you that?" she said. "That Sean was driving?"

"No, but *you* wouldn't have run away. You're a fighter. You wouldn't run away from anything."

"Oh, God." Dorothy came around the table to her. "You're still an idealist, aren't you?" Kneeling, she grasped Margo by the shoulders. "Look at me, Maggie. I *was* driving that car."

"That's exactly what you *would* say—"

"You're right, if Sean had been driving I'd protect him. But in this case it's not necessary. I was driving. Sean wasn't with me. You don't have that tape recorder going, there's no reason for me to lie." Dorothy stressed each word. "I hit those people. I saw them at the last minute and tried to stop, but it was too late. I felt the impact when the car hit them. I heard their screams. Are you listening to me, Margo?"

She waited until Margo nodded.

"And then," said Dorothy, "I floored it and kept going."

"Why didn't you stop and help them? Because you'd been drinking?" Alcohol would have impaired Dorothy's reaction time, and also might have made her more likely to panic.

"Maggie, grow up. I ran because even if I got off legally, a thing like this would have crucified me with my Hispanic constituents. I've spent years building support in that community. You know how tough it was for a gringa like me to gain those people's trust? I wasn't going to let all of that be wiped out by some poor Mexican family running across the San Diego Freeway. That's a disgusting attitude, isn't it? It's alien to every value I used to flatter myself I had. And so what? I did it. I got up and looked at myself in the mirror every morning for a year. It wasn't that hard. I'd have been a damn good congresswoman, too. Well, you'd better eat something, after that tequila. You're not used to it anymore, are you? I'll make sandwiches.

"By the way," said Dorothy, pausing on the way to the kitchen. "I heard you wanted to know about the Baja Nueva Company. Here's a little tip. Ask Harry Rusk about it."

"The labor leader?"

"Harry had some money to invest and he's getting worried about his old age. Guess where he and some of the other union guys invested?"

Even an idealist could see that Dorothy was trying to take the heat off herself by diverting some to her former political ally. Still, Margo felt a stir of excitement, planning to confront Harry Rusk with his involvement in the development . . . and to push for, if not a stay of execution for the colonia, at least some kind of compensation for its residents.

"Tuna or cheddar?" said Dorothy.

"Tuna." Margo had no appetite, but Dorothy was right: she wasn't used to tequila anymore and she'd better eat before she drove.

"One tuna sandwich coming up. Then you can turn on that tape recorder and I'll give you your scoop."

Jaw tight, foot pressing the accelerator to eighty miles an hour, Margo drove south on the Tijuana-Ensenada toll highway. Coming to the toll road after leaving Dorothy's, she'd approached the northbound lane, back to the U.S. But she had turned south instead, somehow compelled to drive deeper into Baja.

Margo had thought she knew Dorothy Troupe, knew what Dorothy was capable of and what was beyond her capability, what was too unethical or too lacking in compassion. It takes one to know one, Dorothy had said, describing Craig LaBerge's instinct for survival. Not only had she committed a hit-and-run and left the people dying, she still wasn't willing to face the consequences of her action.

"You won't be able to prove a thing," she'd said, before Margo started taping. The promised scoop wasn't an admission of her guilt, but a statement that she was getting out of politics "for personal reasons." To avoid having to answer endless questions, she wasn't even coming back to San Diego. She intended to depart from her place in Baja immediately, destination unknown . . . or at least unrevealed to Margo.

"Off the record, where are you going?" Margo had said when she turned off the tape recorder.

"Off the record!" Dorothy snorted. "Don't you get it, Margo? Nothing's off the record with you. If I told you I was going to Iceland, you'd show up with a film crew, it'd be your big break into TV.''

Margo hadn't known what motivated her to drive south, but ten miles from Dorothy's, she pulled over at El Mirador, the viewpoint—where Zeke Holroyd had died. The area had gotten built up lately, with a restaurant and gift shop and half a dozen rounded salmon-stuccoed niches where one could enjoy the view of the bay. She walked uphill to the farthest of the niches and looked over the edge of the cliff at Bahia Salsipuedes below. Lucky for her, she'd arrived just in time for the sunset. Also luckily, there was nobody else around, no one to make her self-conscious about crying.

They had both changed, according to Dorothy. Dorothy, who had become a person Margo wouldn't want around her stepkids. How much had she, Margo, changed? What was she capable of that might have been unthinkable at one time? She had told herself she'd sought out Dorothy to let Dorothy tell her own version of the hit-and-run story. Truth or rationalization? And she was telling herself she had to break the news of Zeke's blackmail, no matter how much pain it caused Lael. She couldn't imagine killing either story; that was out of the question. Would it have been out of the question ten or even five years ago?

However Margo might have changed, it had happened subtly, through a series of small choices, rather than any major decisions. There was no single place she could point to and say, *There! That's where I took a different road.* Hell, she couldn't even say for sure she had taken the wrong road . . . only that she felt she had lost something.

Had something like that happened to Zeke Holroyd? Had he started out simply wanting to help people make spiritual amends for things they felt bad about? Maybe he had crossed the line so gradually—from helping . . . to manipulating . . . to extorting—he had never realized it. Did he believe that he was tempting no retribution, either human or divine? When Craig LaBerge rammed Zeke's car and he sailed over the cliff that stretched in front of Margo, had it been a complete surprise?

The sun sank gloriously into the ocean. Words she hadn't said for years came to Margo's lips.

"Yit gadal veyit kadash shemei raba." She murmured the rest of the Kaddish, the Jewish prayer of mourning. It wasn't the language in which Ezekiel Holroyd prayed. But Zeke wasn't the only one for whom she mourned.